The Clay Endures

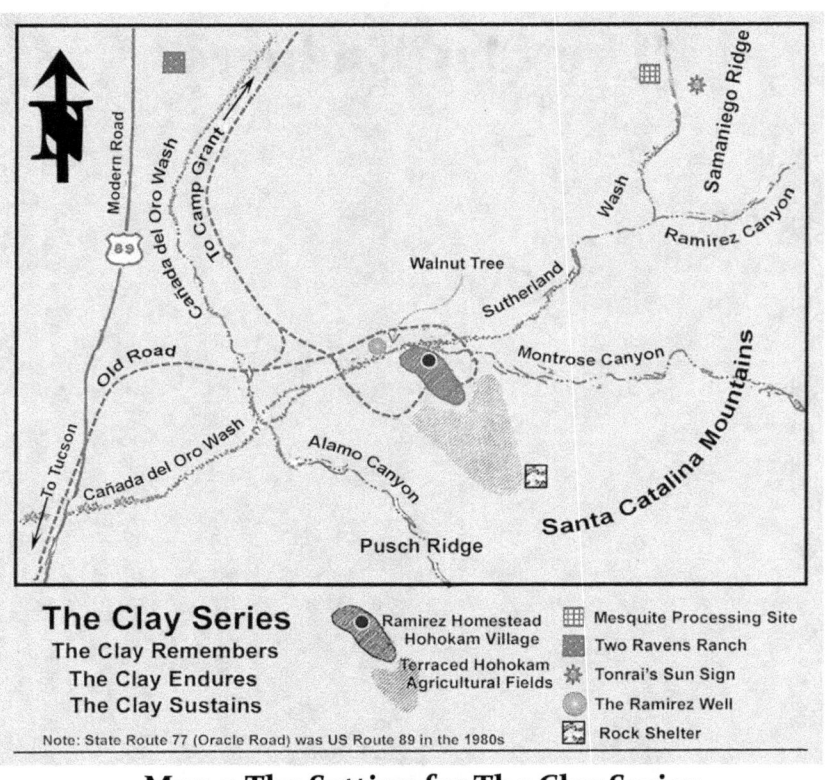

Map 1: The Setting for The Clay Series

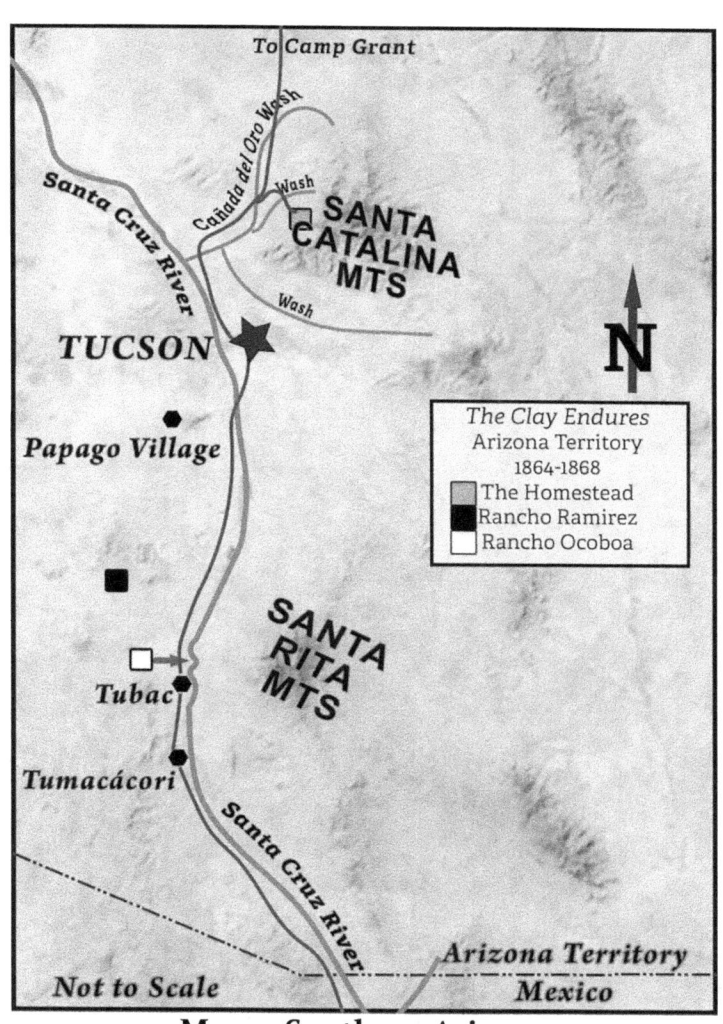

Map 2: Southern Arizona

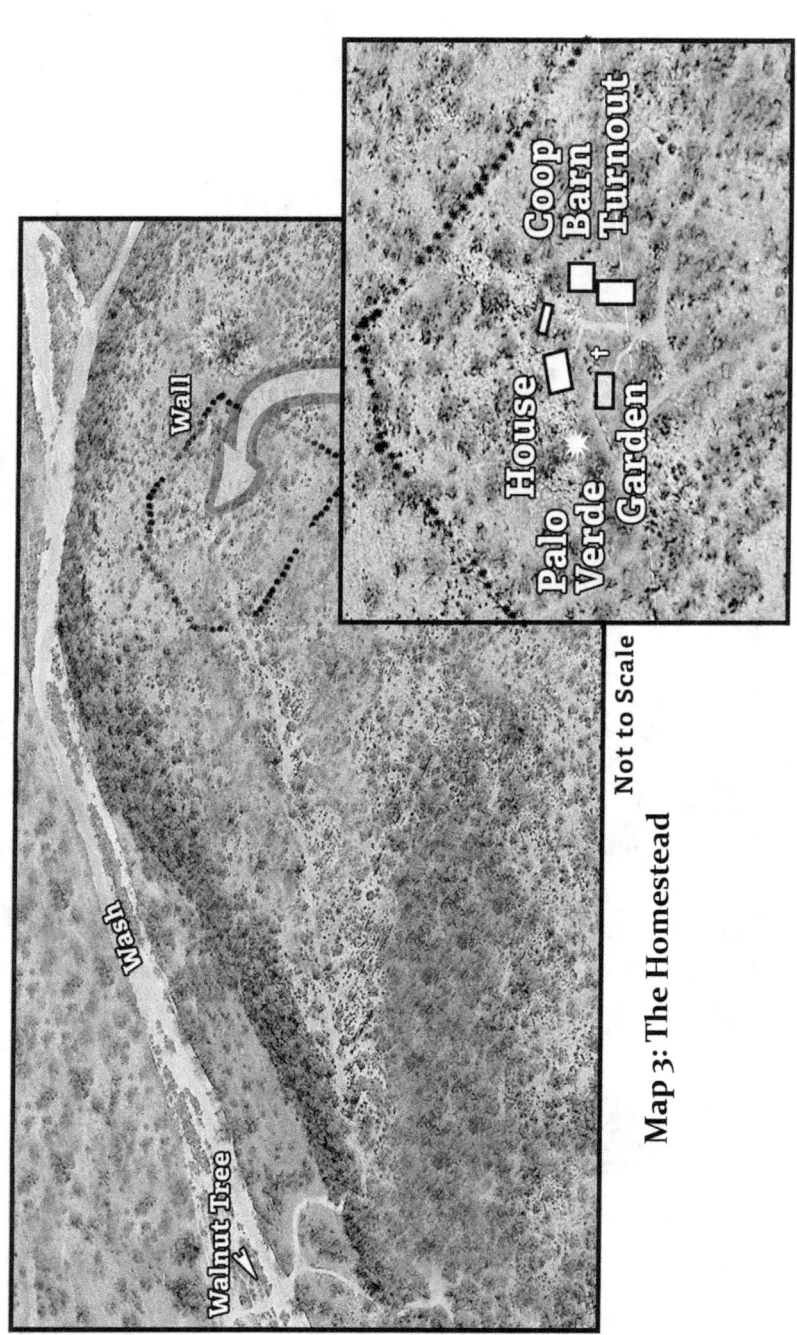

Map 3: The Homestead

Not to Scale

The Clay Endures

BOOK 2 IN THE CLAY SERIES

Sharon K. Miller

Buckskin Books
Tucson, Arizona

Cover design by Juan Carlos Negretti B (JCNB) at www.99designs.com. Email: juannegretti@hotmail.com.

ISBN: 978-0-9961544-3-7 (Print Edition)
ISBN: 978-0-9961544-1-3 (E-Books)

This novel is a work of fiction. The characters of Armando and Esperanza Ramirez are loosely based on Francisco and Victoriana Romero, who lived briefly at what is now known as Romero Ruin in Catalina State Park, north of Tucson, Arizona. This book does not tell their story. All characters, dialogue, and the events described are products of the author's imagination or are used fictitiously. Any resemblance to actual persons living or dead is purely coincidental.

To Jim, my best friend and my love,

and

Paco, my beautiful buckskin gelding, who taught me so much about the beauty of this desert and these mountains that surround us. I miss you.

And, finally, to

Victoriana Romero, whose life on a desolate ridge in the nineteenth century is the mystery that fired my imagination.

The Clay Series

The Clay Remembers
(1986-1992)

The Clay Endures
(1864-1868)

The Clay Sustains
(1158-1162)

Contents

Acknowledgments

My greatest thanks and all my love go to my husband, Jim, for everything he does to allow me to pursue this passion for writing.

Deep appreciation goes to David Neilson, author of *The Prussian Dispatch: Book 1 of The Sophie Rathenau Mysteries*. His keen eye for issues big and small is responsible for much of what is good about this book.

To my advance readers: Linda "Lucy" Fernandez, Suzanne Kirby, Donna Mathews, Linda Murphy, Renee Nanna, Jeannie Waters, Markie Madden, author of the Undead Unit Series (*Book One: Fang and Claw,* and *Book Two: Souls of the Reaper*), and my sister, Betty Ann Hood, I'm grateful for your valuable feedback and suggestions.

Hermania Valenzuela, teacher and Yaqui storyteller, introduced me to the Yoeme culture and the concept of *Sea Takaa* in 1999, and Felipe Molina, Yaqui/Yoeme scholar, provided me with an in-depth education on Yoeme history and culture in 2014. Without their insights, I could not have told this story.

My deepest regard and appreciation go to my friend, Rita Hovey, who advised me on the colloquial use of the Spanish language. All language errors, though, are mine.

To my Scribophile "critters," Bliss Addison, Kristen Kooistra, Maggie Penn, Zamora Strider, and Cassandra Zolotoff, your feedback on selected chapters was extremely valuable.

Andy Ward, pottery instructor extraordinaire, went out of his way to help me collect authentic clay for my replica pots. He taught me how to make the pot that is central to the stories in this series, and even promised to make them for me if mine were a disaster.

The Arizona Historical Society Museum Library and staff, the Arizona State Museum Library and staff, the Pueblo Grande Museum, and the Heard Museum provided access to historical and prehistorical documents and artifacts important to my vision for Esperanza and Armando, their families, and the general culture of nineteenth-century Tucson.

And to my editor, who is also a colleague and friend, Wynne Brown (www.wynnebrown.com), thanks for applying your skill and eagle eye to the manuscript.

Note to Readers

The character of the Apache in this story is not intended to represent the Apache tribe or its cultural traditions. His struggle is the product of my imagination.

While a great deal of research was involved in writing this story, I have, from time to time, taken liberties with the historical record or the timeline of events. Factual errors are mine alone.

*The mother is the earth, the father is the sun.
In Apache, we say you lean toward the father,
but you are with the mother. You lean toward
the sun, but it is in the sky, distant. You touch
the earth and are close to it, part of it.*

Tryntje Van Ness Seymour
The Gift of Changing Woman

Some readers may be curious about various historical events and people in the story or about the use of Spanish and Apache languages. You may refer to Author Notes (organized by chapter) and the Glossary in the back of the book for more specific information.

Prologue

Winter 1865

He stood in the shifting shadows of the palo verde waiting for the woman to appear. Since she and her man came to this place, he watched her many times. She knew.

When they came to this place, he thought she was Anglo. She was not Mexican either. She walked with a straight back, easily—animal-like as if she felt the pull of the Earth, as if she treasured the ground beneath her feet. *She understands and speaks to the spirit world.*

A memory came unbidden. He touched the blunt edges of his hair. Three turnings of seasons had passed, but still he grieved, could not allow his hair to grow. To do so would deny her existence. Anguish walked with him, rode heavily on his back, and tormented his dreams.

Among the *Tin-ne-áh*, a woman's death meant nothing; never think of or speak of her, and, above all, never speak her name. The pain cut through him like a knife.

At *N'aíí'ees*, when she was White Changing Woman, she danced for four days, and her energy never flagged; she wore the blessings of the pollen with dignity and blessed others with it. Standing before him, radiant and happy, she drew her yellow fingers along his cheek. He lifted his hand again, this time to the memory of her touch.

If he closed his eyes, he saw her racing across the desert on her pony, her hair flying—but the image always gave way to blood and wailing and the medicine man's song—to his own medicine's impotence.

With the spirit of a warrior, she had held the promise of his people.

He nearly whispered her name again.

Had he called her back?

He pushed the memory away, and his thoughts returned to this woman—this woman who has come to this place to stand before him, as real as the trees, as real as the mountains, as real as this Earth I tread upon.

Now, she stepped out of the house, rifle in hand and scanned the southern *bajada*, looking for her man. They would allow him to retrieve some of the cows, but the rest would feed his people tonight at *túttsog hadaslin*, Where the Yellow Water Flows.

When she turned, their eyes met, and he held hers in the dark pools of his own.

Part 1: The Beginning

Arizona Territory, 1864

Chapter 1

Spring 1864

Beneath a velvet ash by the river, she stripped ribbons of bark from small branches. With each one, she said, "*Gracias*," and added it to the basket with the *cañaigre* tuber, *pazotillo* stems and flowers, and the spiny tips of the crucifixion thorn. Dappled sun danced through the new leaves, surrounding her with a soft, green glow. She hummed a song she learned from her grandmother when she was a child.

> *Take my hand and walk with me*
> *Walk with me today.*

The song was an invitation to God, so she hoped he would forgive her for singing it for Armando Ramirez, who walked with her after mass the last time the priest came from Tucson. He hadn't taken her hand. People might have whispered. Before the service, he joined her under the ramada, and the expression on Doña María's face reminded her she was not worthy. With him so close, she couldn't focus on the readings, prayers, and responses. She tried not to think about his mother's eyes and the disapproval they communicated. Instead, she concentrated on Armando's broad shoulders, his dark hair, his green eyes, and his hands, wishing he could hold hers but knowing it would be improper during mass.

When she added the last piece of bark to the others and slipped her knife into her pocket, she heard them. Horses coming from the east. If her brothers, Tomás and Manolito, had followed her, they wouldn't come from that direction. She ducked into the bushes, crouched down, and tucked the basket beneath her skirt.

The Apaches slowed, directing their horses into the shallow water to drink. Six. Not enough for a raiding party, but enough to cause trouble. In the shade of the cottonwoods and seep willows leaning over the water, the ponies dipped their noses into the water, drinking and splashing while the men laughed and talked in their strange language.

One man raised his hand. His companions quieted their ponies, holding them motionless even as dappled sunlight danced around them. She held her breath in the silence. Even the birds, which minutes earlier sang and fluttered noisily through the trees, made no sound.

Pressing a knee into the pony's side, the man turned to face her, rifle butt against his leg, barrel pointed to the sky. The others did not move. Through a small opening in the thick brush, she stared at him without blinking. The knife in her pocket would be useless. Even so, she squeezed her fingers around the hilt.

He was young, probably no older than she, his angular face smooth except for a thin, vertical wrinkle between his brows—like her father's worry line. Narrow stripes of black paint crossed each cheek, and he wore a bead-and-bone necklace. Naked but for buckskin moccasins that reached his knees and a loincloth that fell across his thighs from a colorful, woven sash at his waist, his bronze skin glistened in the late morning sun. A brown bandanna loosely wrapped his head, and his tangled, black hair hung straight below his shoulders. When he frowned, the wrinkle deepened. He pressed his pony toward her. One step. Then two. He stopped, tilting his head as if listening.

Did he hear her catch her breath? Could he hear her heart pounding? His eyes bored into hers. *He knows I am here.* She remained perfectly still, praying her brothers had not followed her this morning. She pressed her elbows against her sides, wishing herself as small as the spider weaving a web between leaves inches from her face.

"*Deyaa!*" His voice shattered the silence—the harsh, guttural sound sending a shock through her body. Her shoulders tightened, and she struggled against the rush of energy commanding her to run. She gripped the knife in her pocket and held her breath. She imagined him dragging her from the bushes and—

He spun his horse, splashing across the river and turning northward. The others followed.

Do not move, mi nieta.

She listened until the pounding hooves faded into silence. Her thumping heart quieted, and familiar river sounds reached her ears—water gurgling around rocks a few feet from where she crouched, birds singing above her head, and insects whispering in the brush. Still, she did not move. Unblinking, breathing slowly and deliberately, she settled her heart into a regular rhythm.

Finally, she crawled out of the bushes and stood. A sudden cramp grabbed her leg, and she staggered before gaining her balance. She bent down and massaged her aching muscle. Allowing herself to breathe deeply again, she pressed her palm to her chest and bowed her head. After a moment, she turned to the tree, still unsteady, and placed a trembling hand on its rough trunk.

"*Gracias, el árbol*. My grandmother will draw upon your substance to relieve the discomforts of many people." Before taking the bark, she had asked the tree's permission, and now she must express her gratitude. She had done the same for each plant or root she had collected, leaving the young cañaigre tubers and the fruit-bearing branches of the crucifixion thorn.

Concentrating on Armando and nothing else, she lifted her skirt, crossed the river, and stopped where they had stood the first time he held and kissed her hand. Her stomach fluttered, and her pulse raced, sensations she welcomed, unlike those of moments before. The Apaches were gone. She would not mention this to her parents.

When she reached her grandmother's gate, she turned to face the desert. In the distance, the mountains rose into a clear blue sky above the ribbon of green marking the river's path. She thanked the desert, the river, and the trees for their gifts and for sheltering her.

Abuela Tiva opened the door before she got there. "Come in, mi nieta." She leaned her cane against the wall and took her granddaughter's hand. "I, too, was afraid."

Esperanza wrapped her grandmother's hand in her own. The papery skin was cold, the fingers knotted and arthritic. She didn't know how old her grandmother was, but for as long as she could remember, Abuela Tiva had been short, stooped, and so thin Esperanza feared she might blow away in a strong wind.

"Gracias. You kept me safe."

"Nonsense. You did it yourself." She led her granddaughter to the kitchen still holding her hand.

Putting the basket down, Esperanza smiled. "I don't think so. I didn't see them until they were almost upon me."

Her grandmother nodded. "Seeing is not the same as knowing. You had time to hide."

"But if I had known sooner, I would have come back before they got to the river. Or I might never have gone down there."

"Hah! Don't be so sure."

Esperanza pulled a chair away from the table for her grandmother. At the fireplace, she scooped hot water into a mug and dropped in a pinch of tea leaves.

In spite of what her grandmother said, she didn't believe she shared Abuela Tiva's gift of second sight. Primarily, though, Primitiva Graciela Nuñez Medina was a *curandera*, treating her people's ailments using traditional remedies. Esperanza helped collect the plants and seeds her abuela used to make tonics and poultices, learning how to make them, as well as salves, teas, and other natural medications to treat various illnesses and injuries.

When Abuela Tiva's hands became knotted with arthritis, Esperanza crushed the seeds and the bark into powder, hung the herbs, flowers, and twigs to dry. Once, she had helped treat a little boy who sliced his leg playing with his father's knife. Even though it was infected and the child suffered a terrible fever, he survived. Her grandmother cautioned her, "Wash your hands. Dirt in a wound is bad. Clean bandages. Hot water." The boy might not have recovered without her Grandmother's care. Others had died from such infections.

When she set the mug in front of her, the old woman said, "Hmmph. How'd you know I wanted tea?"

Hands on her hips, Esperanza replied, "Abuela Tiva, I don't need gifts like yours to know when you need a cup of tea."

Her grandmother laughed, wrapped her bony hands around the warm mug, and whispered, "You were right. He knew."

"What? Who?" Did she mean Armando? No. Realization dawned. The Apache. "But if he knew, why didn't he—?"

The old woman shrugged. "I can't say." She sipped her tea and gazed across the mug at something beyond Esperanza's vision. "It was not my spirit that spoke to him."

Chapter 2

Summer 1864

A brutal June sun bore down without mercy. Perspiration trickled down his back, dampening his shirt. He lifted his sombrero and wiped his forehead with his sleeve. Putting it back on, he pulled the wide brim low over his forehead. He shook his canteen. Empty. Sweat soaked Sofi's coat, dripping into the sandy trail as they passed. In spite of the heat, he kept her at a walk, refusing to jeopardize her health to relieve his discomfort. Besides, the sooner he got home, the sooner he would face his parents' anger. Yesterday was *El Día de San Juan* and his eighteenth birthday. He had gone to the Pápago village to see the villagers call down the clouds for the blessing of rains, and he was only now going home.

The Old One always welcomed him, but this time, the elder had invited him to watch a celebration, which he considered an honor. He had met the tribal leader through Felipe, one of his father's ranch hands, whose wife, a Pápago, was also the Ramirez cook. Last winter, he went to the village several times, listening to the Old One share the legends of his people, telling the stories he couldn't tell in the summer when the snakes were awake. Sometimes, he told the tales in Spanish, and sometimes he spoke in their language. Although Armando didn't understand the Pápago words, they hung in the air like music, floating on the breeze, rustling through the scrub, and dancing on the desert floor. The sound was gentle, with no echoes of anger or discord. It was the language of a people whose essence sprang from the earth. He envied their connection with their world, a connection that made him want to learn about this land surrounding his father's ranch.

Throughout the day and into the night, the Indians had danced and chanted, with the men getting drunk on an astonishing amount of saguaro wine. Apparently, drunkenness was essential to the ceremony, but he didn't know why. After he tasted it, he decided he'd best keep a clear head on his shoulders. If they succeeded in calling down the rains, it would be a sign that the summer rains would come to nourish the desert.

But it hadn't rained, and the heat was oppressive. He wiped his brow again.

At the ranch, he rode up to the barn, a sprawling adobe structure that served as housing for the horses and the vaqueros who worked for his father. After getting Sofi a drink, he started to unsaddle her. Felipe stepped up and took over. "*Lo voy a hacer, Señor* Armando."

"Gracias, but I don't mind doing it."

"*Lo sé*, señor. It is my job." The Mexican carried the saddle into the barn and came back with a bucket of water and washed salty sweat from Sofi's shoulders, chest, and back, cooling her down. Watching Felipe care for his horse, Armando wondered why there was so much gray in his mustache, but none in his hair. His thick, dark hair, parted in the middle, fell into his face when he bent over to sponge water on Sofi's legs. From the time Armando was a little boy, he had followed this man around the ranch, asking questions about the cattle, the horses, and the land. The Mexican had always been good to him.

Without looking up, Felipe said, "Your father was like a bull this morning when he discovered you were not here."

Armando rested his forearms on the rail and concentrated on the colors the afternoon sun painted on the rugged peaks of the Santa Ritas beyond the river— the river flowing past Esperanza's home. He sighed. "I'm not surprised. I suppose I must go in and face them." The Mexican did not take his eyes off his work when Armando walked across the bare yard to the house.

Before going inside, he washed his hands and face in the water barrel at the back door. He glanced around, wondering why his mother saw no need to put colorful pots of flowers around the patio like he had seen at Esperanza's house. He sighed and slipped into the kitchen, breathing in the pungent fragrance of mole sauce simmering over the fire.

Ofelia didn't look up from chopping chiles, but she smiled. "*Bienvenido*, señor." Using her forearm, she wiped sweat from her round face, pushing back the loose strands of gray hair escaping from the knot on her head.

"*Hola*, Ofelia." Like Felipe, this woman was special. As a child, he often hid from his brother in the kitchen where she told him the stories that led him to seek out her people. Sometimes he wondered if he loved her and Felipe more than his parents.

"You are hungry?" Her brown eyes sparkled as if she knew he would be.

When he grinned, she reached into the cabinet behind her and handed him a plate. "They're cold. Do you want me to warm them?"

Without waiting, the first *quesadilla* disappeared in a few bites. She handed him a mug of water, and he took his time with the second one. "Gracias, Ofelia. I didn't realize how hungry I was."

"You have been to my village again?"

"*Sí. Ayer fue El Día de San Juan.*"

"I know. You spoke with my grandfather?"

"*Sí.* He allowed me to stay."

As she pushed the chopped chiles from the board to a plate, she sighed and said. "I wish I had been there, but my work is here. I said my prayers for good rains to come."

He cocked an eyebrow at her. "And did you get drunk?"

Even though she frowned, her soft voice betrayed nothing but kindness. "Of course not." She shook her kitchen towel in his direction. "Now shoo. You need to change." She laughed, and her lightly wrinkled face lit with affection. His parents never laughed with him or even smiled at him.

"Where are they?"

"Your father's in his office, and your mother is in the *sala*—waiting for you."

"I suspect she's angry. Maybe I can make it to my room unseen."

Nodding toward the dining room, she said, "Unless Reynaldo is there."

All his life, his oldest brother had bullied him. If Julio, who was the middle son, took up for him, Julio got a whipping. Reynaldo never did anything wrong, and Armando couldn't do anything right. Julio, caught between them, was Armando's best friend.

He took a deep breath, pushed the dining room door open, and peeked in. Empty. After passing his father's office, he hung his hat by the front door and made it safely to his room.

After he stripped off his sweat-soaked shirt, he poured water into the cracked wash basin. While he cleaned up, he rehearsed for his audience with Doña María. He assumed she would scold him for going to the Pápago village and being away all night—always preferable to arguing about Esperanza. He put on a clean shirt and brushed his hair from his forehead, only to have it fall back.

"You wanted to see me, Mother?" The candles in the wrought-iron chandelier cast dancing shadows around the room as he came in the door, resuming their quiet glow when he closed it. The smallest room in the house, the sala was where his mother spent most of her time. A sofa and an armchair, both upholstered in a worn, red velvet pattern, sat in the center of the room. A small library table inside the door held several of his mother's books, along with her Bible.

Her ample weight covered most of the sofa, and she held a small book in her dimpled hands. Because the dim light of the chandelier and the candle on the side table seemed inadequate for reading, Armando assumed she had adopted the pose as a pretense. She did not acknowledge him until he stood before her. The ivory comb holding her thick, dark hair in place on top of her head looked every bit like a crown, approximating the regal air she sought.

After laying her book aside, she held her magnifying glass, polishing the mother-of-pearl handle with dry fingers. She pressed her lips together, her mouth turning down at the corners. He expected their conversation to be unpleasant, but now he knew it would be much worse. The dim candlelight cast her face into shadow, amplifying the ever-present dark circles under her eyes and exaggerating the creases in her cheeks. "Armando, your brother tells me once again you refuse to attend to our expectations. I cannot understand why you must spend your days with those people."

Reynaldo. Determined to be reasonable, he took a breath before answering. "Those people, Mother, are my friends."

"Your *friends*?" Her face reddened, and she lifted her chin, narrowing her eyes. "Your friends? Those people cannot be your friends. They are Mexicans and Indians." Her mouth tightened, and she wrinkled her nose, an expression he had seen whenever she was forced to use language unsuitable for a lady, those times when she was compelled to comment on anyone she considered beneath her. "They are field hands, heathens, and servants." She spit the last word at him.

How should he answer? Should he say he preferred their company over everyone in this house except Julio? He wanted her to understand he was different from his family. He was drawn to the land in different ways. To them, land was a possession, a symbol of status, something giving them power over those they saw as inferior to themselves. Would she understand how the Indians' spiritual view of the earth gave him direction? While he struggled for the words, what she said next brought him back to the moment.

"And they tell me you continue to spend time with the Ocoboa girl even though we forbid it. *Es imperdonable.*"

His first thought was a desire to strangle Reynaldo. She didn't wait for him to comment. "I'm told she rides upon her horse. What's more, she's been seen riding astride, her hair unbound, and her petticoats flying. *¡Es escandaloso!*"

Armando struggled to stifle a smile. It was exactly such behavior that drew him to her. Almost a year ago, he and Julio were on their way to Tubac when three riders came racing toward them at a full gallop. In the lead was a young woman riding astride, her hair unbound and her petticoats flying, just as his mother said. Their own horses, Sofi and Paquito, danced nervously, so they moved to the side of the road to wait. The young woman reined her horse to a sliding stop in front of them and spun around, creating a whirlwind of dust that failed to settle before her brothers came abreast.

One of the young men called out to them, "*Lo siento, Señores.* I'm sorry. You must forgive my sister's lack of grace. She should have been born a boy."

"You are jealous because you don't ride as well as me." Her laughter sang in his ears, and he fell in love at that very moment. He barely glanced at her brothers, and he wouldn't have recognized either one if he ran into them only an hour later. Intoxicated by her beauty, he saw only this girl whose long black hair and petticoats had flown into his heart.

To his mother, he said nothing. He would not make excuses for disobeying their orders not to see her.

"The Ocoboas may have insinuated themselves into polite society, but I know where they come from." She wrinkled her nose again. "Your responsibility is to your father—to this family. I will not permit you to disgrace us!"

"What disgrace, Mother? They have been here longer than us. They came with the missionaries even before our ancestors got here. They are respected members of the community. Her great-grandfather was the governor of Tumacácori, and he served with honor. The region is changing, Mother. Spain hasn't governed us for more than forty years, and Mexico has ceded this part of Sonora to the United States."

Doña María Comadurán de Castillo y Reyes struggled to lift her weight from the threadbare sofa. When she was standing, she took a deep breath and her considerable bosom lifted, straining the seams of her too tight bodice. Her dark, blazing eyes never left those of her son's. "You dare school me on our history? I know of the scoundrels who govern in Mexico and how they have abandoned us, pushed us aside. In spite of them, your father and I will not allow you to sully our lineage. You would do well to respect your ancestors and the sacrifices they made since Nicolás Ramirez, arrived and amassed the wealth our family has guarded through many generations. Your great-grandfather, Don Agustín Ramirez Corella, acquired the grant for this land, our home. We will hold on to our heritage and our dignity."

Because his parents often told this family history, especially when they needed to impress upon others their importance, he needed no reminders. It was a well-rehearsed story she recited without taking a breath.

She continued, "No one—do you understand me?—no one in this family has ever married a Mexican, an Indian, or a *mestizo*." Again, she spit the words out.

Armando stared at the spittle that dripped from the corner of her mouth, and his careful reserve abandoned him. "Mother, please. Do you mean to suggest the Crown sent boat loads of fine Spanish ladies to New Spain to protect our ancestors from breeding with the natives? It defies belief."

Her eyes flashing, Doña María's mouth dropped open. Her face contorted and her dark brows knit together in a scowl.

She shook the magnifying glass in his face. "Your crudeness is beyond contemptible. You expect me to believe the Ocoboa slut is worthy of a Ramirez?"

Now, his face contorted in anger, and before he could stop himself, he said, "No, Mother, it is you whose crudeness is beyond contemptible. I will not allow you or anyone to use such language about Esperanza."

Raising the magnifier above her head, she stepped toward him, and he backed away. "You will not allow me? Who do you think you are?"

Even though she had never struck him—that was his father's job—for a moment, he wasn't sure she wouldn't. And maybe he deserved it.

She lowered both the glass and her voice, speaking through clenched teeth. "Your father will deal with your disrespect. Now, get out of my sight. I will talk to you tomorrow at which time we will discuss our arrangements to send you to Veracruz to your Cousin Vicente." The corners of her lips curled into an icy smile.

"Mother, you cannot be serious. You would send me to Veracruz even though Mexico is in turmoil? I won't go." Once again, he had overstepped, and he steeled himself for her reaction.

"You!" She spit the word at him. "You do not decide anything in this house. You will do what I tell you. Spain will take care of Juarez, and restore order."

Armando wanted to tell her Spain was unlikely to return to Mexico, and that Veracruz was the seat of the liberal, and increasingly unstable, Juarez government. He chose not to correct her.

"You will leave next month, and while there your marriage to Vicente's daughter, María Dolores, will take place. In the meantime, you remain in this house, in your room. You will not see the Ocoboa girl again. Now, get out of my sight." She turned away from him.

Stunned, Armando stared at his mother's stiff back. On leaving the room, he closed the door more forcefully than he should—something that would only increase her anger.

He grabbed his hat and stormed through the front door into the courtyard. When he stopped to get hold of himself, he breathed in the fragrance of the jasmine hanging next to the gate. Such sweetness is out of place here. To the east, the high peaks of the Santa Rita Mountains rose, but his gaze slid along the horizon, turning northward to the range known to him as *L'Iglesia*, the Church. From the distance, it called to him, inviting him to worship beneath its slopes, to make it his home.

In spite of his mother's orders, he saddled Sofi and cantered across the valley to Esperanza, knowing once again his disobedience would have consequences.

Chapter 3

Summer 1864

Frustrated that her embroidered flower looked nothing like those in her garden, she wanted to give up. She hated needlework, but her mother insisted she learn "domestic arts." When her mother used that term, she struggled not to laugh out loud. A future including needles and thread and images of flowers and birds instead of the real thing seemed impossible. She would rather be out riding Pepe, leaving her brothers behind, her hair unpinned and flying.

If her mother noticed she had placed her chair close to the window, she didn't say anything. If she noticed Esperanza repeatedly glanced out the window, she didn't remark on it. She did, however, remark when her daughter put her embroidery aside and yawned.

"Are you tired, *m'hija*?"

"*Sí, Mamá*. May I step outside for some air?"

"Of course. Put a wrap on before you go."

"But it's hot today."

She nodded. "The air will be cooler by the river."

As she was leaving the room, her mother called out, "*Por favor*, say hello to Armando for me."

Esperanza stared, wide-eyed and blushing.

Her mother smiled. "Don't be gone long."

Wrapping her shawl around her shoulders, she raced out the door, pulling the hairpins from her hair, lifting her skirt and petticoats, sweeping dust from the lane into a cloud as she ran to meet him, her hair flying free.

Armando was no sooner on the ground than she threw herself into his arms. "*Buenas días, mi amorita*."

"Why so formal?" She stepped back and scanned his face. "Something is wrong?"

"Sí. My parents have made demands."

She folded her arms across her middle, gripping her elbows, and rubbing her forearms. "What do you mean?"

"They do not approve of us."

Studying the ground between them, she said, "They do not approve of me. I have been expecting this."

"You have?"

"Sí. When you sit with me during mass, I see how your mother looks at me. She dislikes me because of my Yoeme heritage."

He held her to him. "I would spare you this pain, mi amorita."

Together, with Sofi following, they walked to the river, his boots crunching on the gravel while her steps were nearly soundless. Whiptail lizards darted before them on the path, and a collared lizard did push-ups on a rock, showing off for potential mates and warning away the competition. The late afternoon heat had intensified, and a high-pitched whine rose when they passed the acacia and mesquite scrub, the first cicada joined by a second and then a third, until a powerful hum filled the air. When they reached the river's edge, the sound faded, and the air cooled. Holding both her hands, he took a ragged breath. "Please, Espe, never doubt my love for you."

"I could never doubt it." The answer came quickly, but she caught a flicker of sadness in his eyes.

"What haven't you told me?"

"They have made threats."

"What kind of threats?"

As he often did, he lifted her hands to his lips and brushed a light kiss across her knuckles. "They have selected a...proper...bride for me."

Stepping back, she pulled her hands from his, searching his face for understanding. "Who?"

"My cousin. They mean to send me to Veracruz."

"Veracruz? No!" She fell against his chest, sobbing.

"Don't cry." He held her close, resting his chin on her head. "I will leave my family before I leave you."

"You would do that?" She could never make such a choice.

"I would."

She searched his eyes for any sign of doubt, eyes that reminded her of his Spanish descent, eyes that were green instead of brown. Eyes that told her that Doña María Comadurán de Castillo y Reyes was a woman who would never change her mind.

He stroked her cheek softly and lifted her chin, brushing her lips with his own before drawing her to him and kissing her with a desperation he had not yet shared with her. She stood on her toes and wrapped her arms around his neck, returning his kiss with a startling, new passion. An unfamiliar sense of longing and desire rose inside her, and she imagined his naked body next to her own.

Shocked, she stepped away from his embrace, blushing and breathless. "No, I—?"

"Did I do something wrong?"

"No—yes—I mean, no—I mean—" Turning away, she covered her face with her hands.

"I'm sorry if I frightened you, Espe, but I love you so much." He put his hands on her shoulders. "I won't do that again."

She turned and looked into his eyes. "That's the problem." Embarrassed, she struggled to explain. "It's just—I mean—I want you to do that again. In your arms, sometimes I can't get close enough to you. But what if it leads to— something we'll regret, something that—?"

Again, he took both of her hands in his. "Esperanza Luisa de la Luz Ocoboa Herrero, I promise I will never take advantage of you, never shame or embarrass you." He hesitated. "I intend to ask your father for your hand."

Her eyes widened. "Now?"

"Not this very moment and not today, but I will."

"Oh." She pulled her shawl around her shoulders and watched a pair of vermillion flycatchers perform a series of aerial acrobatics, catching insects hovering above the still pools along the bank. "Of course. You must persuade your parents."

"No, I won't even try. They will not change their minds. And yes, I would be pleased if they approved, but no matter what they say or do, you will be my wife."

"Are you sure?"

"Look at the river, Espe." With one hand resting on her shoulder, Armando stood behind her. "The rocks may change the water's direction, but they do not stop it."

The shallow, summer flow sang a gentle melody as it bent the grasses in the channel and wrapped itself around and over rocks and stones to continue its journey northward. Opposite, a velvet ash hung over the water, its reflection shimmering in the afternoon light, its roots reaching into the muddy river bottom. Water bugs skated the surface of still pools along the bank. A deer stepped out of the brush and stopped, head lifted, motionless, watching. When Sofi snorted, he leaped noisily away.

She smiled and leaned against him. "I love it here, especially on hot days like today. Sometimes I come to listen to the river sing, to talk to the deer and the birds, but mostly to be alone and dream."

Armando gripped her shoulders and turned her to face him. "Promise me you won't come here alone again. The Apaches—"

"I'm not afraid." After her close encounter with the six Apaches, she wasn't being entirely honest, but she would not tell him. "Besides, either Tomás or Manolito is always nearby to protect me. They don't think I know, but they aren't good at sneaking around."

"Even so, you're taking a risk, and I don't want to lose you." A breeze lifted a loose strand of her dark hair. He tucked it behind her ear.

She grinned. "Maybe you should teach me to use a gun. I can protect myself and Tomas and Manolito won't have to follow me around."

Looking thoughtful, he said, "I just might."

"But why did you want me to look at the river. What were you getting at?"

"Do you know what happens north of here?"

"No."

"The river disappears."

"Don't be silly. A river can't disappear." She tried to decide if he was teasing. "Can it?"

"Well, not exactly. The river bed continues for a long way—but without any water."

"You're serious?"

"Yes, but it flows again a long way from here. I think there's an underground channel."

"How do you know?"

"Julio and I followed it almost to Tucson, where it turns west and bypasses the town. And we kept going until we found where it rose to the surface again."

She stared at him. "And you warn me about the Apaches? Didn't you think you and your brother were in danger?"

"Maybe, but the river and the mountains kept calling us to explore. We've even gone as far as L'Iglesia and beyond."

"Beyond L'Iglesia?" She couldn't imagine going that far away from home.

"The mountains are beautiful from the other side, and the land is perfect for building a ranch. I will live there someday."

It sounded like a beautiful dream, one she wanted to share. Even if it meant going so far away from her family and everything she had ever known, she was confident she could go with him. She smiled. "You mean we will live there someday."

"I'm not sure how or when, but, yes, we will live there."

Esperanza regarded the river, imagining the strength of its spirit flowing secretly below the ground. "These rocks and grasses may slow it, but they cannot defeat it."

"Like us, Espe. Our dreams will come true. No matter what happens, we will be together."

As they walked back along the path, listening to the cicadas droning again in celebration of summer's heat, she tried to imagine her life with Armando, but images of him leaving for Veracruz intruded.

Chapter 4

Summer 1864

Mother, I understand yesterday was a heathen holiday of some sort." Armando pushed his food around on the plate, unable to taste anything, thinking about Esperanza and his mother's plan when Reynaldo, with his familiar smirk, spoke.

Reynaldo and his wife, Concepción, sat across from him and Julio, while Doña María and Don Jesús sat at either end. His mother presided over the meal, giving orders not just to Ofelia, but also to her husband and her sons. If Julio failed to sit up straight, she chastised him; if Armando dawdled over his dinner, she ordered him to clean his plate. Her demands of the don rarely had an effect; she gave an order and, even though he silently ignored her, she was not dissuaded.

"I don't think so, *mi querido*." She patted his hand. "Yesterday was Armando's birthday." Because neither of his parents had mentioned it, he assumed they forgot.

Even so, he was more irritated to see his mother fawning over Reynaldo, who, unlike him and Julio, did very little work on the ranch. His recent effort to grow a mustache and goatee, both thin and wispy, was a pathetic attempt to imitate Don Jesús.

"Yes, but I understand there was a grand celebration in the heathen village with chanting, dancing, and even drunkenness." He smirked again. "Isn't that right, brother?"

Doña María scooped up frijoles with a tortilla and shoved it into her mouth. She pointed a finger at Armando and, with her mouth full, said, "You were there all night?"

"Yes, Mother." He glared at Reynaldo.

"Even though we disapprove?"

"I enjoy it, Mother. The Pápagos are good people."

Doña María wrinkled her nose.

Concepción glanced at Armando and said, "Isn't Ofelia a Pápago? Doesn't she come from there?" He narrowed his eyes, signaling she should go no further. Her smirk perfectly imitated her husband's.

Doña María lifted her cup to her lips and looked across it at the don. "Perhaps we need to look for a new cook."

Don Jesús grunted.

Damn you, Reynaldo. Damn you and your bitch of a wife. To his mother, he said, "If you don't want me to go to the village again, Mother, I won't."

The rest of the meal passed in an uncomfortable silence with Armando focusing only on the chipped edge of his plate. His mother insisted on using what she called the "good" china for dinner even though many pieces were cracked and missing pieces had been replaced with common ceramics.

As a family rule, no one left the table until Don Jesús put his fork down. Even then, they were to ask permission.

Finally, the don pointed at Armando. "You will join me in my office."

Veracruz. "Yes sir." He stood, nodded to his mother and said, "Excuse me," and waited for her to acknowledge him.

As always, she did not respond right away, but tonight she waited for a few extra beats, not hiding her displeasure. After a sufficient moment, she pursed her lips and lifted an eyebrow. "You may go."

Armando followed his father into the next room. Aside from an ornate desk, there were but two chairs, his father's heavy one, its leather seat worn and sunken with age, behind the desk and an ordinary wooden chair for anyone else. A large trunk, its front carved with conquistadores on horseback bearing the Spanish flag and its domed lid with a Spanish galleon sailing a high sea, stood against one wall. Above the fireplace, his father's elaborate clock ticked on the mantle. The broad base was inlaid with blue-green malachite, and, above the clock face was a detailed gilt carving of a conquistador and his adoring apprentice. His only frivolous possession, he had personally commissioned an artisan in *Ciudad Hermosillo* to make it twenty years ago. Other than the clock, this room was strictly for the business of the ranch and the family and little else.

"Close the door." Don Jesús went behind the desk, opened the humidor and drew out a cigar. Armando waited while his father slid it across his thick mustache, breathing in its fragrance. Apparently satisfied, he clipped the end, put it between his teeth, and walked to the fireplace. The match he struck on the rock frame, flared brightly, and a fragment detached and fell to the floor. As Don Jesús stepped on it, a sulfurous smell filled the room, and he inhaled several times, exhaling gray clouds of smoke with each breath, watching the cigar flare up and then glow red. Armando noted how closely his father's blunt fingers resembled the cigar. After tossing the match into the cold fireplace, the don examined the clock and used his handkerchief to polish the conquistador's helmet.

"Sit." He pointed to the chair.

Chewing the cigar, his father sat behind the desk and closed the ledger. He leaned back and blew out the smoke, filling the space between them. Still, he said nothing. In the silence, the only sound came from the clock.

Armando admired his father's sense of timing, the way he controlled a negotiation, gained the upper hand and disarmed his opponent with silence. Tonight, Don Jesús would find out whether his youngest son had learned any of his skills. He needed to make the case for choosing his own wife—for choosing his own life. And he would need to defend his disrespect of his mother. Never having defied his father before, tonight would be a first.

"What do you have to say for yourself?"

His father expected him to hang himself with an emotional outburst, but he remained calm. "Regarding?" He leveled his gaze at his father, unblinking. Don Jesús was a big man, broad across the shoulders, and round through the middle. His dark hair hung below his collar, and, for the first time, Armando noticed the gray around his ears. Even his mustache and beard were graying; his face, though, other than deep creases along his jowls, betrayed little about his age. The outer corners of his green eyes wore the crow's feet wrinkles Esperanza called laugh lines on her father. The don's, though, were squint lines. Don Jesús seldom laughed, but he squinted with concentration whether he was directing his ranch hands or doing the accounting.

"Among other things," his father replied, "your continuing disobedience. Your mother tells me you treated her with the utmost disrespect this morning."

"Yes, Father, I did. She insulted Esperanza, and I lost my temper."

"I see. We will discuss the Ocoboa girl in a moment. Do you expect your mother and me to stand aside while you squander your opportunities?"

"With all due respect, Father, what opportunities?"

In the silence before his father spoke, the clock ticked off the seconds. Don Jesús's mustache followed the corners of his mouth downward, and his thick eyebrows pushed together above his long aquiline nose. He waved his arm around the room, saying, "I have sacrificed much to make certain my sons want for nothing. I have invested in your future, granting you a secure income for the past ten years—which I would remind you increased handsomely as of yesterday."

Again, Armando was surprised at the reference to his birthday, but then he remembered that it was an accounting issue the don was unlikely to forget.

Don Jesús continued, "Your opportunities? What about your name? This ranch?"

Armando expected his father to make this argument. "This is my home, and I admire your success at building one of the finest ranches in the territory."

When his father did not reply, he went on. "But this ranch is not mine, nor will it ever be mine. Am I to live my life dependent on my brother?" He wanted to point out that his brother hated him, but that was a conversation for another time. Or maybe never. "Can I not make decisions for myself, make my own way in life?"

"Of course, I expect my sons to make their way in life, but I also expect them to uphold the Ramirez traditions. You and your brothers hold the family honor in your hands. Any one of you who brings us dishonor will pay a high price." He drew on the cigar, blew a thick cloud of smoke, and tapped ashes into the ashtray. "The selection of a proper wife is important, which is why we've arranged your marriage to Vicente's daughter. He is desperate to get her out of Veracuz and the mess Juarez has created. She will bring a considerable dowry, one which I will supplement so you can build a ranch of your own."

"Mother told me. My future, then, is a business proposition in which Vicente offers a small fortune to whoever takes his daughter off his hands."

Don Jesús slammed his fist on the desk, leaned forward, and roared. "You will not speak to me with such disrespect. Vicente is an honorable man who wants to protect María Dolores."

Armando hung his head. "I apologize."

"You were disrespectful to your mother and now to me. I will not tolerate such behavior. Give me one reason not to send you to Veracruz tomorrow morning."

"Esperanza." He spoke quietly without meeting his father's glare.

Don Jesús blew out a smoke-filled, exasperated breath and crushed his cigar in the ashtray. "Of course. You continue to see her in spite of our opposition."

"I mean to marry her."

"Marry her? Marry an Indian?" The don rose from his chair and leaned across the desk, his face contorted, and his hands clenched. "No one in this family has ever despoiled our Spanish blood." Armando chose not to repeat what he had said to his mother, to tell his father he believed most locals who claimed Spanish descent, his family included, were actually of mixed blood. "Do you think you will be the first and your mother and I will stand by and do nothing?"

"There is no disgrace in marrying the woman I love." Because he did not want to further anger his father, Armando kept his voice low.

Still standing, Don Jesús started to speak but held his tongue. He twisted his mustache, curling one end up. "Look, son. You seem to believe this is a business transaction, so let's talk in those terms. You have options."

"Which are?"

"Go to Veracruz. Marry this María Dolores, and bring her, along with her dowry, back here. I'll get you started with a place of your own—even give you part of my herd."

Armando started to answer, but his father held up his hand. "Hear me out, son. We can satisfy our expectations for you and help Vicente protect his daughter."

Whatever his father said, he would never agree to go to Veracruz and marry anyone.

"It's simple. Once you get your ranch going, you can hire this Esperanza as a servant, and she can spread her legs for you whenever you want."

This time, it was Armando who stood, his chair crashing to the floor behind him. He was thankful the desk was between them because of the protection it afforded his father. Had it not been there, he would have hit him. Now, he leaned across the desk, just as his father had, looking into his pale eyes. "I will not tolerate either you or my mother speaking of her that way. She is not a whore. I will not go to Veracruz, and I will not marry anyone but Esperanza. Her family is both respected and respectable in the territory, and they are no one's servants." Before continuing, he took a measured breath. "If you and my mother approved, I would be grateful, but I will not change my plans. I do not need to be known as the son of Don Jesús María Ramirez Gonzáles de Ávila and Doña María Comadurán de Castillo y Reyes. I am Armando Ramirez. That's all I need."

The don stared open-mouthed as his son turned to leave the room. At the door, he stopped and said, "I will renounce you and my name before I dishonor her." He slammed the door behind him.

Outside the office, he passed a smirking Reynaldo, who had no doubt been listening at the door. "Say one word, and I'll knock your teeth down your throat. I might not hit my father, but I have no qualms about bloodying your face."

In the barn, while Sofi browsed the hay in her feeder, Armando ignored the heat, the dust, and the flies; he sat on the floor of the stall, his knees up, his arms folded across them, trying to decide what to do. He closed his eyes, picturing them living in a fine house beneath the massive ridge of La Cresta, an enormous boundary of stone and granite protecting them from his parents' interference.

He stared at the ceiling, resting his head against the wall, half-expecting to find the answer hovering just out of reach. A future without Esperanza was unimaginable. How could he ask her father for her hand if he turned his back on his family? How could he ask her to marry him without assuring her parents he could take care of her and give her a home? How far would the money he had saved go? It might be years before he could offer her the kind of future she deserved.

Chapter 5

Summer 1864

Are you all right, Mando?" He didn't hear his brother come in.

"No, but I will be as soon as I leave."

Squatting beside him, Julio asked, "Where will you go?"

He shrugged. "I won't stay here. Since I cannot do what they tell me I must do, I have no choice. I'll find a job in Tucson or hire on as a vaquero somewhere."

"And then what?" Julio rose and reached a hand to his brother.

Armando took it and stood next to the big man his brother had become. Julio had passed Reynaldo in height and girth several years back. From the age of ten, he had ridden with the vaqueros and helped the ranch hands, sharing their work equally. Armando had joined them when he was ten, coming close, but never matching Julio's strength.

He laughed bitterly. "I wish I knew. How can I think about getting married when I have no prospects?" Leaning against Sofi's midsection, he ran his fingers through her mane.

"Whatever you need me to do, I will do." Julio always kept his word, even as a child. He never made a promise he didn't keep.

Armando choked back tears of gratitude. "You're my best friend. You defended me when Reynaldo attacked and taunted me. Every time you got punished for fighting with him, I cried, too. For as long as I can remember, he's hated me, and I don't know why."

"You don't know?"

"What? Do you?"

Julio chuckled. "Your eyes."

Armando frowned. "My eyes? What's wrong with my eyes? Why would he hate—?"

"They're green, like our father's. Reynaldo's are brown, like mine and our mother's. All he got from our father was that long, hooked nose." He laughed. "Fortunately, you and I got our mother's nose."

Armando was too stunned to laugh. "He's jealous of my eyes?"

"Of course. As the eldest, the favored son, he's the one who will inherit everything, and carry forth the Ramirez Spanish banner, so to speak. Even now, he's pretending to be the don. When she thinks no one's around, Concepción calls him, 'Don Reynaldo Enrique Ramirez Comadurán.' But you're the one with perfect Spanish eyes. The undeniable mark of the *gente de razón*, and he hates it."

"And he hates me." Sofi stamped her foot and turned her head. Putting her nose to Armando's chest, she pushed, knocking him off balance and into the wall. He righted himself and laughed.

Julio laughed with him. "I think she's telling you to get over yourself."

Armando massaged Sofi's back, running his fingers along her topline, triggering a shiver. "Does that feel good, mi amiga?" He turned to his brother. "Julio, you're in the same situation. What will you do?"

"They approve of Adelita, and her family approves of me. We've talked about living in Tucson and running cattle along the Santa Cruz where the water comes back to the surface."

"I'd like that, but not along the Santa Cruz."

"North of L'Iglesia?"

"Remember how angry Father was last year when we went up there and stayed two weeks looking for lost treasure?"

They had youthful dreams of being the first to find the treasure from the legendary *Lost Mission of Cirú*. Although they found nothing of the sort, they found what Armando suspected were the remains of *Pueblo Viejo*, an ancient village rather than a mission.

"A fool's errand," Julio said.

"Not at all. Remember those stone walls we found and the old building foundations? I want to use those stones to build a home for Esperanza."

Even though it might be close to Apache territory, he had studied the land and the mountains and sought the connection he learned from the Pápagos. Standing beside those walls, he believed *La Cresta*, the massive ridge, called him to linger beneath its magnificent rock towers and in the embrace of L'Iglesia. A large house, *La Casa de Ramirez* had taken shape in his mind. He imagined gardens, a barn, a corral for many horses, and a herd of cattle foraging on the bajada, with Esperanza and their children living happily in the shadow of the mountains. "I would go there to live today if I could."

Suddenly, he brightened and slapped his thigh. "Julio! I've got it!" His outburst startled Sofi. "Sorry, *mi niña.*" He ran his hand along her back and grinned.

"What?"

"The Homestead Act. I won't need to buy land, and my savings should carry us through the five years we need." His eyes glowed with excitement—as if the ranch were already a reality. "What do you think?"

"You're loco. That's what I think. Look how far out it is—even from Tucson—you'll be isolated with only the Apaches for company. Take your time and think about it. Do you want to take Esperanza up there where the Apaches could attack any time? Besides, are they even taking applications here?"

"I'm not sure. The law passed more than a year ago, so my guess is they are—or they should be. The last time the priest brought the newspaper from Tucson, it said the land office would open soon."

"Slow down, Mando. You wouldn't mind living there, but would Esperanza want to be so far from her family? And what about the Apaches?"

But Armando wasn't listening. He turned to Sofi, running his fingers through her mane. "We're getting out of here, mi niña. We're going to build our ranch."

Gripping his brother's shoulder, Julio warned him, "Ask Esperanza about this first. Don't make any decisions until you talk to her. If she agrees, I'll help you."

During the night, Armando slipped into the kitchen and packed tortillas, jerky, and carrots in his saddlebags and filled two canteens with water from the *olla.* He watered and saddled Sofi, put his rifle into the scabbard, and was on the road to Tucson while the full moon was high. Even leaving this early, it would be dark before he got to Tucson. All told, he would be gone at least three days. If his parents asked where he was, Julio would tell the truth: he went to Tucson to search for opportunities. They would be furious, but they would not doubt his determination.

Riding through the moonlit desert, hearing only the scrape-clop of Sofi's hooves and an occasional owl's call, he kept his eyes on L'Iglesia, waiting on the northern horizon, dark against the pale night sky. The details of the Pápago's creation legend came to him. Elder Brother, *I'itoi*, created the Earth and the creatures and the plants and then the people to live here. For the Pápago, the Earth was a sacred gift, providing everything they need, as well as the gift of "crimson evenings," spectacular desert sunsets to remind them where they came from.

He struggled to see the land through their eyes, to see the ways the Earth cares for all living things, like how a palo verde protects young saguaros so they can grow tall and foretell the coming of the rain. He wanted to understand the natural world in all its complexity and beauty like the Pápagos, but, somehow, it only came to him in bits and pieces. On the other hand, he believed the spirit of L'Iglesia called him, and he would answer that call.

Chapter 6

Summer 1864

The dirt streets and wood-planked sidewalks of Tucson were more lively than he recalled, crowded mostly with Anglos—more than he'd ever seen in Tucson. Many came because of the gold recently discovered in the territory. He wasn't interested in gold. Even though he and Julio had searched for lost treasure, such a quest was no longer his goal. Nor was he concerned about the Apaches. They wouldn't care about a small ranch along the back range.

At the sheriff's office, he asked where to find the territorial land office. The deputy directed him a few doors down the street. Inside, boxes and rolled-up maps were scattered everywhere. A bearded gentleman wearing spectacles on his bald head held a large map of the Arizona Territory against the wall while a younger man stood on a chair and pounded tacks into a corner.

The older man peeked over his shoulder. "Be with you in a minute, sir."

A year earlier, Armando had read about the Homestead Act in the newspaper. Even though it had been law for some time, getting land offices organized was a slow process and, while the states had their offices in place the moment the law went into effect, the territories lagged behind. For him, the timing couldn't be more perfect.

Several maps lay open on the counter, and Armando browsed them, uncovering a map of the area between Tucson and the new border with Mexico. It had been ten years since the Gadsden Purchase made the area part of the United States and a year since the Arizona Territory was carved from the New Mexico Territory. His parents refused to accept the fact that Mexico no longer governed them, having only grudgingly accepted Mexico's independence from Spain. Against all reason, they continued to hope the Crown would once again assert its rule. Even though they insisted they were Spanish, he always saw himself as Mexican. Now, if he understood correctly, he was a citizen of the United States; his parents and others in their generation could cling to their so-called heritage, but he would have no problem renouncing Mexican citizenship.

Unlike his father's map, marking the Ramirez and neighboring land grants, this one included more detail. He found Tubac, Arivaca, Tumacácori, and Guevavi, along with several of the oldest Spanish land grants, even though many were no longer in the possession of their original owners. After locating his father's grant, he compared its rather modest size to some of the others. Drawing his finger across the map to the small curve in the Santa Cruz River where Esperanza lived, he wondered what she would say when he told her.

"Dang it! Henry, hurry up. My arms are getting tired."

"I'm trying sir, but they bend. They won't go into the damned bricks."

"Watch your language," the older man muttered, "we have a customer. And get off the chair. If tacks don't work, we'll have to try nails." When Henry let go of his corner, the map dropped and wrapped around the older man's head.

While Henry extracted his boss from the map, Armando chuckled.

Once he was free, the man straightened the spectacles on his head and held out his hand. "Welcome to the Office of the Surveyor General. I'm John Wasson, and this here is Henry DeHart, my clerk. Sorry for the mess." He gestured to the boxes and rolled up maps. "We're gettin' organized, but I'll tell ya, it's a durn sight quieter here than it was in Nebraska, and hotter, too. This cussed heat is gettin' to me."

Armando shook both men's hands. "Thank you, Mr. Wasson. My name is Armando Ramirez. I'm here to apply for a homestead."

"At the moment, son, your options are limited because of the Apaches. Do you have a location in mind?" Wasson unrolled a map showing Tucson and its environs, anchoring the curled edges under boxes on the counter. After taking the spectacles off his head, he settled them on his nose and wrapped the earpieces around his ears.

"Yes sir." Armando examined the map and pointed to an area north of *La Sierra de la Catarina*, which, on this map, was labeled Santa Catalina Mountains, in English. "Right along here."

Wasson's eyes widened, and his thick, gray eyebrows lifted in surprise. He stared at Armando over his spectacles. "Are you certain? I ain't been here long, but long enough to know that's a far piece from town and unless someone gets rid of the Apaches, you'll be a first-class target." He laid his hand on a stretch of open land between Tucson and the mountains on the north. "How about in this area? The land's available, and you'll be close enough for protection and support."

"I'm certain." He tapped his finger on the map.

Henry Waters peered over his boss's shoulder, shook his head, and went back to unpacking boxes.

"Just 'cause I think you're a durn fool, I've no reason to deny you." While Wasson sorted through piles of papers on the desk, Armando examined the map contours and the path of the wash to locate the small ridge where Pueblo Viejo had stood.

"Henry, hand me the ruler and the scale template." When he had his instruments, he said, "Let's pinpoint it exactly." He slid his glasses down his nose and examined the map. "Section thirty-three." He used the ruler to mark the section boundaries. "We need to identify the one-hundred and sixty acres you want."

With his finger, Armando tracked the road from Tucson, around the point of the mountains and followed it along the base of La Cresta to where both the road and the wash swung northward. His ridge was above a second wash, which came from the east and joined the first where it turned. He pointed to the map contours he was confident represented his future home. "Here." He was so nervous, his heart pounded in his ears.

Wasson, using the ruler and the scale to mark off part of the section along its southern boundary, murmured, "The south half of the southwest quarter and the northwest quarter of the southwest quarter..."

Armando couldn't follow what Wasson was saying, but he thought the boundaries the older man drew appeared correct.

"...in township twelve south in range fourteen...in Arizona..." When he finished drawing the boundaries, Wasson said, "There it is, son. Does it look right to you?"

Armando examined it, pleased it included part of the floodplain below the ridge. He would dig the well down there. Swallowing hard, he nodded.

"And you won't change your mind and apply for something a little closer to town?"

"No." In his mind, he was already building the house.

The older man shook his head and wrote "A. Ramirez, 27 June 1864" inside the lines on the map, saying, "Improvements to the land are required, including a minimum twelve-foot by fourteen-foot dwelling, and you must occupy it for five years before you can claim ownership. You're required to make the land productive, too. In Nebraska, homesteaders grow crops, but the government recognizes the land in Arizona is not always suitable for farming. What is your plan?"

"Does raising cattle qualify?"

"Yes."

"Am I allowed to run cattle on land adjoining the claim if I need to? It takes a lot of desert to provide good forage for livestock."

"For now, you can. Since the land is public, you'll be free to use it as long as no one else claims it for a homestead."

Wasson handed him a blank sheet of paper. "Your application."

Even as Armando tried to take the paper, Mr. Wasson did not release it into his hand. "You won't reconsider?"

"No, sir." The older man shrugged and relinquished the paper, but Armando didn't know what he was supposed to do with it.

"Somewhere in these boxes are printed forms. Would you like to come back after we've unpacked them?" Wasson smiled.

Armando shook his head.

"Can't blame me for tryin'. Don't worry, Mr. Ramirez. I'll tell you what to write, and it'll be perfectly legal." He pushed an inkwell across the counter and gave him a pen. "In the corner, write "Application number 1."

"I'm the first?"

"Yep. The first for this office."

Armando wrote as the older man dictated.

> *Application No. 1 Homestead Land Office*
> *Tucson, Arizona Territory*
> *27 June 1864*
> *I, Armando Esteban Ramirez Comadurán, of Pima County, Arizona Territory, do hereby apply to enter under the provisions of the act of Congress approved May 20th, 1862 entitled, an Act to Secure Homesteads to actual Settlers on the Public Domain....*

Wasson dictated the complicated, physical description of the tract along with the details needed to finalize the petition for the homestead. Armando's hand shook, and he splattered small dots of ink on the page. When the older man asked him to affix his signature beneath his declaration, he exhaled a long breath, relieved to have done it.

While Henry copied the physical description of the property for Armando, the registrar took Armando's declaration and wrote his authorization on it.

> *Land Office at:*
> *Tucson, Arizona Territory*
> *27 June 1864*
> *I, John Wasson, Surveyor General for the Arizona Territory in the United States*

*of America, do hereby certify that the above
application is for land of the Class which the
applicant is legally Entitled to enter under
the Homestead Act of May 20th, 1862...*

Before he left with his paperwork, Armando nodded toward the wall where they tried to hang the map. "You need long, skinny nails, and you should pound them between the bricks. You don't want to break those adobes." After shaking hands with both men, he stepped outside and took a deep breath of the Tucson air, which somehow seemed different, fresher, more alive with hope.

He went to the mercantile and bought Esperanza's wedding presents.

Chapter 7

Summer 1864

Esperanza's mother greeted him with a smile. "Buenas días, Señor Ramirez. Won't you come in?" Her soft, breathy voice reminded him of singing. An attractive woman, she wore her age well. Although her hair was still black, a wide streak of silver swept from her hairline into a thick braid in the back. Her husband said she was still as beautiful as the day he met her.

"Gracias, Señora Ocoboa." Armando appreciated that Esperanza's family ignored Spanish naming customs. Her mother was, in fact, Altagracia María Nuñez Herrero, but she was content to be known as Manuel Ocoboa's wife. "Por favor, may I speak with Esperanza?"

"I'll tell her you're here."

As he approached the Ocoboa home, he'd noted again how different it was from his parents' house; where Casa Ramirez was big and rambling, with rooms added randomly over the course of many years, Casa Ocoboa was more compact. The yard was a profusion of flowers and vines, all blooming at different times of the year, greeting visitors with a colorful welcome. Esperanza tended the flowers and took care of the large vegetable garden behind the house. No color welcomed visitors to Casa Ramirez; even the jasmine was white.

Esperanza came in from the kitchen, hot and flushed, wiping her hands on her apron. She tucked loose strands of her dark hair behind her ears while damp wisps clung to her neck. A streak of flour, pale against her cheek, highlighted the honeyed tone of her complexion.

Because she did not work at it, he suspected she was not aware of her beauty. Long dark hair framed her face with delicate curls that refused to stay pinned back. High cheekbones, a straight, but delicate, nose, full lips, and soft brown eyes would no doubt command the attention of any young men she might encounter. He whispered his thanks that she had chosen him. At seventeen years old, she wasn't obsessed with her looks like other young women, and he had never seen any sign of vanity in her behavior or her attitude. Whether she was dressed for church, working in the garden, or riding Pepe scandalously astride, she always seemed comfortable.

Even so, this morning she seemed perplexed. "I didn't know you were coming." She swept her hands down her soiled apron. "Lupe and the children are here, and we're teaching the girls how to make *empanadas*. I can change if you want."

"No. Don't." He brushed the flour from her cheek. "May we talk outside?"

After hanging her apron by the door, they went out and stood in the shade of a large mesquite. A light breeze stirred the branches, rattling the beans she would soon collect for mesquite flour. Dappled sunlight played across her face and danced in her eyes. This year's resident Gila woodpecker flew back and forth from the tree to her nest in a tall saguaro cactus collecting insects to feed her brood.

"I need to ask you something." He was suddenly nervous about asking her to marry him and to go far away.

"Yes?"

"Esperanza Luisa de la Luz Ocoboa Herrero, I want you to be my wife, and I don't want to wait any longer."

Without a pause, she looked up into his eyes, and, using his full name as he had hers, she replied, "Armando Estaban Ramirez Comadurán, I want more than anything to be your wife."

"Are you sure, Espe? I need to tell you something that might change your mind."

"Why? Don't you believe I love you?"

"Yes, but hear me out and then decide."

Her dark eyebrows drew together, but he pressed gentle fingers against them, smoothing the wrinkles from her forehead, erasing the frown.

"I went to Tucson and applied for a homestead."

The frown returned. "What does that mean?"

"It means the land north of L'Iglesia is ours, and we can start building our home right away."

Wide-eyed, she stepped back. "Right away—now?"

"Yes. Now. My parents can't oppose our marriage any longer because I'm no longer dependent on them. I'm a landowner."

"A landowner?"

"Well, not officially. Not yet. It'll be five years before I own it outright, but in the meantime I'll build our house, and we'll live there and raise cattle. I'll have my own ranch." When he stopped to take a breath, he saw doubt rather than excitement in her eyes. "Don't you understand, Espe? Our dream is about to come true."

Esperanza was speechless. *Now*? Somehow, she had seen his dream of a ranch north of L'Iglesia in the distant future. It never occurred to her it would be so immediate—before they were married. Before he had even spoken to her father. What would her father say if he knew Armando would take her so far from home? How could she live so far from her family?

When Armando lifted her chin, and their eyes met, she saw his fear. His voice was soft. "Espe?"

"Please don't doubt me, Armando. I love you, and I want to be your wife. It's just—"

"Tell me."

She knew what he wanted her to say, but she needed to think. She focused on the woodpecker's swooping flight from the cactus to the tree and back again. Her wings fluttered a few beats before she extended them and sailed up, then she dipped low again with her wings working, then stretching them out, gliding up, all the while calling "ki-ki-ki." What invisible obstacles did she dodge so gracefully? *How can I answer?* Could she overcome whatever challenges lay ahead as effortlessly as the woodpecker?

He gently turned her head back to him. "Tell me."

"It's so sudden."

Armando's stricken expression frightened her. He spun around and slapped the thick, mesquite trunk with his hat. "*Soy un idiota.* I should have talked to you first, but I never imagined you would not agree." His head down, shoulders slumped, he leaned against a low, horizontal limb.

To his back, she said, "I didn't say I don't agree. You took me by surprise."

He ran his fingers through his hair, but he did not turn to face her. "So what do you want?" His voice was low, and the tone was flat.

"First, I'll tell you what I don't want. I don't want you to turn your back on me." Her annoyance faded, her voice quieted, and she laid her hand on his back. "What I want is for us to talk about this. I want to understand what it will be like living up there, what you expect me to do as your wife there. Do you think I can so easily agree—" She choked back tears. "To upending my entire world without knowing anything about that place and how we will live?" In spite of her effort to control them, her tears fell.

He turned and took her into his arms. "I'm sorry, Espe." He stood a full head taller than she, with broad, muscular shoulders narrowing to a slim waist. His physical strength was the product of his willingness to do the physical labor of ranching. Resting his chin on her head, he stroked her hair.

Her ear against his chest, she listened to his heartbeat, willing her own to draw on his strength for the courage she needed to stand with him. "Tell me," she said.

Still holding her, he promised not to take her there until he had dug the well and built the house and a shelter for the horses. "Your home will be small at first. Your kitchen won't be like your mother's—at least not right away—but I will do everything I can to make you comfortable there."

Looking into his green eyes, trying to see his vision of their home, she asked, "How will I cook?"

"In the fireplace."

"What will we eat?"

"Whatever we can grow in the garden, and I'll go to Tucson for supplies and groceries. And Julio will bring us what we need."

"What will I do when you go to Tucson? Will I go with you?"

He hesitated. "I wish you could, of course, but someone must protect the homestead while I am gone."

"Me?" Her dark brows lifted and she leaned away from him, wide-eyed. "What if the Apaches come?"

"Espe, you're a strong woman. You ride a horse better than I do. I'll teach you to shoot. You will never let the Apaches take anything from our home."

Still wide-eyed, she stepped away, trying to find the words she needed. "Are you serious? I will go to battle against the Apaches?" She remembered in vivid detail the moment she had gripped her knife in the scrub and how terrified she was.

"I'm betting you will be better than me with a gun."

Even though it was a fearful thought, she almost grinned.

"Wait here." He walked to Sofi and pulled the rifle from the scabbard and brought it to her. "A wedding present."

She hesitated before taking it, holding it as he had done. "You're giving me your rifle?"

"No. This is your rifle."

"Mine?" Never having handled a rifle, the weight of it pressed on her heart. Even if she learned to shoot, could she kill someone, even an Apache? She remembered the one at the river who chose not to kidnap or kill her.

"It's just like mine. It holds sixteen cartridges, and I'll teach you to shoot."

Holding the rifle made everything real—Armando had her next five years fully planned.

While he carried the rifle back to the scabbard, dozens of questions flew into her head. She needed a better understanding of what the future held for them.

He came back and took her hand. "What do you think, Espe?" His smile melted her resistance, and she forgot her questions.

She laid one hand on his heart and the other on her own. "*Siempre estoy contigo*. I will always be by your side."

"It will not be easy. Are you sure?"

"*Estoy seguro*."

He pulled her into his arms and swung her around in a circle, laughing.

She laughed along with him. "*Será nuestra aventura*."

When he put her down, she stopped laughing. Her brows knit again into a frown. "What if my father says no?"

"Why would he say no? I think he likes me."

"He does, but he is aware your parents dislike me." She hesitated. "I didn't tell you, but Teodoro Ramos spoke to him on behalf of his son, Rosario."

"Rosario? What did your father say?"

"He told him he thought it would be a good match." She looked down. "Even though he knows I'm in love with you, he made the case for Rosario saying your parents will never treat me with respect, and I will be unhappy... Rosario is a nice boy." She glanced at the woodpecker again, praying for the same determination.

"Maybe. But he can't have you. I will be your husband. I will speak to your father today." He started toward the house.

Esperanza laid her hand on his arm. "Don't tell him about the homestead or that we will live so far away. He will surely say no."

"You want me to lie to him?"

"No—yes—I don't know. He will disapprove. I couldn't bear it if he said no." Tears welled again, glittering in her lashes. "He will forgive us, I think.

As they walked inside, she clung to his hand. Her sister was in the front room sewing, and the children were playing on the floor.

Luis glanced up from his toys, but the girls jumped to their feet and flung their arms around Esperanza. "*Tia Espe*, we finished the empanadas without you," Francesca said. "Mamá let me seal them with a fork."

Lupita held up one finger. "And I poked the fork into each one, but only one time."

Esperanza laughed and hugged both of her nieces. "I can smell them baking. Mmmm.... *muy delicioso*."

Lupe laid her sewing aside, smiled at her daughters and her sister, and nodded to Armando.

"Buenas días, Guadalupe," Armando said. "*Como está?*"

"*Bien*, Armando, *bien*. What's going on, Esperanza? You look nervous."

"Armando is going to speak to Papá. Is he here?"

Lupe stood and hugged her sister. She pointed toward her father's office. "I will ask him."

Tapping lightly on the heavy door, she pushed it open just enough to slip inside. In a few moments, she came out. "He will speak to you." To Esperanza, she said, "Let's go to the kitchen and check on the empanadas."

Armando watched them walk away, the girls trailing behind. He was nervous when he applied for the homestead, but this was worse. He knocked on Señor Ocoboa's office door.

"*Venga.*" Manuel Ocoboa's deep voice sounded loud, even through the heavily carved door.

Armando, with his sombrero in his hand, stepped inside. "Buenas días, señor."

The older man stood and greeted Armando with a firm handshake. "Good to see you." He gestured toward a chair. "Por favor."

While Señor Ocoboa went behind the desk to his own chair, Armando took a seat in front of it. For a moment, the scene in his father's office came back to him. He hoped this meeting would be more agreeable.

"What can I do for you?" Esperanza's father was a slender man, beardless with only the slightest hint of a mustache. Armando compared his graceful fingers to his father's thick, stubby ones as he closed his account book and slid it aside, leaning forward and smiling. *Very different from my father*. Like Don Jesús, he had held on to his ranch in spite of Apache depredations and the siege of Tubac, which had only been a few years before. They had fled briefly, taking his elderly mother-in-law with them, but they returned and re-established their home.

"Thank you, Señor Ocoboa. I appreciate the opportunity to speak with you."

"Of course." He waited, a slight smile on his face.

Like my father, he uses silence to his advantage.

Armando cleared his throat, then cleared it again. Finally, he managed to say, "Thank you for allowing me to call on Esperanza. If I may, I'd like to talk with you about her future..."

Chapter 8

Do you know how to find the Ocoboa Ranch?"
Felipe stood before Doña María, holding his hat. "Si, Señora. They live near the old presidio walls at Tubac."

Doña María stared at him and sighed. These useless Mexicans her husband employed were tiring, but finding decent help was next to impossible. "I don't care where it is. I asked if you knew how to find it."

"I do."

"Good. You will take me there. Now."

"Sí, Señora."

Don Jesús had gone with three of his vaqueros to investigate missing cattle. They had been driven off, probably by Apaches, but he hadn't ruled out locals who intended for the Apaches to get the blame. His absence would give her time to implement her plan.

When Felipe brought the carriage to the gate, Doña María, dressed in a black silk dress far too tight around her broad middle, was waiting in the entry fanning herself with a handkerchief. Glaring at him, she demanded, "What took you so long?"

When he started to answer, she cut him off. "No excuses are worth my time."

"Lo siento, Señora." He opened the carriage door and offered his hand. She pursed her lips and wrinkled her nose. Why the don didn't do something about this carriage she didn't know. It had belonged to his grandfather, and the window-glass had fallen out years ago. The once-luxurious leather seats were faded and torn. It was hardly appropriate transportation for a family of their stature.

The doña covered the servant's hand with her handkerchief and allowed him to assist her. Settling into the seat, she laid the soiled handkerchief aside and drew another out of her sleeve. If her plan worked, Don Jesús would forgive her for what she had done.

As the carriage bumped along the Santa Cruz Road, she fingered the heavy bag on her lap, smiling at the dull clinking of the coins inside. Because the dust was unbearable, she pulled the curtain over the window, but she soon raised it again when the heat became insufferable. By the time they arrived at the Ocoboa ranch, her foul mood had reached epic proportions. Not even the music of the coins and her certainty they would soon be rid of the Ocoboa girl cheered her.

The girl was trimming jasmine by the house. Doña María had time to inspect her as Felipe brought the carriage to a halt. She was attractive enough if you liked that sort. Standing in the shade intensified her dark complexion, reminding the doña of the terrible possibility of Ramirez grandchildren that color. *Unthinkable.*

Felipe opened the door and offered assistance. Again, she placed the handkerchief on his hand as she climbed out. Pushing it into her sleeve, she dismissed him with a curt wave.

When the girl wiped her hands on her apron and stood straight, the doña grudgingly conceded she knew how to behave when meeting her betters, but when she smiled and bade her good morning, Doña María frowned. The ninny didn't know enough to be silent until invited to speak.

The older woman closed the distance between them without a word. Dust covered her hair and darkened the streaks of perspiration dripping from the creases in her face. Her dress strained at the seams, and the dust clinging to the dampness under her arms had turned to mud.

Without preamble, Doña María said, "You are to stay away from my son."

Speaking softly, Esperanza replied, "Lo siento, Señora, unless Armando tells me the same, I can't promise."

"You dare to defy me?" Leaning closer, she expected the girl to step back, but, instead, Esperanza met her gaze evenly.

"I do not mean to be disrespectful, but I will consider this after I talk to him."

She lifted her chin and looked down her nose at the girl. "Well, since he leaves for Veracruz tomorrow, you won't have the opportunity."

When the girl caught her breath, the doña assumed victory, but, after a brief moment, Esperanza said, "He told me he would not go."

"He lied. The boy simply can't tell the truth. In fact, he's happy about the marriage we've arranged and delighted he can escape from you." The doña smiled triumphantly and waited for the girl to wilt.

Instead, Esperanza lifted her chin and countered, "If that's true, why are you here? Why would you ask me to stay away from a man who will be miles away tomorrow?"

The doña sputtered. "Well ... of course, his departure is not quite settled, but he will go soon. In the meantime, you are not to see him."

"What shall I do when he comes here?"

Could this child be so stupid? "Why, you must turn him away. Tell your parents to send him home."

Esperanza softened her voice. "I am in love with Armando, and if my father approves, I will marry him.

"What do you mean, 'if your father approves'?"

"Armando has spoken with him."

Momentarily, it was the doña who wilted, but she threw her shoulders back, clenched her fists, and stomped her foot. "That's unacceptable."

The door to the house opened, and Altagracia Ocoboa came out and stood on the stoop.

Doña María glanced at her but edged closer to Esperanza, angling so her back was to the girl's mother. Leaning closer once again, she opened the bag on her wrist and drew out a silver coin, holding it up for the girl to see. "There are sixteen eight-reales coins in this bag. They are yours if you do as I ask."

The coin glinted in the sunlight, and the doña enjoyed the expression of shock she read on the girl's face. No doubt, this was more money than she had ever seen. Victory was within her grasp. The don would be furious, but he would celebrate her success.

"I'm sorry, Señora. The answer is still no."

Speechless, Doña María stood staring, open-mouthed, at the girl's back as she joined her mother on the stoop. She rushed to the carriage, grabbing Felipe's outstretched hand as he helped her inside. She fell against the seat and closed her eyes.

"We must do something." Doña María paced back and forth in Don Jesús's office, wringing her hands while her husband sat silent and stoic at his desk. Apparently, he did not understand the gravity of the situation. "He has already spoken to Manuel Ocoboa about marrying that... that girl."

Deep furrows wrinkled his brow, hooding his pale eyes. "When?"

She shrugged.

"How do you know he spoke to him? Did Armando tell you?"

"Time is not on our side. You must speak with Señor Ocoboa immediately. Tell him he must send our son away when he goes there—to forbid him to come back."

"Don't change the subject. How do you know he spoke to her father?"

Collapsing in the chair before his desk, she did not meet his eyes. Instead, she studied the conquistadores on the trunk against the opposite wall. "The girl told me." Because she didn't get back in time to return the coins to the trunk, she might have to admit what she had done.

When Don Jesús did not reply, she looked up hopefully. He drew a cigar from the humidor and slid it beneath his nose.

Doña María frowned, and when he went to the fireplace and struck a match, she was stunned. "Do you dare smoke in my presence?"

"You are in my office." He blew smoke into the space between them. "I do what I please here."

She fanned the air with her hand. "It's a disgusting habit." Pulling a handkerchief from her sleeve, she covered her nose and glared at him.

Exhaling again in her direction, he shrugged. "When did you speak to the girl?"

Fanning the air again, she slumped her shoulders. "This morning. Felipe drove me. I was confident I could dissuade her."

"I assume you failed."

"The ill-mannered child did not hesitate to say no to every demand. The girl has no breeding."

"Did you think you're so intimidating she would cave in to your demands?" He inhaled a long drag from the cigar and blew smoke in her direction.

She swept both the question and the smoke away with her handkerchief. "Must you be a lout and smoke that awful thing?" She dabbed her watery eyes. "Will you not make him go to Veracruz?"

"How many times can you avoid my questions? The Ocoboas may not be of our class, but they are, as Armando pointed out so forcefully to me, no one's servants. What made you think you could persuade her?"

Involuntarily, she glanced at the trunk. He narrowed his eyes. "What did you do?"

"Nothing! I—"

Don Jesús laid the cigar in the ashtray, went to the trunk, and examined the lock. He slipped a key from his vest pocket and unlocked it.

The cigar smoke curling around her head made Doña María's eyes water. She dabbed them but focused on the wooden box he lifted out of the trunk and carried to the desk. Would he notice how many were missing? If he didn't, she would return them later, and he would never know. Pressing the handkerchief against her nose, she stared at the floor.

The box was old and scarred from handling by generation after generation of the Ramirez family. No one knew its age or which Ramirez first used it to hold

Nicolás Ramirez's treasure. The don opened the box and ran his fingers through the rough-cut, silver coins. The dull clinking echoed in her ears. "How many?"

His voice was so quiet, she wasn't sure she heard.

"Answer me, woman. How many?"

"Sixteen." She held her breath.

"Sixteen?" His green eyes blazed. "Are you mad?"

Now, she struck back. "Yes, I broke into your precious treasure. What have you done to stop this cursed marriage? Someone needed to do something."

"Make no excuses, woman. You stole from me, putting our wealth at risk. How did you get into the trunk?

As a wave of pride washed over her, she lifted her chin and looked him in the eye. "A hairpin. I used a hairpin."

"A hairpin?" He stared at the lock on the trunk and then back at her. "You opened the lock with a hairpin?"

Pleased that she had made a fool of him, she squared her shoulders and smiled proudly.

Even though she had never seen such rage in his eyes, when he stepped closer, she met his gaze and waited.

The slap resounded through the room. Her head jerked backward and a sharp pain radiated from her neck down her back. Her cheek stung and involuntary tears flooded over the hands she held to her face. Gasping for breath, she sobbed loudly.

"Quit blubbering. Do you think I won't hurt you again because you weep like a child?" Don Jesús grabbed her wrist and twisted her arm. "Where are they?"

Whimpering, she took the bag from her pocket and handed it to him.

He dumped the coins out and counted them, dropping them one by one into the chest. "Fortunately—for you— the girl declined your offer. Did it not occur to you she might take the money and still refuse your demands?"

"No. I didn't—" She drew out her handkerchief again and wiped her tears and blew her nose.

"Perhaps, then, she is more honorable than you."

She stared at him, unbelieving. *How dare he suggest—?*

"You will never touch these coins again. My father and grandfather and those who came before have protected Nicolás Ramirez's treasure from the mine at Guevavi for generations. He paid his due to the crown and passed this to his descendants. Our wealth and position sprang from this treasure. We do not spend this silver. This ranch earns its own money. Tapping into this reserve will signal our demise."

He closed the box and returned it to the trunk, twisting the hasp on the lock. Turning to her, he said through clenched teeth, "If you meddle with this trunk again, you will have no need for hairpins. I will tear your hair out by the roots. Do you understand?" He sat again behind the desk and picked up his cigar.

To get back into his good graces, she pretended to be contrite. "Sí, Don Jesús. I understand."

"Now, may we get back to the matter of our son?" He blew another cloud of smoke in her direction.

"Sí." She held the handkerchief against her wrinkled nose.

"The boy is determined." He tapped ashes into the ashtray. "A rather admirable trait in someone other than my son."

Relieved to have the issue of the coins behind them, as painful as it was, she pushed forward. "For the last ten years, you have paid him a generous stipend. If you allow him to use that money to marry this girl, you will look a fool."

Crushing his cigar, Don Jesús asked, "Are you suggesting he surrender that money?"

Doña María brightened. "Yes. An excellent idea." She fanned the last of the smoke away and pasted a smile on her face.

He shook his head. "No."

"No? Why not? Surely he will do as we say rather than give up that money." How could this man be so obtuse?

"Don't underestimate his determination. Besides, my honor is at stake now."

"What do you mean? How is this about you?"

"I don't expect you—a woman—to understand, so I will explain as simply as I can. If I disown him and cast him out penniless, the responsibility is on my shoulders. Others will not remember—or care about—his disobedience. The failure of Don Jesús María Ramirez Gonzalez de Bonillas' son would be my failure.

"So what will you do?"

"Allow him to make his own decision."

Outraged, Doña María screamed, "And marry an Indian?" She stood and leaned across the desk. "A heathen?"

He leaned toward her, his face inches from hers. Quietly, he said, "You are the one who proved this 'heathen' is more honorable than her future mother-in-law."

Doña María stood back, stunned. "Have you lost your mind?"

"Take care, woman. You will not speak to me in that tone."

She fell into the chair behind her, made the sign, and began to pray.

"Shut up. Your prayers mean nothing to me." He opened the door and said, "You may go to your bedroom, or you may go to the sala. This conversation is over."

Chapter 9

Winter 1864

The winter rains came early, and the rain-swollen river rushed past them. "I don't want rain on our wedding day."

He kissed her hand. "The weather will be perfect."

So much had happened since Armando applied for the homestead. Not the least of which was that Armando's parents no longer opposed their marriage. When she refused the doña's demands and even her money, she assumed she had lost him forever, that their opposition would double. Surprisingly, Armando said his father gave him permission to make his own decisions, and his mother said nothing more on the issue.

Julio and Adelita married in September, and now she and Armando would wed in just one week. Theirs would be a small wedding under the ramada at the Ocoboa ranch when the priest came from Tucson.

Now, standing beside the river, Armando took her in his arms and kissed her, generating the physical longing she happily anticipated. She allowed him to cup her buttocks and pull her against his rising desire. He traced kisses down her throat, pushing her shawl aside, kissing the swell of her breast. Her breathing became more urgent, and she pressed herself into him, but Armando gently released her from his embrace. "Slowly, mi amorita. I promised."

Color rose in her face, changing her honey-gold complexion to pale mahogany. "Gracias. But sometimes I can't get close enough to you." She pulled her shawl tight against the cool air that followed his warm embrace.

"I have to struggle, too."

Changing the subject, she turned and said, "Even the river is in such a hurry that the rocks and grasses can't slow it."

Behind her, he wrapped her in his arms, and together they watched the water flowing past. On the other bank, the yellow leaves of the velvet ash dropped lazily into the river and floated hurriedly toward an unknown destination.

"¡Mira!" Esperanza pointed to a glossy black bird picking berries out of a cluster of mistletoe at the top of a nearly leafless mesquite tree. He gazed at them with elegant red eyes, his sharp crest rising. After singing a series of trills, he went back to his meal. "El pájaro negro always comes back this time of year. The females come later. I suppose he must find a place to build a nest even before he chooses a wife."

"Like me. I chose our home before I met you. I always planned to bring my wife to live beneath La Cresta."

She turned to face him. "When you call it La Cresta, you make it sound like something different from an ordinary ridge." If she learned more about the place he would take her, she would be less frightened.

Gazing into the distance, he said, "Our home will be on a small ridge, which is one of many. La Cresta is different, though, not just because it's so massive, but because I'm drawn to it. *Es muy bella.*" When he paused, she explored his eyes, trying to see what he saw. "The western end of the mountains, which, on clear days, we can see from here, only hints at what the other side is like. Those south-facing slopes are softer, scattered with desert scrub and cactus all the way to the top. You'll see it when we move to Tucson. But when you ride around the point of the mountains, you discover a rugged ridge of rock walls, towers, pinnacles, and jagged peaks reaching for the sky, reaching for..." He hesitated. "I wish I could find the words to explain how I feel. Sometimes, I'm overcome. It calls me, telling me it's my place in this world. I draw strength from it." He took her hand. "I could never have defied my parents if I hadn't found La Cresta. We might not be together now..."

For the first time, Esperanza understood the power that place had over him, the depth of his commitment to living there. More than anything, she wanted to share his dream, even if she was afraid. "But we are."

Lifting her chin, he brushed her lips with a gentle kiss.

A song called them back to the bird.

"I used to think of him as a priest-bird because of his shiny black robe, but now I believe he's far too flashy. His is not a humble spirit."

The sun glinted off the bird's silky feathers, reflecting a mosaic of greens and purples. Armando nodded. "Who knew black could be so colorful?"

"He's telling us we can find light, color, and hope even in the darkest moments. I thought we might never find our way together, but look at us now."

As if on cue, the bird regarded them again, sang another series of trills, and flew away with a flash of white under his wings.

Watching him out of sight, she asked, "Do you think he knows we're about to be married?"

"Of course. And speaking of our wedding, I have a present for you."

He took a small box from his saddlebag.

She untied the white ribbon, lifted the lid, and gasped at the sight of an exquisite, silver crucifix with a delicately carved figure of *Jesucristo* on the cross. She wove the chain through her fingers and held it up. Reflected sunlight cast beads of light into Armando's eyes. Standing on her tiptoes, she kissed him.

As he opened the clasp, she turned and held her hair out of the way. After he put it around her neck, she sighed and leaned back into him. "I will never take it off."

Esperanza kissed her grandmother on the cheek. "Mamá sent you something." Abuela Primitiva examined the contents of the basket, bending close and running a bony finger over a chunk of cheese and a stack of tortillas.

"Gracias. These hands won't let me make tortillas anymore." Her voice was hushed and, at times, almost breathless.

In the kitchen, her grandmother pointed to a chair and said, "Sit, mi nieta. I have somethin' to say."

"First, let me tend the fire." Every day, Tomás or Manolito came to make sure she was well, to take care of her fire in the morning and at night. Because her brothers had ridden to Tubac with their father this morning, it fell to her.

After she added firewood and the warmth spread through the kitchen, she took Abuela Tiva's shawl from a hook and wrapped the old woman's bony shoulders. She sat in the chair next to her, taking one of her grandmother's hands in her own.

The old woman wasted no time getting to the point. "You are about to be married, mi nieta. When your husband wants to lie with you, you cannot deny him. Married women must submit."

The blunt statement took her by surprise, and she blushed. Was this why her mother sent her this morning?

"You will not always like it." She took a wheezing breath.

I won't? She believed the desire she felt in Armando's arms was a promise of pleasure. She was looking forward to finding out for herself when they married. *Will it be so bad?*

Her grandmother knew what she was thinking. Laying her other hand on Esperanza's, she said, "Pay attention, child—I said 'not always.'"

Although she was curious, she waited for her grandmother to explain.

"A man can give his wife pleasure if he wants to, but most men only care about themselves. He will be selfish if you let him. Do not allow him to be selfish."

"How?"

"By knowing you are doing the most natural thing in the world. There is no shame. For either of you. Invite him to give you pleasure and you give it in return." The old woman looked off into an unknown distance, a faint smile playing along her thin lips.

Again, heat rose in Esperanza's face, embarrassed for herself but also for imagining Abuela Tiva as a beautiful, vibrant woman lying with Abuelo Jorge. "I will try."

"Good." The old woman smiled a toothless smile and continued. "But that's not all. Where you are going, you must not have children.

"Tucson?"

"No. Not Tucson."

Esperanza searched the old woman's face. "I should know better than to try to keep a secret from you."

"You do not want children."

"But I do."

"Of course you do, child, but you don't want your babies born there, do you?"

"No. I'm terrified." Within a year of her marriage, Lupe gave birth to Luis, and since then, Francesca and Lupita were born, and now she was expecting another. Four children in less than six years for her sister. How would she be able to avoid getting pregnant for five years at the homestead?

Using the table to push herself up, Abuela Tiva made her way to a cabinet and brought out a small cloth bag tied with string.

At the table, she handed it to Esperanza, who looked inside. "Wild carrot seeds?"

"Chew them the next mornin'. And maybe a few more the second mornin.'"

"They will keep me from—?"

Abuela Tiva shrugged her bony shoulders. "Can't promise every time." She tapped the table with a long fingernail. "Plant some, so you don't run out."

Esperanza stared at them. "I collected these for you. Why didn't you tell me what they were for?"

"No reason I should tell you until now. They're not enough, though. Armando has to help."

"What do you mean?"

"Pull out in time."

Heat rose again to her face. "What do you mean?"

Her grandmother smiled and patted her hand. "You will know when you have lain with him."

Esperanza had a vague notion of what sex involved. More than once she was aware of Armando's physical desire, and she understood where her desire was located in her body. More than once she had struggled against it; more than once she wished she had lost the struggle; more than once she was grateful for Armando's promise.

"What about what the priest said? Will we be committing a sin if we do... things to prevent—?"

Her grandmother's rheumy eyes hinted at a long-ago sorrow Esperanza knew nothing about. "Hah," she said. "Priests don't get pregnant."

Part 2: La Cresta

Arizona Territory 1865-1866

Chapter 10

Summer 1865

Esperanza rose before the sun. She lit the candle, kissed her rosary, and made the sign, whispering a prayer to Our Lady. She picked up the other picture. The photographer had set up his equipment and spent a long time situating them. Armando sat on a chair, and she stood beside him with a hand resting on his shoulder. They were to look at the camera and hold perfectly still for minutes at a time. In spite of their happiness, they were not to smile. At last, it was over, and they were released from the photographer's captivity to join their family at the ramada to celebrate. She wished the image really reflected how they felt. Tracing her finger on the crucifix in the picture, she did the same with the one she wore. She whispered another prayer—one of thanks for Armando's love.

She filled the wooden basin with enough water to rinse the sleep from her eyes and mouth. After pulling on her long petticoat and blue skirt and buttoning her long-sleeved blouse, she sat on the edge of the bed and nudged him. "Time to get up. The sun does not wait."

While he dressed, she put on her boots, wrapped her shawl around her shoulders, and stepped into the chill morning air.

Above the eastern ridge, the sky brightened, dimming the stars. In the south, the dark silhouette of La Cresta emerged from the darkness. At times, those granite walls pressed in on her, an impenetrable boundary between where she would be by choice, and where she must be by obligation.

The massive slopes and canyons of La Sierra de la Santa Catarina wrapped around them to the south and to the east, posing, for her, an awesome contradiction. At first sight, they mesmerized, their rugged beauty masking hidden dangers and inviting men like Armando to linger in their shadows and to settle on their slopes. He loved these mountains, and although she wanted to share his devotion to this place, she struggled to understand why it was somehow alien to her. When she lowered her gaze, she understood the truth of this land—its indifference to their struggle.

The road to Camp Grant passed on the west, following a wash flowing from the north. Few riders or wagons avoided an Apache ambush along the road, but, for now, Armando's trips south to Tucson were uneventful.

They came here in May—eleven months after he applied for the homestead and six months after they were married. While they lived in town, she had studied the front range, trying to imagine the view from the other side based on his description. She failed. Her first glimpse of La Cresta came when they rounded the point of the mountains and Armando stopped the wagon to give her time to take it all in.

"Isn't it beautiful, Espe?"

The expression on his face told her how much he wanted her to agree with him. "Yes..." Like him, she struggled to find the words. *It is beautiful*. But she could not see what he saw; she could find no welcome in its rock towers and peaks. The rugged ridge, stood cold before her on this hottest of days, daring her to find peace and joy in its shadow. As each mile took her farther from her sister in Tucson, as well as an impossible distance from her parents and brothers, the more fervently she prayed five years would pass quickly. Could she compete with these mountains for her husband's devotion? Afraid of being unfair to him, she vowed to share his passion.

This place was nothing like she imagined. Before he brought her here, in her mind's eye, she saw a quaint little house surrounded by gardens, not unlike her parents' home. Here, she lived in a two-room rock house with a dirt floor and a fireplace.

In addition to the small house, Armando and his brother had built a shelter for the horses, which, like the house, was a simple stone structure, hardly worthy of being called a barn. It was barely big enough for two horses. The makeshift feeders inside and the barrel for water would serve until Armando could build a proper barn. It was dark and dank inside with the only air and light coming through long narrow openings under the roofline. Little air circulated for the horses at night when they had to be locked inside.

He had used stones from an old wall that completely surrounded the foundations he and Julio had discovered when they roamed here looking for treasure. He believed the wall surrounded some kind of compound where people had lived many years ago. Now that wall surrounded them.

He had rebuilt parts of the wall as a potential defense against the Apaches, also hoping to keep the javelinas out of the garden. Still, there were several areas where it was still in disrepair. The southern boundary, facing La Cresta was mostly collapsed. Armando had promised to use those rocks for her "real" house.

"Someday," he often said, "I will build you a home with ten rooms—maybe twenty."

Whenever he said this, she nodded. "I know."

"We will have muchos vaqueros working for us. You will have servants and will not need to work so hard. *Prometo.*"

Someday...

The summer heat wore her down, and the wide open sky intensified the violence of the thunder and lightning that came with the monsoon rains. She didn't remember either being so fierce at home.

He came up behind her and pushed her hair aside, kissing the back of her neck. Momentarily, she tensed, but then relaxed, giving in to the warmth spreading through her.

Beside her, with his arm around her shoulders, he surveyed the yard and La Cresta, towering before them, visible in the rising light. The sun, still behind the mountain to the east, cast its rays through the canyon, illuminating the pinnacles and casting deep creases into shadow.

She watched him as he scanned the bajada, standing erect, his shoulders squared. She was struck again by how handsome he was, his complexion somewhat lighter than her own, who, unlike other men, wore his dark hair fairly short and grew no mustache or beard. Since he didn't shave every day, his whiskers often left a rash on her chin after making love. She smiled, remembering that after he learned the cause of her rash, he sometimes shaved after dinner, an indication of what he had in mind for later. He pushed his hair off his forehead, only to have it fall back again.

She loved his pride and determination, and she accepted his commitment to this place. As his wife, she would endure whatever came her way. Even though she suspected she understood this place far better than he did, she would help him tame this land.

The sun climbed higher, bathing the distant *cordones*, the finger ridges that lay between them and La Cresta, in pale morning light, its warmth pushing cold air down from the mountain heights. She tightened her shawl around her shoulders, watching as he tried to count the brown specks in the distance.

"*Treinta y siete*? I'll ride out after breakfast." Even then, thirty-seven animals wouldn't be an accurate count since the cattle roamed across several ridges.

The Apaches constantly stole their cattle, but they had not yet caused trouble at the house. He spent part of nearly every day riding out among the cattle, checking for problems, but if he saw the Indians on the bajada, he went after them. She feared they would kill him. Why couldn't he just let them take a few cows once in a while?

She turned to him in the rising light. "I want to start enlarging the garden. I'll make breakfast later."

Armando went into the house to fetch the shovel and her wide-brimmed hat.

She laid her shawl aside on a collection of rocks tossed out of the garden and started digging. He turned her around, took her into his arms and kissed her softly. "*Muchas gracias, mi querida.*"

"¿Por que?"

"For believing in me. You believed when no one else did. You believed when my parents threatened to disown me for wanting to marry you. *Tú eres mi alma*—my soul."

She lifted his hand to her chest, their fingers resting on the crucifix. "*Y tú eres mio.*"

He kissed her again and pressed his body against hers. His need rose, and her own yearning settled low inside. She wondered if they were going to go back into the house. But he released her and turned to his own chores.

As he did every morning, he would feed, water, and groom the horses and saddle both of them, leaving them saddled all day in case he needed to ride out after Apaches trying to steal his cattle. He often used Esperanza's horse, Pepe, to make sure he got regular exercise. Sometimes, When Armando was working in the yard, Esperanza rode Pepe around the inside of the perimeter wall for her own enjoyment and to exercise him, but it wasn't the same as racing down the road with the wind in her ears.

After getting the horses ready, Armando would clean the rifles and check the ammunition supply. This, more than anything, signaled the need to go to Tucson for supplies. When his regular morning routine was done, he would turn to other chores. Today, he planned to shore up the north wall of the house.

Her garden, which she had established soon after they arrived, didn't provide as much as she hoped. She had tilled aged horse manure into the soil and planted corn, beans, and squash, what she called the sister crops. She began with the corn that would grow tall enough for the beans to climb. The broad leaves of squash would help shade the soil for its sisters. She considered planting amaranth, one of her favorite green vegetables, until she discovered it grew wild on the floodplain below their ridge.

Today, she pulled weeds and dug out small brittlebushes. The endless supply of rocks in the garden failed to discourage her. She added them to a pile Armando would use later.

Next, she dug along the southern edge. Yesterday's rainfall might make today's job easier. Winter rains—the female rains—nourished the desert, often soaking deep into the soil, but summer rains—the male rains—were full of noise and bluster, coming too hard and too fast to soak in. Only a few inches down, she encountered dry, hard earth. Most of the rain had run off the slope.

On the other side of the house, he whistled a tune while he gathered rocks from the old wall, putting them back into place to raise its height or to fill in low spots. *He's happy here. He doesn't mind the isolation.* For her, though, it weighed heavily. Some days being so far from town, so far from her family brought on a painful depression. She could never tell Armando, but sometimes, even when he was here, she was deeply alone. Because it kept her in close contact with the Earth, gardening helped. She loved to turn the soil and prepare it to receive the seeds that would provide the nourishment that would sustain them through the coming months.

Even though digging into the packed earth took all her strength as well as her weight to break through the hard surface, she did not resent her aching muscles at the end of the day. She was in her element. She had made scant progress when, suddenly, the shovel slid easily into the ground, the surface crust giving way to a darker, loamier soil. Now, turning it was almost effortless. Extending the boundaries would be easy.

She worked her way toward the old wall, happy not to work so hard when the shovel struck something. She sighed. Most likely another rock—or, with luck, a stone tool. When she first dug the garden, she found a *metate,* an old grinding stone, that she used as a doorstop from time to time.

Broken pieces of pottery scattered the ground all across the ridge. Each fragment reminded her that other women had lived in this place. Occasionally, she found a decorated piece, which she slipped into her pocket. She kept a small collection on the kitchen shelf. At times, she looked at a fragment and drew her finger along a painted line, trying to imagine the whole vessel and how the design came together.

Now, with the sun high above, she wiped perspiration from her forehead with her sleeve and knelt, uncovering what appeared to be a large piece of pottery. Curious, she brushed away the dirt, revealing red lines against brown clay. The more she uncovered, the more it looked like a whole pot.

Eventually, she released it from the ground and held it before her in the sunlight. A red, geometric pattern showed beneath the layers of dirt clinging to its sides. Not big, but not small, either. Maybe sixteen centimeters across with an opening of about half that. She cradled it easily in her hands. The inside was packed with dirt, which she guessed was the reason it wasn't broken. As she held it up to the morning sun, a strange sensation swept over her, a presence she had not felt before and her loneliness lifted. She glanced toward the palo verde to confirm the Apache was not there. Besides, when Armando was here, the Apache never came.

The woman whose hands first caressed the sides of this pot, the woman who shaped it from raw clay, who painted the lines on the outside—that woman once lived in this place. Her spirit still lived in this pot.

She carried it to the barn and rinsed it in the water bucket revealing clear red lines and geometric scrolls encircling it. After cleaning the dirt out of the inside, she slid her fingers along the shoulder and imagined the woman whose hands made it. She turned it over, taking note of the almost round shape, and the neck tucked in and rising to an almost imperceptible flared rim. The bottom was plain. As she slid her thumb along the interior, she turned it around, examining the design on the outside. Her thumb came to rest in a small depression, the thumbprint of the potter.

> *She did not think about her work; her dark hands simply molded the clay. Dipping her fingers into the precious water, she shaped the neck evenly and flared the rim only slightly, turning the vessel in her hands. With a small, smooth stone, she polished the outside, already seeing the red lines she would paint once it was ready.*

In that moment, Esperanza knew the maker. This pot and her presence here were gifts. In the house, she set it on the table, standing back to study it. "Tell me about the woman who made you. What was her life like in this place?"

Armando came through the door. "Who are you talking to, Espe?"

She laughed. "No one. Look what I found in the garden."

"It looks old."

"I think it's very old. It's more proof that Pueblo Viejo was real. People lived in this place long before we came."

"In spite of the Apaches, I'm glad we're here," he said, putting his arms around her.

The Apaches. She leaned into his chest, her head barely reaching his chin, listening to his heartbeat and willing hers to beat in concert with his. Why didn't she tell him about the one who watched her from the palo verde?

Chapter 11

Summer 1865

This morning, as she did every morning, she wiped dust from the table, the shelves, and the clothing chest. When the wind blew, sand sifted through the open crevices and covered everything. She carried the bedding outside to shake before remaking the bed.

Smoothing his side of the sheets, she picked up her one-sided conversation with him from his last trip to town, "Once again, Mando, I will sleep alone tonight. I think I miss you more at night than during the day." She laughed. "I know what you think, but it's not only because of the pleasures we share. When you wrap me in your arms, I feel safe and loved."

Being alone during the day was difficult, but at night, she lay awake listening to the night sounds—coyotes yipping and howling, an owl hooting, something rustling through the bushes. Sometimes her imagination got away from her, and she wondered if the sounds were Apaches signaling to one another and closing in for an attack. The possibility remained in the back of her mind.

She swept the hard-packed, dirt floor and, talking out loud, asked her absent husband, "Did you remember to bring a mat for the floor?" In her mind, he always answered, "Sí and look what else I've brought you." She didn't know what she'd like, but she would be pleased if he surprised her now and then.

"Armando," she said, "these walls need plaster to keep out the wind and the dust. That, and a mat on the floor, would make the house easier to keep clean, and I can decorate."

She tried to imagine color in this dull room. "I'll hang a chile ristra by the door. Do you remember those big paper flowers Lupita and Francesca made for our wedding? I'd put them over there." She pointed to the wall behind the bed.

Her wedding. Her happiness that day had been tempered by guilt. They had not told her parents about Armando's homestead and that he would take her so far away. During the ceremony, when her father placed her hand in Armando's, she realized she was saying goodbye to her parents and brothers, and sadness intruded on her happiness. She had turned back to her father and fell against him crying. He held her in his strong arms and wept with her. Her plea for forgiveness went unvoiced.

In Tucson, she was happy living in a small house near Lupe while Armando and Julio regularly traveled to the homestead to dig the well and build the house and barn. When it was finally ready for them to move in, they had no choice but to tell her parents what they were about to do.

That was three months ago, and it was the last time she saw her family.

"He's going to be furious with me, and he has every right. Not telling him our plans was the same as a lie." Armando did not look forward to her parents' reaction.

With Easter approaching, they were on their way to her parents' house from Tucson, where, after a Lenten celebration, they would tell them goodbye. Because she had promised Armando she would stay to protect the homestead whenever he went to Tucson for supplies, she did not expect to see her family again for five years.

As the wagon bounced across a dry wash a few miles from Tubac, she laid her hand on his knee. They had ridden in an uncomfortable silence while she rehearsed how she would break the news to them. "I begged you not to tell him. He should blame me, not you."

"No. If he's angry at anyone, it should be me. I didn't have to listen to you. I was less than honorable."

"We both were."

"Well, do you want to tell them right away? Or when we're ready to leave?"

"It's cowardly, but could we wait until Sunday, after mass?"

"Whoa, Sofi, Pepe, whoa." Armando reined in the horses and set the brake on the wagon. He turned to his wife. "If we don't tell them sooner rather than later, you will not enjoy this time with your parents. You'll fret and be unhappy. You said your father would forgive us. Do you believe it?"

"I want to."

"Espe, your father is a good man. He will understand." She leaned against him, and he put his arm around her shoulders. "I should tell him. His anger should be directed at me, not you."

"But—"

"No. I owe him my honesty."

He picked up the reins and released the brake. "Hyah! Sofi! Pepe!"

In spite of her resolve, she cried and clung to her mother as soon as they arrived.

"What's wrong, m'hija?" Her mother held her while she sobbed.

Señor Ocoboa cast a questioning glance at Armando.

"May we sit? There is something we must tell you."

Even as Esperanza and her mother sat together on the sofa, the men remained standing.

Twisting his hat in his hands, he said, "First, I need to apologize to both of you. I failed to tell you the plans I had made for us when I asked for her hand."

Señor Ocoboa frowned, the crease between his brows deepening. "What do you mean?

"Before I spoke to you, I applied for, and was granted, a homestead."

"That's good, isn't it? You knew you couldn't depend on your father. I assume you will be building my daughter a home."

"Yes sir, but the land is north of L'Iglesia. On the other side of the mountains."

Her eyes wet with tears, Esperanza watched her father's face as he registered this news. Her mother turned to her. "Espe?"

"Sí, Mamá."

Manuel Ocoboa's face contorted, and he grabbed Armando by the shirt, yanking him close. "You will take my daughter into Apache territory?"

Esperanza jumped to her feet, grabbing her father's arm before he could swing. "Papá, No! I begged him not to tell you. Don't blame him, please." Her tears began to fall again.

Her father did not release his son-in-law, who had made no move to defend himself. "You will let your wife bear the guilt of your deception?"

"No sir. I am the one at fault. I deceived you, but I swear I have never deceived your daughter."

"It's true, Papá. I knew. I'm excited about our adventure."

"Adventure? *Adventure?!* Among the Apaches?" He stepped away from Armando, his fists still balled, his knuckles white. He glared at his son-in-law, the crease between his brows deepening, but when he looked at his daughter, his brows relaxed and his anger seemed to dissipate into resignation. "Are you sure about this, m'hija?"

"Sí, Papá." She lifted her father's and Armando's hands to the crucifix at her neck. With their three hands together, touching the cross, she said, "We will be careful. We promise, *antes de Dio.*"

Tears filled her father's eyes while Señora Ocoboa wept openly. She made the sign and whispered a prayer.

To Armando, he said, "You will drive your cattle up there?"

"Sí. There is a lot of desert for them to forage."

"You'll be a long way from Tucson. You'll need to travel back and forth for supplies. Won't that be dangerous?" Señor Ocoboa's worry line deepened with his frown.

"My brother, Julio, will come out regularly to bring supplies and to help me with some of the heavy work, and I'll go to Tucson maybe once a month for supplies."

"And leave my daughter alone? You don't think she's vulnerable to an Apache attack if she's there by herself?"

"If necessary, she will defend herself and our home."

"How?" He looked at Esperanza.

She smiled through her tears. "We are both prepared, Papá. Armando taught me to shoot. He bought me a rifle."

He shook his head. "I should have known. Your brothers say you should have been born a boy. They may be right."

Armando laughed. "I, for one, am glad she was not. She rides a horse better than me. You won't be surprised she also shoots better than me."

Señor Ocoboa had taken her into his arms. "Nothing she does surprises me, but I'll be no less worried about my baby girl."

Now, remembering, a tear slid from her eye. She wiped it away with her sleeve. *Stop it. You promised your husband you would stay here when he was gone. You know we can't leave this place unattended. The Apaches would take everything. Quit feeling sorry for yourself, and get back to work.*

Armando did not miss his parents, but not seeing her family was painful. Her sister had always been her best friend, and she loved Lupe's children, Francesca, Lupita, Luis, and baby Mateo. She missed Tomás's wedding, and she suspected Manolito, too, would be married before they claimed the deed for the homestead. Some days five years stretched like an eternity before her.

As she returned to her household chores, she thought of her mother's attention to the "domestic arts," insisting her daughters learn practical sewing skills, as well as embroidery, along with cooking, cleaning, and gardening. Although loneliness plagued her from time to time, she was well prepared to keep house, even in this place.

This morning, at dawn, Armando had driven out in the wagon for what should be a routine trip. With Armando and both horses gone, it would be doubly lonely. But he would be back tomorrow She hated it when he needed to be gone longer. As usual, she gave him letters for her family.

It occurred to her that Julio might stay here once in a while so she could go to Tucson with Armando, but she decided it would be selfish to ask him to give up even more of his time away from Adelita and his own cattle. So she never brought it up, and Armando never mentioned it as a possibility.

Each time he prepared to leave, she wished she could go along. But leaving the homestead untended for even a short time was risky.

Even so, he might at least ask her if she wanted to go. She wouldn't, of course, knowing her responsibility here, but she wished he would ask.

Before going outside, she picked up the rifle, checked to make sure a cartridge was in the chamber. She remembered when he took her to the river to teach her to shoot.

"This is the best rifle I can get for now," he told her, "but it is a little unstable, so you need to be extra careful." He showed her how to use the lever action to eject a spent cartridge and how it forced the next one into the chamber. "As soon as you lock it, the hammer is in the firing position, which means you can accidentally discharge it."

She practiced picking it up, propping it against a tree or a wall, and putting it down, and never aiming at herself or anything she didn't intend to shoot. As a repeater, it would make short work of any Apaches within range.

He tested her on loading the cartridges and shooting targets against a high bank. As he watched her bring the rifle to her shoulder, he said, "I wonder what my mother would say about this."

Without answering, she focused on the sight, shifted left, and honed in on the target. She squeezed the trigger, and the tin can flew in the air with a perfect hole in its center. Lowering the rifle, she rubbed her shoulder. At first, the kick bruised her, but as she continued to practice, she got used to it. She grinned. "Doña María would be scandalized."

He affected his mother's sophisticated tone. "'Ladies do not handle firearms.'"

They laughed as they set up a new row of targets.

Before long, she proved him right. She did shoot better than he did. From almost any distance, she consistently hit what she aimed at, although she was less accurate with moving targets. Armando assured her he wouldn't ask her to hunt big or small game. He didn't have to mention a moving target might be an Apache

Today, she made her usual circuit around the yard, looking for anything out of place, any sign of an intruder. She scanned the bajada and saw nothing unusual.

As she turned to go into the house, she sensed someone watching her. She scanned the perimeter, her heart pounding, and she almost missed him. But for the red bandana tied around his head, he blended into the low-hanging branches around him. Involuntarily, she met his gaze—again—as she had done before. He watched from beneath the large palo verde beyond the garden, some fifty paces from where she stood.

Her heart slowed, and she took a half-step forward. She was tempted to take a closer look at the bead and bone medallion he wore, but she resisted. The large knife tucked into his belt might be a warning, but she ignored it. If he meant to harm her, he would have done it by now. His black hair, streaked with gray, had been chopped unevenly, hanging nearly to his shoulder on one side, but only to his ear on the other. The creases in his copper-colored face suggested he might be her father's age. She was shocked to think of her father and the Apache in the same thought.

Looking across the distance into his dark eyes, she whispered, "*¿Que quieres?*"

Chapter 12

Fall 1865

E spe!"
By the time she ran out the door, rifle in hand, the dust had settled from his mad dash. She whispered a prayer and listened to Sofi, racing down the rutted track and out of hearing as they rounded the base of the ridge. A man alone fighting even a small band of Apaches did not stand a chance. She made the sign, holding her breath, and praying to see him and Sofi rise up on the next ridge.

Not far to the east, Apaches had separated a few cattle from the herd. Armando disappeared into a gully before cresting the next rise and stopping. When he raised his rifle to his shoulder and fired, the report echoed off the mountains. He pushed it into the scabbard and kicked Sofi into a gallop. Another shot. Again, she held her breath—

There he is. She allowed herself to breathe again.

Armando bent low over Sofi's neck as they dashed through the brush, his left hand on the reins, his right hand ready to draw the Henry. He reined Sofi to a halt and took off his hat. They might be waiting for him. He nudged the horse forward a slow step at a time, pressing her into a side pass so only his head would emerge first. When he peered over the ridge, a shot rang out. He ducked, and the bullet whistled past him. "*¡Los Bastardos!*"

Back below the ridge, he slid from the saddle, wrapping Sofi's reins around a sturdy branch. "Shhh... Sofi. Be quiet." He stroked her nose and hung his hat on the saddle horn. Crouching low, making his way through the brush, the wicked thorns of an acacia tore his sleeve. *Damn catclaw!* When he pulled loose, the branch swung back and sliced his cheek.

"*Mierda.*" He dragged his hand across his bloody face. Pulling himself through the persistent acacia, he had to yank his shirt, as well as his arms, free of the vicious thorns. By the time he reached friendlier scrub, his shirt sleeve was torn, his arm and cheek bleeding. He peered through the branches at the top of the ridge and spotted two Apaches driving three cows eastward. The third man was nowhere in sight. Armando squatted, raised the Henry to his shoulder, and drew a bead on one of the pair. Before he could pull the trigger, a searing pain jolted through him.

He tumbled sideways, dropping the rifle, and gasping for breath. As a wave of dizziness engulfed him, he tried to make sense of a world suddenly tipped over. When he put his hand on his side, where the pain settled, he found an arrow lodged in his side, just above his waist.

"*Madre de Dios.*" It was hard to tell how deep the arrow had gone, but he struggled to his knees. He twisted around to see where it went in. Dizziness and heat engulfed him.

I can't pass out. I've got to get back to Esperanza.

Once he got his breath, he took his shirt off, slipping it over the arrow inch by inch, stopping only when the slightest movement slammed him with excruciating pain. *Jesucristo, help me.* With the shirt out of the way, he pressed his fingers around the entry, feeling for the point, and gasping with each touch. *Not deep. Good.* He clenched his teeth and explored the point's position. It had angled into his side and could have passed through without doing much damage. Pulling a thick branch between his teeth and biting down on it, he took a breath and yanked the arrow from his side. Screaming, he fell forward, catching himself with one hand.

He used the Henry to push himself upright. *Got to get back...* The arrow lay on the ground at his feet. As much as he wanted to pick it up and break it over his knee, getting home was more important. He staggered down the slope to Sofi, barely noticing the catclaw tearing his shoulder.

The mare was standing where he left her. *Eres bella.*

He slid the Henry into the scabbard and turned her parallel to the ridge so he was standing uphill. He dragged himself into the saddle and let Sofi take him home. He tried to keep one hand pressed against his bleeding side.

When Esperanza heard Sofi making her way up the hill, she ran to meet them. Armando was shirtless, leaning forward against Sofi's neck, and blood covered his hand and ran down his pants leg. "Armando, what happened?"

"I'll be all right." He slid from the saddle and fell to his knees. Esperanza tried to help him rise, but he brushed her away. "Take care of Sofi."

She led the mare to the hitching rail where Pepe stood watching. After tying her, she moved the bucket of water within her reach and loosened her cinch.

She went back to her husband. As he struggled to stand, he groaned. She bent her knees and lifted his arm around her shoulders, straining under his weight and trying to stand straight while he got his feet underneath him. With each step forward, he winced and caught his breath. "You'll be fine, Armando. Let's get inside." Twice, she almost stumbled under his weight, but she finally got him into the house, where she sat him in a chair by the table.

At the fireplace, she swung the kettle from over the fire and filled a large wooden bowl with hot water, as well as a smaller basin for washing her hands. She took clean rags from the chest and dropped two of them into the hot water and put a bucket of cold water on the floor next to her husband.

She washed the blood from around his wound, tossing the bloody rag into the bucket, and using a second one to repeat the process, each time exchanging the bloody cloth with the one in the cold water, which quickly turned a pale red.

"The bleeding has slowed." She bent closer. "It's an ugly cut, but not deep enough to cause major damage."

Armando winced when she pushed the edges of the skin together and applied pressure. "You couldn't have done this on catclaw. What happened?"

"An Apache arrow." He winced again when she jerked her hand away from him and stood straight.

"An Apache shot you?"

"Grazed me." He touched his cheek. "This one was catclaw."

"He did more than graze you." She applied pressure again, and he winced again. Taking a breath, she reminded herself to be gentle, even if she wanted to strangle him.

Now that she knew he was injured by an Apache arrow, she would need to be alert for signs of infection. She said a prayer of thanks for the lessons she had learned from Abuela Tiva.

She covered the wound with the ointment the doctor in Tucson had given her, pressed a wad of bandaging against it, and wrapped a long strip of cloth around his middle to keep the dressing in place. After cleaning the scratches on his cheek and arm, she applied more ointment. When she was finished, she stood behind him, looking down at his dark hair and bare shoulders. *Will the day come when he rides out and doesn't come back? Will I need to search for his body?* Tears welled in her eyes and she murmured a quick, but silent, prayer to Our Lady.

"Lie down and rest, *mi amor*."

While he rested, she tended to the horses. Even though it was still early, she unsaddled them and put the tack away. She hung the bridles on a peg and took the curry comb, brush, and hoof pick outside. Avoiding thoughts of her husband's death, she focused only on Pepe and Sofi. He was lucky this time. But next time...?

She brushed them until their coats shone in the afternoon light and, using a clean, wet cloth, she cleaned their eyes, nostrils, and inside their ears. She cleaned their hooves and checked for pain, tapping the pick against the sole and the sides. An abscess would bring the horse up lame, and a split hoof would be trouble. Finally, she applied a generous coat of pine tar to each one. Their hooves would need to be trimmed soon.

Satisfied the horses were sound, she turned them into the small enclosure.

After feeding them and filling their half-barrel with fresh water, she started back to the house to check on Armando. He had pushed the shutter open and stood watching her.

She reached for his hand. "You should be lying down, Mando. You might start to bleed again."

"You shouldn't have to work so hard, Espe. I'm supposed to take care of you and the horses.

She opened her mouth to say something, but she held her tongue. She stepped back and put her hands on her hips.

"Armando, when have I complained?"

"Never, but—"

"Did I not promise to share your life and your dream?"

"Yes, but—"

"You want me to complain? I will. This isn't the first time you've come back from the bajada with an injury, but it's the most serious one. Treating those injuries is the hardest thing I have to do." In spite of her intention not to lose her temper, her anger rose. "Until now, you've had scratches and scrapes. Those are nothing. But today they attacked you. Every day, I face the possibility of your death. And you're feeling guilty about me taking care of the horses?" Tears spilled down her cheeks. "Go ahead and feel guilty if you want, but not about the horses or what I do to help you build your dream here!"

She turned and stalked across the yard.

Armando came and stood stiffly beside her. "I'm sorry."

She didn't answer, and she didn't look at him. If she did, she'd either cry or lash out again.

He took her hand and traced the callouses on her palm. "Before we got married, you never had callouses like these. And your hands were soft. I loved holding them."

That was hardly what she wanted to hear. She tried to pull her hand away from him.

He didn't let go. "Your hands are still beautiful, Espe. Every callous is a testament to the kind of woman—the kind of wife—you are, to what you're willing to do for me. To how you sacrifice your needs for mine."

"There is nothing I need more than you, Armando. You *must* believe that."

"And you need to know there is nothing in this world I need more than you. Not this ranch, not those cattle out there"—he swept his arm in the direction of the bajada—" not these mountains. Nothing is more important to me than you."

She searched his eyes—those green eyes she loved so much in spite of his mother. Did he mean it? "This ranch is your dream, Armando, and I promised to help. I will not fail you, but promise me you will not take foolish chances out there." She nodded in the direction of the bajada.

"I promise. I will protect the herd, but I will not be reckless."

She leaned against him. "Gracias." She put her arms around him, but when she hugged him, he flinched, his jaw tight.

She jumped back. "I'm sorry, Armando."

"I'm fine, Espe. I deserved it."

Chapter 13

Winter 1865

More than four years. She stood in the doorway of the house, counting the time that lay ahead.

As their first Christmas on the ridge approached, Esperanza grew melancholy. She had not seen her family in more than six months and years would pass before she would see them again. She refused to take her obligation to Armando's dream lightly. She had promised to help him build his ranch in this place, and she would not ask more of Julio than he was already giving. So she would wait while time passed so slowly

Lupe's children must be growing fast, and baby Mateo might be walking soon. Esperanza had sat with Lupe through her labor and delivery, and the midwife, satisfied Mateo's howling indicated good health, allowed her to cut the cord, wash him, and wrap him in a soft blanket while she delivered and wrapped the afterbirth.

As Esperanza held him, his now quiet, but inquisitive eyes searched her own, and her heart swelled with love. When she placed him in Lupe's arms, she experienced a terrible stab of jealousy. Tears of longing mixed with tears of self-pity. Lupe reached for her hand and said, "Do not weep, Espe. Your turn will come."

"Lo sé. But not now. I cannot raise a child out there." They were just weeks from moving to the homestead. Watching the baby suckle tore at her heart. "Five years, Lupe, we must live there five years before the land is ours. That's how long I must wait for my first child."

Now, she went to the storage room and filled a small pail with chicken feed. Armando brought fifteen chicks from Tucson a month ago and built a coop with a wire enclosure. Surprisingly, they made her days alone more interesting. She talked to them, and she liked to think they talked back, clucking, cocking their heads, and inspecting her with one eye. Armando wouldn't need to bring eggs from Tucson, that is, if the chicks survived. Between coyotes and hawks, they had lost three, which meant she had to keep a constant eye on them.

Carrying the Henry with her, she leaned it against the coop and sang out, "*Aqui*, chick-chick-chick," scattering the feed on the ground inside the enclosure. With the rifle in hand, she walked the perimeter, looking out across the bajada. She didn't try to count the cattle.

Against a pale, winter sky, snow covered the highest ridges of the mountains to the east and frosted the jagged peaks of La Cresta. Curvebills sang from leafless mesquites and palo verdes around the house, staking out nesting territories. Again, beneath his tree, the Apache watched, motionless, expressionless. With the rifle loose in her hand, the barrel pointing down, she heard sparrows singing and the chicks pecking, scratching, and peeping.

Inside, she asked herself, "Why don't I fear him? Am I making a deadly mistake?" He was not a young man, maybe her father's age, maybe not a warrior—at least not now, although she didn't know if Apaches got too old to go to war. *Does he love his children as much as my father loves his? Does he have children?*

Again, it startled her to think of this Apache and her father in the same breath. She missed her father.

Her guilt about keeping their plans secret still haunted her. She hoped he had forgiven them.

He had always spoiled her, allowing her to run with her brothers and to race against them on horseback—races she often won. He rarely scolded her for her willfulness. Once, he caught her riding Pepe bareback and astride, wearing a pair of her brother's trousers, her hair flying. She smiled at the memory.

His stern expression was one he reserved for when she misbehaved. "Esperanza Luisa, go to your room and dress properly. I will speak to you on the patio."

Moments later, she stepped out the door, with her hair pinned up, prepared to apologize and promise to behave. He stood, looking out at the mountains and smoking a cigar. She waited. He blew a gray cloud of smoke that enveloped his head and shoulders before drifting away on a light breeze. He turned. For a few moments, he said nothing.

She suspected he couldn't stay angry. A big man, taller than her by a foot, his brown eyes always found a twinkle for his adventurous daughter. For the first time, she saw his creased forehead and loose skin pouched beneath his eyes. *When did my father get old?*

He shoved the cigar into a colorful pot of sand; her mother did not permit cigars in the house. "Esperanza

Luisa, m'hija *linda*, what will I do with you? What would your mother say?"

He raised his hand, cutting off her response. "No. We both know what she would say and what she would demand of you in penance. I will not tell her, but you must promise you will never wear your brother's trousers again." He suppressed a smile. "At least not where you are likely to be seen."

Esperanza ran the few steps between them and threw her arms around his neck as he picked her up and spun around one turn. "Guard your spirit, my daughter. Be cautious about who you share it with."

And now, on this winter's day in this place, she murmured aloud, "I love you, Papá. I'm sorry we deceived you, but I believe I made the right decision."

As much as she missed her family, she didn't believe she would ever regret sharing her spirit with Armando even in this lonely place.

At dusk, when she heard the horses and wagon rattling up the track, she ran outside. Armando jumped from the wagon and grabbed her in his arms, kissing her face and neck.

"*Mi amorita, te adoro.*" He kissed her again. "Sometimes when I'm on my way home, I begin to think something awful might have happened."

"Don't worry, Mando. Nothing will happen. I am fine here." She actually believed it.

"I have letters and a surprise for you."

Wide-eyed, she said, "A surprise?"

"Your Christmas present." Armando turned to the wagon and lifted a box from under the seat. He put it on the ground and opened it.

Inside, two shining eyes looked at her. She glanced up in disbelief and reached for the puppy. He was black and fuzzy with a white blaze on his nose, a white chest, and his right front leg was white. Laughing, she wrapped him in her arms and let him lick her face.

"I brought gifts from your family and mine, but we will wait until Christmas to open them."

Her brow furrowed, and she lowered her chin to the pup's head. "We have nothing to give to them."

"I gave Julio some money and asked him to buy presents for everyone from us. He and Adelita will do it, and Lupe will take our presents to your parents and brothers."

"It's not the same. We won't even know what we gave them." She slid her hand through the pup's soft fur, comforted by his warmth.

Armando laid one hand on hers and the other on the puppy's head. "He'll keep you company when I must go to Tucson. You won't be so alone here."

"Gracias."

"We will train him to warn us if the Apaches are near. He will protect the chickens from coyotes and predators. But he will also be your protector, your friend, your watchdog, watching every moment for any threat."

She held him up, looking into his face. "Since you will be my guardian, I shall call you 'Goyo'"

When Armando turned to the wagon, Esperanza tucked him under her chin, stroking his soft fur and whispering, "How will you behave with my Apache? And what will he do when he meets you?"

She put the pup on the ground and helped Armando unload the supplies she asked him to bring: *masa* for tamales, dried beef, spices, potatoes, and onions for *cazuela*, the soup her mother always made at Christmas.

"Lupe sent flour and sugar. She said it wouldn't be Christmas without *buñuelos*."

Goyo, happy to be out of the box, sniffed around in the yard and relieved himself. When he spotted the chicks, he crouched low, inching toward them. Esperanza laughed, pleased to see he knew his job. To Armando, she said, "We need to keep an eye on him while he's too little to defend himself against coyotes." She called to him, and he ran to follow her into the house.

During dinner, Armando told her Adelita and Julio were expecting their first child. "Julio is crazy with excitement."

Her throat closed, and she choked back tears. "I'm happy for them."

Armando placed his hand on hers. "We will have children, Espe."

After dinner, with Goyo curled up at her feet, she opened the letters Armando brought her. She read Lupe's letter first.

> *Dearest Little Sister,*
>
> *I hope this letter finds you well. Armando tells us the Apaches continue to raid the herd, but they have not come near the house. I pray that continues to be the case. He told us how much he depends on you and how hard you work. Please be careful, Espe. I hope you are not overdoing things.*
>
> *We are well. The children are growing fast. Luis and Francesca are attending school at the church. Francesca is proving to be an excellent student. She loves to read, but I fear Luis is lazy. Sister Encarnación tells us he's very smart, but she has sent two letters home reporting he often fails to complete his arithmetic drills. We make him do them*

*every afternoon, but he pouts and dawdles.
It's exasperating because he knows how to do
them. He doesn't put his mind to it.*

*Lupita is growing tall, and I think she
takes after her Tia Espe. She insists on riding
the horse with Alejandro and is begging for
one of her own. She can run, too. I think
even Luis will lose to her in a footrace soon.
And Mateo. What can I say about this lovely
child? He is sweet and good natured. Even
teething has not been difficult. He had a cold
a few weeks ago but came through it with no
problems. He's growing fast, too.*

*We went to see Mamá and Papá last
weekend and went to the service with them
on Sunday. They are both well, but they do
worry so about you. The Apaches are making
things difficult for everyone. They might need
to abandon their home again. If they do, they
will bring Abuela Primativa with them. I gave
Armando letters from them.*

*God be with you now and always,
Your loving sister,
Lupe*

Training Goyo proved to be both easy and entertaining.
He seemed to want to please them, and he learned
quickly. Esperanza started with the "stay" command.
She didn't want him to follow Armando down the track
when he left. His job was to remain near the house, even
when she walked down to the wash to strip bark from
the walnut tree to make medicines for pain and infection,
or into the desert to collect medicinal plants for other

remedies, or to gather amaranth for dinner.

Every day, after the horses were fed and saddled, and the chickens fed, Armando and Esperanza made a game of training the dog. A playful pup, he loved attention. She would bring him to the middle of the yard, hold her hand, palm out, in front of him and say, "*¡Estancia!*" Then she would walk back to the house, or Armando would walk down the track. If he moved to follow, she would hold her hand out again, and repeat the command. It did not take him long to get the idea that he must wait for the command, "Venga," before moving. Sometimes she gave him a bit of tortilla as a treat or she scratched his ears and praised him.

The laughter Goyo brought with him filled a void in her life. She couldn't remember laughing so much—certainly not since coming to this place. Every morning, when she stirred, Goyo jumped on the bed and stepped on her stomach on his way to lick her face. She'd wrap her arms around him and pull him down between them, pushing Armando out of bed. He would growl good-naturedly about being replaced by a dog.

When they went out, Armando to tend to the horses and ride out to check the herd, and Esperanza to let the chickens out of the coop, Goyo remained at her side. It made each day much brighter and happier. But he had not yet met the Apache.

Two days before Christmas, she made the tamales, setting them in the kettle on a woven steamer basket. When they were cooked, she covered them with a damp cloth to cool and put them into the storeroom. On Christmas Eve, while the soup simmered, she made buñuelos and baked them on the hearth in her grandmother's Dutch oven.

When Armando came in from feeding Sofi and Pepe and closing the chickens in, he said, "Something smells muy delicioso."

Goyo sidled up to her and stretched his nose to the edge of the table. "No, Goyo." To Armando, she said. "He'll soon be big enough to reach for anything he wants here." She prepared a bowl of dried beef she had pounded, soaked, and saved for him. "Merry Christmas." She placed it on the floor and told him to sit. He waited for her signal. "*Ahora.*" Once he had permission, he devoured his Christmas meal.

Behind her, Armando wrapped her in his arms, kissing her neck. "*Feliz Navidad, mi amorita. Te amo.*"

"*Y tu.*"

He held her hand, and they bowed their heads, saying a prayer of thanks for their first Christmas here.

After dinner, while Esperanza put the leftover soup and tamales into the cold storeroom, Armando took the Bible from the shelf, along with her rosary. He found the Christmas passage and waited for her to join him. She wrapped the rosary around her hands and fingered the beads. Goyo sat at her feet, leaning against her leg.

He read, "*Aconteció en aquellos días que salió un edicto de parte de César Augusto, para levantar un censo de todo el mundo habitado...*"

After he finished reading, they opened their gifts. Lupe sent Esperanza writing paper and ink; her parents sent a small daguerreotype of them in a silver frame. She drew her finger across the image. Tears threatened. "I do miss them so, Armando."

"I miss them, too. They mean more to me than my own parents." He breathed soft kisses across her knuckles. "Our time here will pass, and you will see them again, I promise."

Outside, the moonless, night sky shimmered with stars. They held hands, searching for the brightest ones and for the shapes her father taught her to look for in the sky. Esperanza pointed. "That is *Orión*. Those three stars in a row. They're his belt. His sword hangs below it—that fuzzy cluster. Papá used to take us out to look at the sky. He showed us the constellations and told us stories about their names. Orión bragged that, as the greatest hunter, he would kill all the animals in the world. I am thankful he didn't succeed."

As if to make her point, an owl hooted somewhere and received an answer from a nearby tree. Coyotes howled and yipped out in the desert. The dog stood and pricked his ears toward the sound.

"Yes, Goyo. Coyotes are your enemy. You must not let them visit the chickens. And the owl? He and the hawks are also interested in having a nice chicken dinner. You must not let them."

Armando pointed. "Ah! Look! A shooting star! If we make a wish on a shooting star, it will come true." He tightened his arm around her shoulder, pulling her close. "God has been good to us, Espe. I am thankful for this land and for you. I love you more than life itself, and I wish good fortune for us here and for our someday children."

Chapter 14

Spring 1866

The sound bounced off the mountains and echoed across the desert. She didn't know who fired, but she doubted Armando could get off a shot at a full gallop.

He had ridden after the Apaches who were, once again, stealing cattle. She lost sight of him but followed his track by the dust rising from the scrub. Goyo stood by her side, leaning against her leg.

She searched for the Apaches. They were moving around in slow circles watching Armando close in on them instead of hurrying to drive the cattle they separated from the herd.

"Madre de Dios." A trap. Normally, they kept out of range of his rifle.

He came back into sight riding along an open ridge, rifle in his hand, pushing Sofi hard. Before she had time for relief at spotting him, another shot echoed and

Armando fell from the mare. "*¡Ah, Dios!*" She ran to the gelding and shoved her rifle into the scabbard. Hiking her skirt high, she threw her right leg over the high cantle and pressed into the stirrups, pausing only to shout at Goyo. "*¡Estancia!*"

They dashed down the track through the brush. Mesquite branches and acacia grabbed her skirt and petticoat, but she did not slow. She wasn't sure where Armando went down. Here, below the ridge, the trail went up and down and around larger trees and cactus.

As she rounded a turn in the trail, the mare came thundering toward her, dragging her reins. "Whoa" Esperanza turned the gelding across the trail and raised her arm. "*¡Sofi!* Whoa!" The frantic horse slid to a stop, heaving and blowing. Esperanza sidled close to her, leaning out to grab the reins. She pulled her around and started in the direction the horse came from. At first, Sofi resisted. She wanted to go home.

"*¡Vámanos!* Sofi, come on!" Choosing not to be left alone, the mare ran along beside her. "'Mando!" She drew Pepe up, settled the horses, and listened.

"*¡Espe, estoy aqui!*"

She worked her way through the brush, stopping to listen from time to time. She found him sitting on the ground, blood dripping from his forehead, and looking a little dazed.

Esperanza started to dismount, but he raised his hand and told her to stay in the saddle.

"*Estoy bien, Espe.*" He stood and slid the rifle into the scabbard, grabbed his hat, shook the dirt out of it, and jammed it on his head. "They missed me," he said. After mounting his horse, he patted her on the neck. "And then I fell off."

Relieved, she suppressed a laugh. "How many cattle did we lose?"

"I'm not sure. Lying on my back in the trail didn't exactly give me a good view of them." He dragged his arm across his forehead, wiping blood on his sleeve.

"It doesn't look bad, Mando. You'll have a headache." She was glad he could joke.

She reached for his hand, and he sidestepped Sofi close, kissed her, and said, "They've had time to get away. Let's go count cows."

They turned their horses and rode across the bajada.

Even though she might have ridden out here before, Armando insisted she stay at the house, and he wouldn't hear of her riding out alone. So for her, this was a rare opportunity to explore the surrounding landscape. Spring had come early, and the winter rains had provided for a colorful display of yellow poppies with a scattering of blue lupine. Great expanses of flowers covered south-facing slopes, and in the distance, hillsides glowed golden in the sunlight.

She drew Pepe to a halt at the top of a narrow ridge. "I had no idea how beautiful it is."

"Sometimes I'm so focused on the cattle and the Apaches I forget."

"I can understand why you fell in love with this place. Out here, closer to those massive rock towers, I feel their power, the spell they cast." All the time she had been here, the spirits of the mountains and the desert had failed to speak to her, but today, she thought she heard them whisper.

At the house, Goyo laid near the chicken yard, his black paw crossed over his white one, chin resting on them, and watching the chickens do what chickens do.

"Good boy!" When Esperanza called, he got up, wagging his tail, and followed them to the hitching rail. After dismounting, she knelt and wrapped her arms around him, burying her face in the warmth of his dark fur.

While Armando tended to the horses, Esperanza went inside and stripped off her skirt and petticoat. Examining the damage, she sighed. *Mamá's sewing lessons will be tested.* She folded them both and laid them in the chest. When she dug through her clothes, she came across her brother's trousers. She held them up and decided if she had been wearing these, her clothes wouldn't be in shreds. On a whim, she put them on, tightened the waist with a length of twine, and went outside.

In the garden, she pulled the weeds that seemed to appear overnight, thankful the rain gave the cilantro and onions a healthy start, and wishing the weeds didn't enjoy the same benefit. She would soon need to hand water because little rain would fall between now and the start of the monsoon.

The corn's thin green leaves reached upward. Soon, when she planted the beans, they would climb the stalks and hold them steady in the wind. Then, the broad leaves of the squash would shade the soil and hold moisture for the others. Armando had started building a rock wall around the garden because the javelinas still came through the collapsed southern wall. Of course, birds were a big problem. Thrashers were notorious for stealing the seeds and new sprouts before they took hold.

Periodically, Goyo came to check on her. When she shooed the birds, he joined in, trampling through the tilled soil, seeded rows, and young plants, barking at the fleeing birds.

She laughed. "Gracias, Goyo, but perhaps you can learn to chase them without undoing my work." She traced his white blaze with her thumb and softly caressed his head. He wagged his tail.

"I think I should put up a scarecrow or two. I'll ask Armando to make some poles, and I'll tie on strips of cloth that will blow in the breeze. My petticoat is already in rags."

"Who are you talking to?" Armando came around the house and stopped short, staring at her.

"Goyo. We're going to put up scarecrows."

"What in God's name are you wearing?"

"Manolito's trousers. If I wore them more often, especially when I need to chase after you, I wouldn't need to mend my skirt." Looking down at her brother's clothes, the legs rolled at her ankles, she burst out laughing, grabbing the pants on each side and executing a deep curtsy. "May I introduce myself, kind sir? I'm Countess Esperanza of El Rancho Ramirez. Welcome to our fine estate."

Armando laughed and strode to her. He bowed low, saying, "I'm pleased to make your acquaintance, Countess." Standing, he lifted her hand to his lips, brushing a gentle kiss across her knuckles the way he had not done for a long time.

She stepped into his arms. He pulled her close and kissed her, probing her mouth with his tongue. Cupping her buttocks, he held her against him, and she wrapped her legs around his body, giving in to the passion he offered. She answered his tongue with her own, and hooked her ankles together behind his back, pressing her need against his. He slipped her legs from around him and carried her into the house.

"I can't believe how beautiful you are—even in men's trousers, but you've made my work here more difficult. I can find my way beneath your skirt, but this is new."

She grinned. "A problem I'm all too familiar with. Keep trying."

He untied the twine and unbuttoned the trousers, letting them fall to the floor. She stepped out of them and pushed her boots off. He pulled her close, and his calloused hands, rough against her buttocks made her shiver with need. She tugged his shirt open, kissing his bare chest. She pressed her naked body against him, rubbing her own callouses along his back.

She led him to the bed and drew the blanket down and sat. After unbuttoning his pants, she pulled them to his knees and pleasured him. When she laid back, Armando hurried to pull off his boots with his trousers tangled around them. Esperanza laughed as he danced around the room with trousers and boots half off. Laughing with her, he lay down, pulled her on top of him, and whispered, "Espe, *mi amor, tú eres mi vida.*"

"*Y tú eres* mía." Nothing else in the world mattered. Not the hard work. Not the loneliness here. *Nada.*

Chapter 15

Spring 1866

In the morning, Armando left for Tucson. She gave him letters to her family and a list of groceries and household things she needed. He promised her he would bring plaster to do the inside walls and floor.

She and Goyo watched as the wagon disappeared down the track, listening until he crossed the wash and headed out to the Tucson Road. Making the sign, she said a quick prayer for his safe return.

In the house, she chewed the seeds Abuela Tiva had given her, grateful they continued to work. She resolved to plant some so she would not run out. Then, she brought a bag from the store room and dumped it out on the table. The walnut bark strips had dried nicely, so it was time to prepare them for making poultices or tea in case of another emergency. She had made Armando drink walnut bark tea to ward off infection from last week's injury.

She took several strips and laid them aside for tea, and broke the rest into smaller pieces for grinding. Using an old tin bowl and a smooth hand stone, she ground the bark into a fine powder and returned it to the bag. If she needed it, all she would have to do is to mix the powder with a bit of water, smear it on a bandage, and she'd have a poultice that would relieve pain.

Later, in the barn, dust motes floated in narrow shafts of light from the windows along the roof line while she raked manure into a pile and scooped it into a bucket. She made several trips to the far side of the garden where she dumped it. After she finished in the barn, she collected manure from the turnout.

Because she didn't want the horses standing in urine-soaked soil, she tackled the urine puddles while the ground had time to dry. In the dim light, the rank, ammonia smell made her eyes water. She shoveled the wet soil into the bucket and disposed of it beyond the perimeter wall. When she was finished, she left the door open to let air circulate. Tomorrow, she would fill the holes with dry soil, and the barn would be clean when Armando got back.

Goyo divided his attention between her and the chickens.

Exhausted, she shooed the chickens into the coop, and called Goyo to come inside. After a light meal of tortillas and tea, she fed the dog and collapsed on the bed. Goyo hopped onto the bed and curled himself against her. She laid her arm across him and fell into a sound sleep.

In the morning, even though she felt rested, her shoulder muscles ached. She decided today would be a quiet day with no heavy work. After feeding the chickens and leaving Goyo to tend them, she went back inside and filled the large basin with hot water. She stripped and washed all over, taking pleasure in the warmth as she rubbed the wash rag over her body, but shivering when the water cooled on her skin.

Instead of her usual skirt and blouse, she put on her green calico dress, the only dress she brought with her. It buttoned in the front from an open neckline to the waist, with narrow bands of lace trimming the neckline and the sleeves. Since it was gathered more fully in the back than in front, the skirt was a little slimmer than most of her skirts. Armando liked it and would be pleased to see her wearing it when he got back tonight.

She filled a pitcher with warm water, dropping in a small cloth bag of lavender leaves to steep. She filled a basin and went outside to wash her hair. When she was finished, she poured the lavender water through it, toweled it, and then combed it.

She went inside to get Armando's shirts and her torn skirt from the chest. She wouldn't mend the petticoat since she had decided to keep it for the scarecrows, as well as for bandages she hoped she would not need.

She carried a chair outside. Her hair would dry while she mended clothes. She propped the Henry against the house and sewed a button on the shirt. It was a peaceful day, with a clear blue sky. A pair of quail hopped up on top of the old wall, the male calling, "puk-KWA-ca-ha, puk-KWAH-ca-ha." When she was a little girl, Abuela Tiva told her they were calling, "*Los Pápagos. Los Pápagos.*" Sometimes, they sang a three-note call, sounding like *Cuidado! Cuidado!* They explored the ground along the wall, prospecting for a nesting spot and chattering to one another. Sparrows fluttered through the surrounding scrub, and a cactus wren began building her nest in a cholla across the yard.

Goyo took his position near the chicken yard, but a whiptail lizard darted past his nose, and he chased it into the rocks, sniffing and snuffling, searching for it, his black, fuzzy tail wagging happily. When he realized he wouldn't find it, he gave up and went back to guarding the chickens.

Humming a tuneless melody, Esperanza focused on rips in the skirt, barely noticing when the shadows began to lengthen. A slight breeze interrupted her work, and she stopped humming.

What is that song? Where have I heard it?

In the center of the yard, Goyo sat motionless, staring at the palo verde. The soft melody drifted to her and caught her attention.

His hands lifted, palms up, his eyes closed, face inclined to the sky, the Apache chanted softly. Goyo tilted his head and perked his ears at a subtle change in the melody. He lay down, crossed his front feet the black one over the white one, and rested his chin on them, his eyes never leaving the Apache.

She wondered how long he had been there chanting—even as she hummed along.

Dajídíl slipped into the shadows. At the bottom of the ridge, he crossed the wash, barely disturbing the water's flow. His pony waited under the walnut tree, where he tied a small, downy eagle feather to a low-hanging branch. He led the pony to the wash and squatted, scooping water into his mouth while the pony drank.

He swung easily to the pony's back.

> *Morning star clears away the clouds.*
> *The clouds hide from morning star.*
> *Morning star welcomes the sun.*

He rode eastward, his pony's hooves soundless on the desert floor, with only the sounds of birds chattering in the scrub as he passed by.

Images of his daughter floated before him and mingled with those of the woman. Had he called her spirit from the darkness to taunt him when he whispered her name? And what dangers lay ahead because he sang her song? He was as helpless now as when she passed from this world. When she was taken.

Her birth had been a gift to his people. When the time came for her puberty ceremony, more than any other girl of the tribe, she would *be* White Changing Woman—the first woman in the world. The woman who came before them all. But they did not know.

In the mountains, he had spent five days and nights in a rock shelter. With no food or drink, he depended on the spirits to give him sustenance. He scattered sacred pollen to the four directions and chanted steadily.

In his vision, a girl child, surrounded by a dazzling light, ran beside the river, her black hair flying. Dark clouds hung low in the sky. She carried a spear, much too long for a child of her size, but she carried it with grace. When she threw the spear, he followed its arc, soaring into the sky, through the clouds, scattering them into the four directions with a blinding flash of light. The spear landed in the midst of an enemy camp. A great cloud of dust rose, obscuring everything on Earth. When the dust cleared, a beautiful young woman stood in place of the spear. The enemies lay dead around her. She raised one hand to the east and began to dance, shuffling her feet and chanting, the fringes on her buckskin dress dancing with her, creating the music White Changing Woman gave his people for the girls of the tribe.

While she chanted, the sun climbed above the mountain, its light blending with the light surrounding her.

Remaining dark clouds thinned and scattered, absorbing her light and merging with the light of the sun.

Then, all ll faded into nothingness.

When he returned to his village, he entered his wikiup, and his first woman, the one who had never given him a child, knelt before him, offering bread. He took a bite, broke off a piece, and handed it to her. After she ate, he said. "We will have a girl child. She will be called Morning Star."

In time, his sister brought him news that his woman gave birth to a girl child. He answered, "I know." A single cloud crossed the sun's path, casting his village into shadow.

Throughout her childhood, he killed many deer, some of which spoke to his spirit on her behalf. Each time, his prayer of thanks rose more forcefully, and the sprinkling of the sacred pollen to the four directions held a greater meaning. He saved these precious hides for her dress, tanning and softening them in anticipation of her womanhood ceremony.

As the girl grew, he shaped the pale, cream-colored poncho from the best hide. Two hides made the arm-length fringes hanging from the shoulder and the shorter ones hanging at the hem. Two more made the skirt, and the last one provided the layers of fringes encircling the hem.

He shaped hundreds of metal cones with his own hands. Into each one, he sang his own medicine songs, and, as he attached them to the fringes, he heard the exquisite music of his vision once again. He added bands of beadwork and yellow paint to strengthen her spirit and to please White Changing Woman.

When her blood flowed three summers past, she spoke quietly to her mother, "It is time."

Her mother nodded and led her to the dwelling of her godmother. She Sings at Night prepared her for the ceremony. Word spread quickly among the band. Morning Star would become a woman.

In her godmother's shelter, she sat, contemplating the coming ceremony. She Sings at Night sent her two small sons to her sister's wikiup and dispatched her husband to prepare the ceremonial plaza. At a distance from the main camp, he built a circle of rocks for the bonfire and led a group of young men to find slender trees to strip and bind together for Changing Woman's ceremonial home. They constructed brush shelters for her parents and godparents.

When her flow ceased, her godmother dressed the girl in the ceremonial dress made by her father. She held up the drinking tube. "During the ceremony, you may drink water, but you must drink only through the tube."

"Yes, Aunt. I understand."

She showed her the scratching stick. "You must not scratch with your hand. You will keep your body untouched and respect your sacred nature."

"Yes, Aunt. I understand."

Morning Star lowered her head while She Sings at Night placed the thong holding these sacred tools around her neck. The girl lifted the stick and touched it to her shoulder, satisfied.

Once Morning Star was dressed, her godmother handed her the ceremonial cane, a peeled stick with a crook, held by a length of rawhide, on one end. A downy eagle feather, an owl wing feather, and two cone tinklers hung from the cane, along with four ribbons: black, green, yellow, and tan, representing the four sacred directions.

Finally, She Sings at Night brushed Morning Star's hair and braided it loosely, entwining rawhide thongs through each braid. Her godmother hung a downy eagle feather in her hair. The final adornment was a beaded headband with a shell fragment hanging in the center of her forehead.

She was ready to assume the power of White Changing Woman. She would honor her people's way of life and strengthen them for whatever trials they might face.

His daughter stepped into the light of the rising sun. In her dancing, he saw the future of his people. She would be a strong, warrior woman. In her youth, she competed with boys her age and older, always winning the races, on foot or on horseback. She could throw a spear with accuracy and fire seven arrows from her bow before the boys could load five. Through her, his people would prevail over those who would steal their lives and their freedom.

On the third day, she and her godmother faced the rising sun while the people gathered behind her and began to chant. She danced in place, shuffling her feet and pounding her cane on the ground. The tinklers on the cane and the dress sang in harmony. The drums beat a cadence during the recitation of the creation story, and she listened, rapt.

The people danced while women massaged and molded her into a woman, and she danced again. When it was time to run, she did so with grace and speed; she never faltered. When the Gaan came down from the mountains and danced the four sacred directions, they celebrated the people's balance with the Earth. Because her heart was pure, Morning Star brought them together in unity and strength.

...and now this woman. In this place. Did Ussen mean to taunt him? Did Ussen mean to test him?

As he rode quietly through the desert back to his village, he tried to understand the challenge that had been laid before him. What did Ussen intend? What should he do about this woman and her man? Had he offended Ussen by allowing them to live? Must she forfeit blood to atone for his disloyalty?

Chapter 16

Spring 1866

Esperanza was weeding the garden when Armando's wagon came into the yard. She was surprised to see Julio, on Paquito, following, and even more surprised to see two more riders behind him.

She stood, transfixed, unbelieving. Her father and Manolito. *Papá?*

"Papá!" She dropped a handful of weeds and ran to meet him. He was off his horse in mere moments, and she flung herself into his arms, fearful that she was dreaming and he would disappear.

As he lifted her off the ground, his strong arms told her he was real. "Papá, you're really here?" Her tears blended with his when she kissed his cheek.

"M'hija, I've missed you. Mamá sends her love."

He stood her on her feet, and she reached for her brother who wrapped his arms around her. "Lito! You're so tall. Look at you!" When she last saw him, he was only a little taller than her. Now he was nearly as tall as their father. "I fear you've grown up since I saw you."

He grinned. "Did you see my new horse?" He nodded toward the fleabitten gray Armando was tying at the rail. "I think Sucio and I can beat you and Pepe now."

"Sucio? You call your horse 'Dirty'?"

"Sí. He looks like he's been splattered with mud."

She clung to his hand, as well as her father's, afraid to let go. "I'd love to race you again. But I think my Pepe can beat your dirty horse."

When she looked around at Armando and Julio, their smiles were as wide as she'd ever seen.

"How did you—?" She couldn't find the words she needed.

Julio explained that Manolito had stopped to see him a month ago, right after Armando had been in Tucson. "He asked me when Armando might be back and if I thought he and your father could join him on his next trip back to the ridge. They came to Tucson two days ago ready to come with us."

She looked at her father. "Who's with Mamá and Abuela Tiva?"

"Tomás and Javiela are there. By the way, they will be parents themselves in the fall."

Again, a familiar jealousy stabbed at her heart, but she tried to ignore it. "I'm happy for them."

Goyo circled the small group, sniffing the strangers' trousers.

Esperanza introduced him to her father and brother. "He guards the chickens and keeps me company when Armando is gone." Manolito bent to pet him.

Armando, back from tying the horses, said, "Take them inside. Julio and I will handle the supplies."

"I need to get dinner. Did you bring meat?"

"I did better than that." He took a box out of the wagon. "Empanadas from Lupe."

Julio handed a large, covered pot to Manolito. "And cazuela from Adelita."

In the house, after hanging the pot of soup in the fireplace and stirring the fire, she turned to find her father and brother scanning the room, studying the unplastered walls and the dirt floor. For a moment, she was ashamed. "I know it's not much, but we are all right here."

"Don't worry, m'hija. I wasn't expecting to see a fine Spanish hacienda. But—"

"Armando's going to plaster the walls and floor and we'll have a mat on the floor soon. It won't look so bad, then."

He took her hand and turned it over, tracing the callouses with a forefinger. "You work hard here."

"I do, Papá, but I promised to help Armando achieve his dream. I am his wife. You would not expect me to do less."

While they talked, Manolito explored the small house. He examined the things on the shelf with her Bible and went into the storage room. He came back to the door and said, "Papá, look. They have everything they need right here."

She led her father to the store room, which was nearly as large as the room where they lived. "Armando brings water up from the well and siphons it into this barrel. It's very handy for me. We keep the harnesses and tack in here, too, along with everything we don't want to lose to the—" She stopped herself.

Her father finished for her. "The Apaches. Have they been a problem?"

"Armando's lost several cows to them, but we've had no trouble near the house." She couldn't say none had been here, only that there'd been no trouble.

Manuel Ocoboa's brows drew together, deepening the crease between them. "Armando leaves you alone regularly. Does he not worry about an Apache attack during his absence?"

"Of course, Papá. But I have Goyo and my rifle."

Before he could answer, Armando and Julio came in to put the tack and supplies away.

"What's this?" Manolito was standing at the table holding the old pot.

"I found that in the garden. The stories about Pueblo Viejo are true. People lived here a long time ago. I'm always finding broken pieces outside."

"I saw them on the shelf."

When Armando came out of the storage room, he said, "The soup smells good and I'm starving. Let's eat."

After dinner, Esperanza looked around the small room in a minor panic. "How will we all sleep tonight?"

Julio laughed. "We worked that out on the way here. Your father will sleep in here, using the pallet I use when I come, and Manolito and I will sleep in the wagon."

"Are you sure? We can push the table back and try to make room on the floor."

"Our horses will be in the turnout all night, so it's best if we're out there with them."

While Esperanza cleared the dishes from the table, the men went outside.

"You've been very quiet, Armando." Manuel Ocoboa didn't look at his son-in-law. Instead, he gazed at La Cresta. They had walked to the south end of the yard beside the old wall while Julio and Manolito fed the horses and prepared their beds in the wagon.

"Yes sir." Armando didn't quite know what to say. He feared he was being judged and found wanting. Seen through the eyes of her family, the house he had built for Esperanza was primitive and crude. And had her father really forgiven them? Him? "No disrespect intended, sir."

"None taken." Manuel Ocoboa withdrew two cigars from his pocket and handed one to Armando. He struck the match on the rock wall, lit his own cigar, and handed the still burning match to the younger man. Armando drew on the cigar, exhaling the smoke as the cigar flamed up. He dropped the match on the ground and stepped on it.

"It's beautiful here, son." He shifted his gaze from La Cresta to the mountains to the east. "Very different from looking at these mountains from Tucson."

Armando's relief at being called "son" blended with his sense of pride. "It's what first drew me here. The cattle do well on the bajada." He gestured in that direction. "And we have a view all the way around us here."

"And the Apaches? Any threats?"

"Other than stealing cattle, none so far. I try to protect the herd, but once they've cut a few out, it's hard to get them back. I try. I might retrieve one or two."

"It's a big area for one man to manage—and dangerous when you go after them alone."

"Yes sir. I keep my distance. Their guns are not as good as mine."

"Having lost some cattle, have you made up for it with calves?"

"Not really. At least not yet. The mountain lions and the coyotes have taken five of the seven that were born this year. None of those survivors are male, so I don't have to worry about castrating them. If I have any male survivors, Julio will help me with that."

Now, Señor Ocoboa turned to face his son-in-law. "And Esperanza? How is she really doing?"

Again, Armando felt he was being judged. "You can be proud of her, sir. She works hard and she's not afraid."

"Even when she's here alone?" He lifted his chin and blew a cloud of smoke into the air above their heads.

Before Armando could answer, Julio and Manolito, with Goyo running circles around him, joined them.

The older man handed Julio a cigar and a match. "Thank you both for bringing us here. I'm surprised you've been able to travel back and forth so freely in spite of the Apaches. I pray that continues."

Armando nodded. "We have been fortunate. I'd like to think that we don't have much to offer except the cattle."

Again, the crease between Manuel Ocoboa's brows deepened. "I doubt that. You have two fine horses. If nothing else, I suspect they'd be interested in stealing them."

Slightly irritated, Armando replied, "That's true. I lock them in the barn at night, but they—and we—are vulnerable during the day. I'm very aware of that."

Esperanza came out of the house and joined them. The sun hung low in the western sky casting La Cresta in stark relief and long shadows across the yard. She took her father's hand, and he put his arm around her, drawing her close to his tall frame.

Manolito, examining several pieces of pottery he found on the ground and not looking at his father, said, "I'm going to help get rid of the Apaches. I'll kill as many as I can."

His father frowned again. "We've been over this many times, Lito. You are not going out on your own—or with a bunch of young upstarts with no experience—to fight the Apaches. We must let the Territorial government handle them."

"But they're doing nothing. The United States pulled their army out of the presidio to fight their war with each other. So who's going to defend us? We have to do it ourselves."

His father sighed. "You may be right, but you're going nowhere—at least not yet."

Esperanza listened to this exchange with a growing sense of alarm. Her little brother, only a year younger than she, was bent on going to battle. She shuddered to think of his death at the hands of a hostile band of Apaches. And she tried not to think of the one who watched her.

In the morning, Esperanza made a big breakfast while the men made preparations to leave. When they came inside, Armando said, "After we eat, Julio and I are taking Manolito out to the bajada to check on the cattle. When we get back in, they'll leave for Tucson."

"Won't that make it late when you get back?" She looked to her father.

He nodded. "Manolito wants to explore this countryside first, and I want to spend more time with you, m'hija."

Over breakfast, Manolito pointed his fork at Esperanza and grinned. "Funny thing, Espe. Right after you moved out, I seem to have lost a pair of trousers. You wouldn't know where they went, would you?"

She glanced at Armando and blushed. "I'm sure I don't know what you're talking about, Lito."

Her father kept eating but didn't succeed at hiding his smile.

Later, they sat together at the table. "Tell me the truth, m'hija. Are you happy here."

"I am happy to be Armando's wife." She picked up the old pot, rested it in her lap, and traced the lines with her finger.

Her father spoke softly. "That's not what I asked. Are you happy here."

She looked at the unplastered walls and the dirt floor. "It's not much, I know, and I miss you and Mamá and my sister and brothers every day. Sometimes I'm lonely, but I have this pot, and it helps."

She handed him the pot, and he turned it over in his hands, examining the design. "How?"

"I found it when I was digging the garden...it's old, going back, I think, to when the people of Pueblo Viejo lived here. It seems to carry the spirit of the woman who made it. We talk. She keeps me company."

"I see. You and your grandmother are very much alike."

She took the pot and put it back on the table. "Let's go feed the chickens."

When the men came back from the bajada, Manolito was excited. "Papá, you should have come with us. You can see for miles. We're used to seeing the mountains around Tucson and Tubac, but there are more mountains far west of here." He swung his arm in that direction. "I'd like to fill my saddlebags and just ride as far as I can go." His eyes shone with excitement and with the mystery of what might lie so far to the west.

"Maybe someday, son," his father said. "For now, we need to head back to Tucson so we can start home tomorrow." He shook hands with Armando. "Take care of my girl."

"Yes sir. I will."

Wrapping his daughter in his arms, he said, "I love you, m'hija. Stay strong."

"I love you, too, Papá. Give my love to Mamá and to Tomás and Javiela."

Esperanza took her brother's hands and kissed his cheek. "Be good, Lito. I love you."

"Y tu, Espe."

When the three men were mounted and ready to leave, she reached for Julio's hand. "Thank you for bringing my father and brother here."

"*De nada.*" They turned and started down the track.

Armando and Esperanza stood together watching them go. When her father and Lito looked over their shoulders and waved before disappearing from sight, her tears overflowed.

Armando held her. "Maybe they will come back again."

"*Eso espero.* I hope so."

Chapter 17

Spring 1866

Esperanza passed through the opening in an unfamiliar, well-built cobble wall, pausing only to ask the desert's permission before entering. She walked toward La Cresta along a surprisingly well-worn path. She frequently went this way when she collected herbs and seeds. But today, she found fresh tracks, from flat footwear different from her own boots or Armando's, and among them, barefoot tracks, small, like children's.

When did a child pass here? Why didn't we see him?

When the path curved around a tall saguaro, she came upon an unfamiliar structure. Like a house, but not quite like a house, it rose from the desert to a height

*of about five feet with mud-plastered walls
and roof. She walked around it and found a
low, open entrance. She ducked her head and
stepped into the opening. Inside, she stood
straight; the floor was below ground level.*

*As her eyes adjusted to the gloom, she
noticed a fire pit in front of the entry, with
glowing embers. The smell of burning
mesquite filled the room, and a thin cloud of
smoke drifted toward the doorway. Several
pots and ollas of various sizes sat around
the room and woven mats covered parts of
the floor. The interior walls were unplastered,
revealing branches and limbs of varying
sizes. Two sturdy mesquite trunks on either
side of the fire pit held up the heavy ceiling.
On one, a small olla full of water hung from
a short limb.*

Someone lives here. I have intruded on
their home.

Just then, indistinct voices filled the air.

Armando? No. Women's voices.

*Stepping into the sunlight, she blinked
and squinted, trying to find the women.*

*She hadn't seen it before, but now a
ramada and other dwellings like this one
surrounded her. Beyond them, an opening in
the cobble wall faced La Cresta.*

*The voices grew louder, among them, the
shouts of children. In the courtyard, a handful
of dark boys and girls, naked and barefoot,
threw sticks for a brown dog to chase and
bring back to them. Several women sat in a
circle under the ramada. She approached, but
they took no notice. Naked from the waist up,*

their dark skin glistened in the reflected light,
their breasts danced with the movement of
their hands as they transformed clay into
pots.

One woman...

Her thick, black hair hung over her
shoulders. On either side of her mouth, blue
lines stretched downward to her chin. She
concentrated on the unfinished clay pot in
her hands. Her dark eyes focused only on her
work. She smoothed the clay, and, holding a
small rock inside and pounding the outside
with a flat piece of wood, she thinned the
walls and shaped the pot.

Esperanza gasped. "My pot."

Startled, the woman looked up. When
their eyes met, the world began to spin. Faster
and faster it went until everything was a blur.
Desperate and dizzy, she reached out, trying
to find something—anything—to hold on to,
something to slow her, to stop the whirling.
A hand took hers and the world slowed to a
motionless silence. She no longer stood in the
desert. La Cresta had disappeared.

In the distance, unfamiliar, exotic flowers
climbed surrounding hillsides and reached
into a golden sky; nearby, familiar flowers
enveloped her in a riot of brilliant colors.

An ocotillo bent above her, pouring a
flood of red from its blossoms around her,
the red filling her mouth and blistering her
tongue.

When she could stand it no longer, from
behind, mariposa lilies and desert marigolds
surged into the red, transforming it to orange

and then a brilliant yellow, extinguishing the fire in her mouth.

Morning glories threaded around her, wrapping her in a soft, blue cloud, cooling her tongue.

Gentle breezes blew the cloud away, revealing a single amaranth growing at her feet.

The hand holding hers was dark—darker than her own honey-brown skin. The woman who stood before her picked the tender, green leaves from the amaranth and fed them to her, nourishing her with new strength and energy.

The woman spoke into the silence. "In the Sea Ania, the Flower World, you are welcome."

"I have no offering, nothing to give."

"You bring your sea takaa, the power of your spirit. It surrounds and protects you. These flowers are your spirit, that which is beautiful and good in you. Your heart is pure and your spirit is strong.

The corners of her mouth lifted slightly, and the blue chin lines curved with her smile. When her dark eyes penetrated Esperanza's, the world around them shifted. She found herself standing beside the ramada, still held by the woman's gaze.

"Gracias."

"¿Por que?" Armando rolled over to face his wife. "You are talking in your sleep, mi amorita." Sliding his arm under her, he pulled her close and curled himself against her back. She snuggled against him, their knees bent, their bodies molded into one. She drifted into a dreamless sleep.

Chapter 18

Spring 1866

The next morning, they rose and set about their work as they did every morning, but Esperanza couldn't concentrate. She needed to find something, but it wouldn't come into focus. She went outside hoping something would spark her memory.

The horses, as always, were tied at the rail, saddled and ready in case the Apaches raided the cattle again. Armando was enlarging the turnout, creating a fence from bare ocotillo branches he had cut last winter. She stared at them, seeing, in her mind's eye, the green leaves and red flowers they would wear when they grew as a living fence. Something burned her tongue.

She lifted her gaze to La Cresta and started walking. She stepped around the rocks and cobbles from the collapsed part of the wall and stopped, examining the desert floor and looking at the open spaces between the prickly pears and mesquites. Something teased the edges of her memory.

Several saguaros, their arms twisting in every direction, pointing up and pointing down, grew there. As she passed them, parts of the dream came back in flashing, vivid images, too quickly at first to make sense.

The dwelling.

The children.

The women.

Images took shape, images of this place many years ago. *How long ago?*

The people of Pueblo Viejo. They built mud houses, and they raised children who laughed and shouted and played with dogs. The women made pottery. And sometimes someone dropped a pot and left the broken pieces where they fell. Even as she thought it, she glanced down to see potsherds at her feet.

She picked one up. Plain, not decorated like the pot from the garden. She remembered the woman in her dream. The blue lines on either side of her mouth lifting with her smile, her thick black hair hanging over her shoulders as she shaped the vessel. Her dark eyes gazed into Esperanza's and invited her to linger a moment with her spirit, assuring her she would never be alone here.

The woman's words came back to her: "Your heart is pure, and your spirit is strong." She had heard those words before. It was the last time she saw Abuela Tiva. The day after they told her parents about the homestead, she and her mother went to see her grandmother.

"Does Lupe know what you and Armando are doing."

"Sí, Mamá."

"Why didn't she tell me?

"I asked her not to. It was up to us to tell you."

Her mother sighed. "If you are bound for this 'adventure,' as you call it, there are things you must plan for."

Esperanza raised her eyebrows. "You sent me to Abuela Tiva for that, didn't you?"

"Not that." Her smile was strained. "What will you do if you or Armando gets sick, or worse, is injured?"

"Abuela Tiva taught me what to do, and I made an appointment with Dr. Matas in Tucson. Since we will be living so far from town, he was kind enough to provide me with ointments and even a small vial of laudanum."

"Laudanum? He gave your laudanum?"

"He gave me strict warnings about how to use it." The doctor had also lectured her on the foolishness of leaving the safety of Tucson, but she didn't tell her mother everything he said. Only after he understood she would not take his advice on the matter, did he offer his counsel. "He was more than helpful."

"I'm glad, but I'll feel better after my mother talks to you." She took her daughter's hand, and they followed the path to Abuela Tiva's small house.

The old woman was waiting for them. "Venga." Using her cane, she led them to the kitchen where a basket waited on the table. "Sit." She passed the basket to Esperanza. "You know what these are and how to use them?"

Esperanza examined the bags of seeds, dried leaves, herbs, and crushed bark. She nodded. "I think so."

"Good. I 'spect you won't have a cook stove—tricky to cook over an open fire in the fireplace. Your mamá never had to do that." Dabbing her rheumy eyes with her apron, she said, "Make sure your man gets the right kettles, pots, and tools you need. You'll need to swing pots in and out of the fire." She paused. "Hmmph! What do men know of cookin'?" Mother and daughter laughed. "You'll need a pot big enough for a steady supply of hot water all the time—not just for cooking, but for emergencies, too." She showed her how to cook with a cast iron Dutch oven. "Take mine. I have little use for it now."

As they were saying their farewells, Abuela Tiva took her granddaughter's hand, closed her milky eyes, and whispered something in the old language. Altagracia Ocoboa's eyes filled with tears. On the way home, Esperanza asked her mother what her grandmother had said.

She recited it for her daughter.

Go, my child.
Be one with the earth.
Use her gifts wisely and well.
Your heart is pure.
Your spirit is strong.
You will not falter.

Chapter 19

Summer 1866

Goyo abandoned his dinner and ran to the door, barking.

Outside, the cacophony of rumbling wagons, accompanied by shouting drivers and outriders, along with braying mules, announced the arrival of Ochoa-Tully freight wagons on the way to Camp Grant. It reminded Esperanza there were others in the world, even if they were all men.

"Goyo, wait!" The dog spun around in the yard and came to stand beside Armando at the door.

She grabbed her shawl and ran outside. The dog jumped up, pressing his front feet against her apron. She scratched his ears, saying, "I know, Goyo. I'm excited, too. You can come with us this time."

Armando took her hand, and, together, with Goyo running circles around them, they walked down the hill.

Besides Julio's regular visits bringing supplies or coming out to help Armando with some big project, her only connection to the outside world came from the regular passage of the freight wagons, some of them pulled by as many as ten mules, on their way to Camp Grant with supplies and provisions. At best, hauling heavy loads, they might make fifteen miles on the first day out, aiming to camp below the Ramirez ridge where the two washes meet.

Armando remembered Estevan Ochoa from Tubac, where he first began his local freighting business. Now he worked out of Tucson with his partner, hauling freight for the army. If he had room in a wagon, he also brought supplies for Armando.

It was impressive to see the orderly way the muleskinners and drivers directed the heavy wagons into a circle for the night and how quickly other men raised picket lines between the larger trees. After the wagons were in position, amidst a rising cloud of dust, several men unhitched the mules, took them to the wash for a drink, and picketed them. Other men took care of the horses, taking them for water and picketing them on a separate line. Two men spread hay along both lines.

Inside the circle, the cook and his helpers began preparing a meal at the chuck wagon. On this night, they'd eat well; most nights, dinner would be jerky, cold tortillas, and biscuits. Armed sentries on horseback rode the perimeter, rifles at the ready in case of attack.

Esperanza welcomed this intrusion on her life here, and she loved watching the chaos. Estevan Ochoa strode about the encampment, stopping at each wagon, examining the huge wheels. He squatted down beside a rear wheel and slid his hand around the hub.

She glanced at Armando. "Do you think there's something wrong?"

He shrugged.

When Ochoa stood, he waved in their direction and, after speaking to one of his teamsters and pointing to the hub, he joined them.

He tipped his hat, inclined forward, and took Esperanza's hand. "*Buenos tardes, señora. ¿Coma està?*"

"*Muy bien, gracias, y usted?*"

"Bien, bien." The dark brush of his mustache lifted with his smile.

Turning to Armando, he shook his hand. "How are things out here?" His dusty suit coat and necktie suggested he would likely go back to Tucson in the morning after sending the freighters on their way.

"Not bad. Actually, I haven't lost so many cattle in the past few weeks. I did lose two calves to a mountain lion."

"How many are left?"

"Less than forty." Esperanza admired her husband for telling the truth. She suspected he hated to admit his losses. He was a proud man who wanted to prove he could start a successful cattle ranch.

"Well, if you need to replace any, let me know. My broker can bring some up from Sonora."

"Gracias, I appreciate it."

Goyo sat quietly beside Esperanza. He was now tall enough that she could rest her hand on his head without bending down. The older man looked at the dog who was watching him closely. "I have not met your friend, Señora."

"*Este es Goyo.*"

The dog lifted his paw, and Ochoa smiled, bowed, and took it. "*Encantada de conocerte*, Goyo." To Esperanza, he said, "Your guard dog and protector, I think?"

"Sí."

The teamster who examined the wheel approached and waited to speak to his boss. Goyo stood, hackles raised, and rumbled a low growl in his throat.

"*Está bien*, Goyo." Esperanza ran her hand along Goyo's back, feeling the tension in his shoulders. Axle grease smeared the man's hands and pants, and he wore a battered hat pulled down over his forehead. She sensed his eyes on her in the gathering darkness. A shiver ran down her back, and she wrapped her shawl more tightly around her shoulders.

"Mister Ochoa," the man said, frowning at the dog, "that wheel is no good. The hub is cracked."

"Gracias, Sam, I'll take a look." He turned back to Armando. "I'll see you in the morning, Señor Ramirez." He shook his hand again and nodded to Esperanza.

As the two men walked away, Goyo remained standing, tense, hackles up, and growling. When the teamster glanced over his shoulder at her, Esperanza squeezed her elbows against her sides and held her forearms against her midsection. "I don't like him."

"Who?"

"The teamster. Goyo doesn't like him either."

Ochoa and the Anglo squatted beside the wheel.

"He may be harmless enough. Ochoa picks good men. Maybe it was the odor of the grease."

"Maybe." The man glanced in her direction again when Armando turned. Again, she shivered.

Armando took her hand. "Let's go home."

When they reached the yard, he pointed. "Look." He put his arm around her shoulders and drew her against him.

Behind the eastern ridge, the full moon brightened the sky in anticipation of its rising. As the first sliver of the moon crested the tree-lined ridge, the pines cast silhouettes across its face, the shadow image widening and narrowing again as the moon climbed higher. Above the trees now, it bathed the yard in soft shadows and light.

Armando took her in his arms and kissed her, and she molded her body to his. It had been weeks—or so it seemed—since they had made love. On most nights they fell into bed exhausted from long days of work. Now, he traced kisses down her cheek, along her neck, and cupped her breast in his hand, lifting it to kiss the swell. He untied her blouse and let it and her shawl fall away from her shoulders, kissing her breasts, sucking a nipple, and circling the other with his thumb. She moaned and arched her back, her breathing faster and more urgent. He swept her up in his arms and carried her to the house.

Inside, in front of the fireplace, he slowly undressed her. The flickering light danced across her bare skin as Armando covered her body with kisses. "You are the most beautiful woman in the world."

He removed his boots and dropped his trousers on the floor. On the bed, he knelt between her legs, bent down, and flicked his tongue in her crease.

She writhed, lifting her hips to him, weaving her fingers into his hair and moaning. He slid his tongue across her belly and to her breasts. He caressed them and kissed her neck, pressing the length of his body to hers, and as he entered her, she kissed him and tasted herself on his mouth. She pulled her knees up and answered every thrust with one of her own until she was overcome with wave after wave of pleasure—the sensation mercilessly pounding every part of her body.

For a brief moment, Armando collapsed on her, his labored breathing matching her own. When he slid to the side, she felt a rush of wetness between her legs. In spite of realizing he did not pull out, she reveled in the overwhelming sensation she had experienced. *This is what Abuela Tiva meant when she said a man could give a woman pleasure.*

When he gathered her into his arms, their bodies slick with sweat and the essence of their love, she nestled her head under his chin and fell into a contented sleep.

During the night, she dreamed that Goyo stirred from his usual place on the floor and stood at the door growling. In the dream, Armando rose from the bed and pulled on his pants and boots. Her dream-self mumbled, "What's wrong?"

"Shhh—" Armando picked up his rifle.

Suddenly awake, Esperanza pulled on her chemise, picked up her own rifle and stood aside as Armando opened the door. The moon bathed the yard in pale light. Nothing moved, no sign of anyone or anything. To Goyo, he said, "¡Ahora!"

The dog shot out the door and ran past the barn barking. Armando stepped out and followed. Something—or someone—scrambled through the brush and down the back of the ridge. Goyo stopped at the edge of the yard to await his next signal, but he continued to growl, a low throaty sound indicating the danger may have passed. He sniffed the air for any lingering smells suggesting otherwise. Armando called to the horses, "Sofi, Pepe, it's all right." At the sound of his voice, they quieted.

Armando patted Goyo on the head. "Gracias, *mi amigo*. Good job." He, too, sniffed the air noting the absence of the smell of javelinas raiding the garden or of a skunk looking for eggs. A mountain lion would stir up the horses. A coyote would have the chickens in an uproar. He sniffed again. The odor was familiar. *Axle grease*. "*Hijo de puta*, what was he after?"

He turned to go back to the house with Goyo following. Esperanza waited in the doorway watching them cross the yard. "What was it?"

"Coyotes. They're gone now."

Armando rose before the sun, dressed, and left Esperanza sleeping. When he opened the barn, he found a black streak on the lock. Axle grease. He wiped it off with his finger.

Below the ridge, Ochoa's outfit prepared for their early morning departure.

He harnessed the horses and drove down the hill, parking the wagon along the Tucson Road behind the freighters. Ochoa glanced his way and nodded when he joined him.

He suspected Ochoa would see any mistakes the men might make as they prepared to start out. Once the wagons were in line, the muleskinners took their positions beside their teams to wait for the signal to move out.

"Excuse me. I'll speak with you shortly." Ochoa and his foreman strode along one side of the train and back down the other side checking wheels, wagon springs, and mules. The two men spoke briefly and shook hands.

The foreman mounted his horse, loped to the front, raised his arm and shouted, "Ho-o-o-o!" Muleskinners, one by one, lifted their whips and whistled down the line as each team of mules, straining against the traces, put the wagons into motion one after the other.

Ochoa returned to stand beside Armando, thumbs hooked in his lapels, looking like a proud father as the wagons rumbled down the road.

When the last muleskinner directed his driver to set out, Armando said, "Quite an impressive sight."

"Indeed it is, my boy." He turned to the younger man and pointed to the pile of fence posts he brought. "May I help load those on your wagon?"

"No, gracias. I know you need to get back to town. I appreciate your bringing these more than I can say." He hesitated. "I need to tell you something, and I hope you won't take offense."

Ochoa raised his eyebrows. "What is it?"

"Last night, we had an intruder near the house. Goyo chased him away."

"You suspect one of my men?" Ochoa narrowed his eyes, his graying brows pulling together over his long nose.

"Yes sir, I do." He sensed the older man expected him to continue. "The odor of axle grease was in the air, and I found this on the barn lock when I opened it this morning." He held up his hand.

The older man frowned again. "Sam. I can't say I'm surprised. I've been wary of him since I hired him. He's a good mechanic—one of the best—and I need the best. My regular mechanic broke his arm and is out of commission."

"I'm sorry. I thought it was important."

"It is. Indeed, it is. I will take care of him as soon as the train comes back. He won't be with us in the future."

"Gracias."

They shook hands and Ochoa mounted and turned toward Tucson, riding away alone, something not many men did in an area known for Apache attacks. He was one of the most honorable men in town. He would keep his promise.

Chapter 20

Summer 1866

"You're sure you want to do this while I'm gone?"

"Yes. Don't worry, Mando."

"How about waiting until I come back. I hate to see you working so hard."

She smiled. "You won't be here to see me."

With the rising sun reflected in his eyes, he lifted her chin and kissed her lightly. "I don't know why you put up with me."

"Could it be your beautiful green eyes—?" She stood on tiptoes and brushed a kiss along his temple and another against his ear. "Your strong shoulders—?" She ran her hands from his shoulders to his biceps and squeezed. "Or your—"

She reached for his groin, and he groaned. "You're making it harder for me to leave this morning."

"Mmm-hmm, it's much harder now." She grinned wickedly.

He wrapped his arms around her and laughed, "Behave yourself, my beautiful wife. When I come back, I will allow you to explore every part of my body to identify those parts most dear to you."

"I hope so. You've been neglecting me for the past month."

He gently pushed her away and took her hands, holding both to his lips. "I'm sorry, but I promise to make up for it when I come back—that is, if Julio doesn't come back with me."

She sighed. "Of course. You need to repair the barn roof."

He nodded and kissed her. "*Adios*, for now, my love."

He climbed into the wagon and took up the reins.

"*Vaya con Dios*." She wove her fingers together and held her hands to her lips as he disappeared down the track. She made the sign and offered a quick prayer to Our Lady.

She remembered the last time they made love, and her insides fluttered pleasantly. Something happened, something different—and astonishing. Armando was a generous lover, and, thanks to Abuela Tiva's wise counsel, he was always gentle and gave her pleasure. But the last time went beyond anything she had yet experienced. Even now, as she remembered the sensations surging through her body, she flushed, and desire settled low in her belly and between her legs.

"Stop," she said aloud. "I'll never finish the laundry if I keep thinking about that."

The day was already warming; she needed to wash the clothes and put them out to dry. The afternoon might bring a thunderstorm.

She threaded a length of hose to the water barrel through the opening to the storage room. With one end in her mouth, she drew water into the hose. As soon as it reached her mouth, she aimed the hose into one of the tubs, filling it. She siphoned more water into the second tub to half full.

In spite of the rising temperature, she had built up the fire to heat water in the large kettle. She made several trips carrying hot water from the house to the tub. On another day, if Armando were here to help, they would build a fire outside to heat the water, but for now, this lukewarm water would do. The bedclothes and Armando's heavy trousers would wait. She trimmed slivers from a bar of lye soap into the water.

She put her chemise, nightdress, and second petticoat into the tub. Using her laundry bat, a length of mesquite wood Armando had cut and smoothed for her, she stirred the wet clothes. After rinsing them, she wrung them out and hung them on bushes in the sun.

As she put Armando's shirts into the warm water, Goyo, who had been keeping an eye on the chickens, leaped up and ran across the yard chasing a rabbit. "Goyo," she shouted, "leave the bunny alone."

He gave up the chase but came to stand beside her, leaning forward, his ears pricked, and his eyes on the path to the wash.

"What is it, Goyo?"

He growled, and his hackles lifted. A battered hat came into view, followed by the head of the man who wore it. When he saw them, he ducked into the brush. She picked up the Henry. Goyo continued to growl, and the man stepped out into the open, coming up the path, and stopping short of the yard. The dog quieted but remained alert.

"Howdy, ma'am." The man took off his battered hat and held it against his chest. He frowned at the dog." I wonder, could I trouble you for a drink of water."

"Why didn't you get it at the wash, sir? It would have saved you a walk up the hill." When he put his hat on, he pulled the brim low. She knew where she had seen him before.

"Well, yes ma'am, you're right." He smiled, revealing the absence of several teeth behind his dirty, unshaven face. "But when I got to the wash, I remembered someone lived up here who might offer me a bit of hospitality." He took a few steps sideward as if to circle the yard. Goyo growled and took two steps toward him, hackles raised, teeth bared. The man stopped.

Esperanza did not answer.

"You wouldn't turn a tired and dusty traveler away, now would ya?" When she didn't answer, he said, "Could ya tell yer dog to back off? I don't mean no harm."

"You work for Ochoa. I didn't hear the freighters." With the rifle across her body, her right forefinger rested above the trigger, fingers of her right hand through the pump lever. She held the barrel in her left hand, pointed upward for now. She had never shot a man, and she prayed she wouldn't have to—he might be harmless after all.

"No ma'am. I don't work for Ochoa no more. Somebody told him a lie about me, so I'm lookin' for a job. Mebbe your husband needs a ranch hand?"

Esperanza almost laughed. "I don't think so, although I do appreciate your offer. Now, you need to move along."

"Mebbe I could talk to him?" Grinning, he said, "He is here, ain't he?"

She heard the edge in his voice. *He knows he's not here.*

"He's out on the bajada with the cattle. He'll be back shortly, and I don't think he'll appreciate finding you here."

The man chuckled. "He ain't out there. An' he won't be back anytime soon."

Esperanza's heart almost stopped, but she refused to let him see her fear. "What makes you think so?"

"I saw him leave this mornin' in the wagon. I spect he's gonna be in Tucson for a couple of days."

Esperanza allowed her heart to beat again. "Where's your horse? I don't think you walked here from Tucson."

"I left him down below tied to a tree."

"Mmm-hmm. You figured you'd sneak up on me."

He grinned. "Yes ma'am. You're right. Now, how 'bout you put the gun away. I reckon you don't even know how to use it." He started toward her. "I came here fer some hospitality, and I aim to git it."

"¡Goyo, ahora!" The dog sprang, knocking the man to the ground, tearing his sleeve and biting into his flesh. Screaming, the man tried to put his hands around Goyo's throat, but the dog clamped down on his arm, drawing blood.

"Get him off me! Get him off!"

"¡Goyo, *basta!*" Standing closer, she had the rifle at the ready when the dog backed off.

"God damn you, you Mexican bitch! Look what your dog did to me! He held his bloody arm. "I didn't do nothin' to you."

"No, you didn't. And you won't." She raised the Henry. "I can shoot a fly off your shoulder at twenty-five feet and barely crease your shirt. Get out of here and don't come back."

She glanced at Goyo. "Sit." The dog sat but never took his eyes off the man as he scrambled to his feet, picked up his hat, and started down the track. He looked over his shoulder once, still holding his bloody arm, and disappeared below the ridge.

Esperanza allowed herself to breathe again, but both she and the dog kept watch in case he came back.

She propped the rifle beside the door and knelt, wrapping trembling arms around Goyo's neck and whispering her thanks into his warm fur.

Still shaking, she stumbled around the corner of the house and vomited until there was nothing left to come up. After she caught her breath, she took Armando's shirts from the tub, rinsed them, wrung them out, and laid them over the bushes. She fed the chickens and gathered eggs from the coop; she mucked out the barn and the horses' enclosure, piling the manure near the garden.

Later, she collected the dry clothes and held them up. *They are too wrinkled. I wish I had an iron.* She sighed, smoothed them, folded them, and put them back into the chest.

She stayed busy for the remainder of the day but kept the gun handy in case the man came back.

It was just after dark the next night when she heard the horses pounding up the track. Without setting the brake, Armando leaped from the wagon and grabbed her. "Espe, you're all right!" He held her in his arms so tightly she couldn't breathe.

"What's wrong?" *He can't know about my visitor.* But she could see he had driven the horses hard; they were both lathered and heaving.

"I was afraid something happened to you."

"Why?"

"That man, the man from Ochoa's crew—I thought he might have been here."

Even though she wondered why he thought it, she answered simply. "He was."

"My God. Are you all right?" He wrapped his arms around her again.

"I'm fine. Let's unload the supplies and take care of the horses, Mando. They need our attention right now.

We can talk over dinner." She assumed Armando had encountered him on the road.

While Armando rubbed Sofi and Pepe down, checked their hooves, stabled, and fed them, Esperanza put the ammunition and supplies he brought into the store room and started dinner.

Later, he explained that Julio, riding Paquito, had been with him. "Before we came around the point of the mountains, we found a man lying in the middle of the road and a horse browsing the weeds nearby. We thought his horse had thrown him, and he was only knocked out, but when we turned him over, we found an Apache arrow in his chest and the broken shaft underneath him. His arm was mangled, too, like he'd been attacked by an animal."

She nodded. "I thought the Apaches didn't go around the point of the mountain. You travel that road all the time."

"I always felt a little safer once I got to the other side— but now...." He hesitated. "You said he was here?"

"Yes."

Armando slid off his chair to his knees beside his wife. He took her hands. "What happened?"

She described everything and how Goyo protected her. "To tell you the truth, I was terrified I might have to shoot him."

"I'm to blame, Espe. I got him fired from his job."

"You what?"

"Remember the night the freight wagons camped below, and I told you Goyo went after coyotes?"

"Yes."

"It was the Anglo wagon mechanic. I found axle grease on the barn lock. I told Ochoa in the morning, and he promised to fire him."

"He knew you were gone. He saw you leave yesterday morning, so he must have been hanging around down below. He said someone lied to Ochoa about him and he lost his job. Maybe he hoped to get even with you for getting him fired."

"I never thought I'd say this, but I'm glad the Apaches killed him. I don't understand why they didn't take his horse."

Esperanza drew in a sharp breath, but she dismissed the thought before it formed fully in her mind.

"Julio took him back to town?" She lifted the pot from the table and held it in her lap, absently tracing the design with a forefinger while he talked.

"Yes. After we caught his horse, who didn't like having a body strapped across his saddle. If Julio hadn't brought Paquito, I'd have had to turn back to Tucson with the body." He pulled his chair closer, taking her hand again. "I'd never forgive myself if something happened to you."

She set the pot back on the table, wrapped both hands around his, and leaned toward him. "Do you think I am a woman who is helpless without my husband beside me at all times?

"I am a man. I'm supposed to take care of you."

"Armando, who taught me to shoot?"

"I did, but—"

"And why did you teach me to shoot?"

"To protect yourself and to help protect the ranch, but—"

She held up her hand. "Did I agree to build a home here with you?"

"You did, but—"

She cut him off again. "Did I not know you would leave me here alone from time to time, and I might need to defend myself?"

"Of course, but—"

"Armando, we don't live in Tucson, and I don't spend afternoons having tea with the fine ladies of the city—if there are such. And besides, I can't abide gossipy females."

He laughed. "My mother might believe it's a more suitable activity for her daughter-in-law."

She pressed his fingers against the crucifix. "Did I not pledge you my love, my spirit, and my future?"

"You did, and I pledged the same." He leaned in and kissed her.

"I am here for you, Armando. I would not be anywhere if you were not with me." She touched the crucifix. "I admit it's hard, and sometimes I'm lonely, but I would not choose otherwise. I am who I am because you asked me to help you build this ranch. If I must kill a man to protect your dream, I will do it."

Chapter 21

Summer 1866

She searched the desert on either side of the path. It had to be here. The woman lived somewhere near here. She needed to find her.

She walked past the scattered cobbles from the old wall and saw a flat-topped shelter different from the one she had seen before. As she crept closer, she heard women's voices and laughter. Circling it, she found the entry and stepped inside.

In the dim interior, five women sat on woven mats around the hearth, and another stood to the side holding a basket.

They paid no attention to her. One of the seated women spoke, "Look at you, Sister, your belly is fat and round. It's been several turnings of the moon since you joined us here. Your baby will be coming soon."

The standing woman replied in a musical voice. "I think two more and my son will be here."

The other woman spoke. "A son? Can you be so sure?"

"Yes, Sister, I am sure. In the Flower World, I met a little boy. He laughed and called me Mother before he ran away."

"Don't be so sure. You always think you know more than anyone else," the other woman answered.

Without responding to the comment, Ha-wani put the basket on the floor. "I will bring more food in the morning."

When she passed Esperanza, their eyes met, and she sensed the warmth of the woman's spirit. She followed her out of the shelter. The women continued to chatter and laugh behind them.

Ha-wani stood tall, looking toward the mountains, her dark eyes glistening in the afternoon light. She began to sing.

Ayamansu seyewailo huyatanaisukunisu
Enchine taluka enchine haliwa
Empo taabwikoseewa
Empo sewailo taabwikoseewa

Ha-wani cradled her belly with both hands but wore an expression of profound sadness. Esperanza watched her pass through

the opening in the cobble wall, now standing
several feet high.

Esperanza followed, but the woman was
gone, and when she looked again at the wall,
it lay collapsed and scattered at her feet.

Ha-wani's musical voice carried on the
light breeze.

Over yonder in the flower-covered wilderness
    world
I lost you, and I am looking for you
You are the bird of paradise flower
You are the little flower world's bird of paradise
    flower

Chapter 22

Fall 1866

Again, Armando raced out to chase the Apaches. Esperanza sighed, torn between her fear for her husband and her certainty that no matter what he did, he would never defeat them. She made the sign, whispered a prayer, and opened her Bible to the page marked by her rosary.

El amor es paciente y amable.

She tried to remember this, to remind herself every day not to be impatient with Armando's obsession with this place. Although she appreciated the beauty of the mountains and La Cresta, their spirits spoke differently to her. Even so, she was determined to make a good home for him.

Amor...does not insist on its own way; it is not irritable or resentful. Too often she failed with this. Sometimes, she resented the cattle, the absence of plaster on the rock walls around her, the absence of a mat on the floor, and the presence of the pack rat who stole their beans and raided the horses' grain. Even though he promised he would bring plaster from Tucson, he always forgot.

Love bears all things, believes all things, hopes all things, endures all things.

Shots echoed off the mountains, startling her silent meditation. She resisted running outside, closing her eyes and praying, counting the beads of her rosary. "*Ayúdame, Señor, a ser una mejor esposa. Déme la fuerza para durar.*"

Glad there were no more gunshots from the bajada, she continued to read and pray. When Goyo barked, she put down the Bible, reached for the Henry, and peeked out the door. Sofi, her saddle empty, crossed the yard heading for the water barrel. She ran out to find Goyo standing over Armando, lying in a heap at the top of the track.

She knelt beside him and turned him over. He was unconscious, and his shoulder and arm were drenched in blood. She laid her hand on his chest, relieved to find his heart still beating. She tore his shirt open and found blood pouring from a bullet hole in his shoulder. Ripping a layer from her petticoat, she wadded it and pressed hard on the bleeding.

Although he flinched and moaned, she was grateful he could respond to pain. She slid her other hand behind his shoulder, feeling for the exit wound.

Finding none, she whispered, "Ah, Dios."

She stood, lifted her skirt and pulled off her petticoat, tearing long strips, making one into a pad to cover the wound. She struggled to lift him high enough to wrap the rest around him to hold the padding in place and to keep his upper arm bound to his side.

Armando groaned and sucked in his breath.

"I'm sorry, my love."

As soon as she secured the bandages, she ran into the house and brought out the blanket, which she spread on the ground beside him. Fearful she might make the injury worse, she didn't want to roll him to his stomach. Tucking as much as she could under him, she rolled him to his uninjured side on the blanket. She held him steady with one hand while pushing her other beneath him to find the blanket's edge. Once she got a grip, she pulled, scraping her hand raw on the hard-packed ground, switching hands when the pain was too much. After what seemed an eternity, she had it under his upper body. She stood and straddled him, using his belt to lift him to the blanket, pausing only when he gasped in pain or cried out.

She wrapped the corners of the blanket around her hands and started dragging him to the house. After only a few feet, she lost her hold on the blanket and fell. She massaged her hands to restore circulation, and again, she gripped the blanket and pulled, muttering, "I can do this. I have to do this."

Three more times, she fell, but she wouldn't quit. Goyo ran back and forth, barking, apparently confused and concerned. "Don't worry, Goyo. We'll get him inside."

In the house, she pushed the bed aside and pulled the remaining bedclothes down to cover him on the floor. After sliding a pillow under his head, she brushed his hair away from his forehead. Goyo lay down beside him.

She lit the lantern, added more wood to the fire, and put hot water in the basin to wash her hands. The lye soap burned, but she reminded herself that her pain didn't compare to Armando's. *Abuela Primitiva. Help me do what I need to do.*

He groaned and thrashed around, crying out. She poured a few drops of laudanum into a cup and added water. Kneeling beside him, she held it to his lips, but he turned his head away. When she persisted, he coughed and swallowed.

Soon, he quieted, and she cut away the bandages, uncovering an angry, jagged hole. The bleeding had stopped, but she knew he might die. She filled the basin again and, this time, washed the wound.

She held the lantern up, casting light on his shoulder. Steeling her courage, she touched the wound, hesitating only a moment before pushing her finger into the opening. He cried out when she touched the bullet, only a few centimeters down. Should she try to take it out? Or should she just keep him comfortable? But doing nothing wasn't an option. If he got an infection, he would likely die.

You have to take it out, mi nieta.

"I can't."

You can.

She set the lantern aside and smeared honey on his wound to head off infections, and she applied a hot, damp, bandage. After washing her hands again, she took her small knife from her sewing kit, never having dreamed she would use it to dig a bullet from her beloved's shoulder. Pouring whiskey into a small bowl, she dropped her knife in—open—to soak.

She ripped more bandages from another petticoat and laid them within reach. Dragging the chest near him, she set the lantern down and checked his heartbeat again—too slow, not like the strong beat when they were making love. She rose and washed her hands once more, setting the bowl with the knife next to the lantern.

"Goyo, move over." The dog got up and lay down between Armando's head and the wall, staying close.

She knelt beside him and uncovered the wound. The bleeding had stopped, but she found torn threads from his shirt embedded in the ragged skin. She pulled them out, dipped a cloth in the whiskey, and cleaned the area around the injury, allowing some to drip into the opening.

She unbuckled his belt and strapped his forearm to his side to limit movement while she probed for the bullet. Taking a deep breath, she slipped the blade into the hole, measuring the depth. He jerked, and she lost her grip on the knife. If she couldn't hold him still, she might make his injury worse. She pressed her knee against the inside of his elbow and put her left hand on his collar bone, leaning her weight on him while she probed again. He struggled against it, but she managed to hold him still. The knife reached beyond the bullet, but how could she move it up and out?

Her own heart pounded in her ears, and a dizzying wave of heat washed over her.

"Help me, Abuela Tiva."

Do it, mi nieta.

Taking another breath, she swept her arm across her forehead, clearing the sweat dripping into her eyes. She gritted her teeth and slid the blade past the bullet, first on one side and then on the other. He began to bleed again, but maybe the flow would cleanse it. *But please, God, not too much blood.*

Now, she slid the blade past the bullet and tried to push it under—just a tiny fraction. Armando sucked in his breath and moaned. Goyo licked Armando's forehead and put his head down keeping his eyes on her.

"Hold on, my love. Hold on."

She continued to slide the knife past the bullet, lifting by tiny increments. With each effort, she used less blade, but the opening enlarged and the bleeding worsened. At last, the dark shape of the bullet showed through the veil of blood.

"Almost there. Almost..." With one final lift of the blade, the bullet broke free of the opening, but the bleeding intensified. After blotting the wound, she wrapped the bullet in a bloody rag and put it on the chest. She washed the wound again, applying pressure to stanch the bleeding. In spite of Armando's moans, she pressed hard until the flow slowed and stopped.

After applying another coating of honey along with a hot, clean compress, she touched the crucifix at her neck and whispered a prayer of thanks, adding, "Thank you, too, Abuela Tiva."

Sitting back on her heels, she focused on her husband's shallow breathing. Had she given him too much laudanum? Would he wake up?

Wearily, she rose to her feet, dropped her knife into the whiskey and carried the lantern back to the table. She washed her bloody hands and put the knife in the soapy water, tossing the whiskey out the door.

"Come, Goyo," she said.

The dog followed her out and went to the edge of the yard to urinate. She realized her own bladder was full, so she walked around the corner of the house, lifted her skirt and squatted. When she stood, she saw Pepe still tied at the rail, but she didn't see Sofi anywhere.

"Ah, Dios." The sun had reached the western horizon. It would soon be dark.

"Sofi! ¿Dónde estás?" She ran to the barn. Inside, the mare waited.

"Sofi." Esperanza put her arms around the horse's neck and cried. Goyo sat beside her, leaning against her leg.

When she caught her breath, she said aloud, "Stop it. You don't have time to waste on hysteria." She brought Armando's rifle into the house. She watched his chest rise and fall evenly. Back outside, she unsaddled the horses and carried their tack to the storeroom. After giving them a ration of grain and a bundle of hay, she checked their water supply and locked the barn.

The feathers scattered around the chicken coop meant a hawk must have taken one—or more—she didn't count them as she shooed them into the coop and secured the door.

When she and Goyo went into the house, Armando was restless and moaning.

"That's good," she said to the dog. "The laudanum is wearing off." Goyo tilted his head in response.

She prepared another dose, with one less drop than before, holding the cup to his lips until he swallowed.

She put food into a bowl for Goyo, but he didn't leave Armando's side. She dropped the bar across the door, filled the kettle again with water, banked the fire, turned down the wick in the lantern, and, exhausted, collapsed on the bed. She reached down for her husband's hand, and fell into a troubled sleep.

Chapter 23

Fall 1866

During the night, Armando woke several times. By the dim light of the fire, Esperanza gave him sips of water. She didn't want to give him more laudanum; keeping him knocked out might not be a good idea. If he came to, maybe he could help her do what she needed to do. *He's a strong man. He can handle this. Unless...* No. She refused to think infection.

She got up before the sun, stirred the fire, and lit the lantern. Armando was asleep, his chest rising and falling with each breath. She went out to feed and water the horses, while Goyo made a circuit around the yard, relieved himself, and came to watch what she was doing

She wished she could take Armando to Tucson, to a real doctor, but she would never be able to lift him into the wagon. The freight wagons passed not long ago. They should be coming back soon, but when? She sighed and went inside.

She knelt and brushed his hair from his forehead, testing for heat. Not yet. She lifted the bandage. The hole was ugly, but no longer bleeding.

When she picked up last night's bloody bandages to soak, the bullet fell out and rolled across the floor, coming to rest against the table leg. She didn't pick it up.

Armando moaned and tried to rise.

She hurried to his side, kneeling. "Be still, my love. Give yourself time."

"What happened?" His voice was weak and hoarse.

"You were shot."

"Shot?" He winced when he tried to lift his arm, which was still strapped to his side.

"Try not to move."

"*Tengo que hacer pis.*"

Esperanza smiled, hoping it was a good sign. Supporting his uninjured arm, she helped him stand, unbuttoned his trousers, and slid them down. He swayed.

"Dizzy—"

"Sit. On the bed. Sit." She held his good arm, slowing his descent.

She pulled his boots and trousers off and put the small chamber pot between his knees. At first, his body did not want to let go, but he finally passed a long stream of urine.

His face paled, and he swayed again. "Hurts—"

"Lie down, my love." His face contorted as she helped him lie back and lifted his feet to the bed. She covered him with the blanket. Goyo came to sit beside him, resting his chin on the edge of the bed.

In spite of her reservations, she prepared another dose of laudanum, a little less than before. He needed to rest.

After he quieted, she made a walnut bark poultice. It would help to relieve his pain. She removed the bandage from his shoulder and stared at the opening. Her grandmother had sewn the little boy's injury closed, but she was afraid if she tried, she might make it worse. She cleansed it again and applied the poultice.

Laying her hand on his forehead, her heart sank. Hot.

Outside, she turned the horses into the enclosure and let the chickens out to scratch in their yard. "Keep your eye on them, Goyo, and don't let me forget to put them back in tonight," she said. The dog lay down and rested his head on his front paws. When she went into the coop to collect the eggs, she heard a rumbling and whistling from below. She stepped out into the yard and listened. The freighters.

"Goyo, stay!" She ran down the path. At the wash, she lifted her skirt and splashed through, waving her hands and shouting. Ochoa's foreman, riding beside a wagon, raised his hand, calling for a halt. He turned his horse toward her.

Esperanza stopped to catch her breath.

"Mornin', Señora Ramirez." The foreman tipped his hat. "Somethin' wrong?" Lucero Rodriguez was a tall man with a ready smile.

"My husband is injured, and I'm afraid he's getting an infection."

Lucero dismounted and shouted to one of the muleskinners. "Keep the wagons here, and tell Emiliano I need him now. And tell him to bring his kit."

Leading his horse, they started up the hill. "Are you all right, Señora Ramirez?" She was breathless from running.

"I'm fine. I knew you'd be on your way back from Camp Grant soon, but I didn't expect you this morning."

"We got a late start yesterday, so we ended up campin' north of the crossin' a ways back. Otherwise, we would've been here last night."

Esperanza hoped it was good fortune they were here now and not bad fortune they hadn't arrived last night. "I'm just glad you're here now." Goyo greeted them in the yard, his tail wagging. Lucero patted the dog's head and tied his horse to the rail.

As Esperanza led him into the house, he asked, "What happened?"

"He was shot."

"Good God. How bad?"

"In the shoulder. I took the bullet out, but I'm afraid he's getting an infection." She laid her hand on Armando's forehead.

Lucero stared at her, silent for a moment. "You took—?"

A man with a black valise stepped through the door. He was older and much shorter than the foreman.

"Señora Ramirez, this here is Emiliano Gutierrez. He ain't a doctor, but he's the next best thing. He keeps our men in good shape when they need a bit of doctorin' on the road."

Emiliano took his valise to the table, removed his hat and hung it on a chair back. "May I wash my hands, Señora Ramirez?"

"Of course." She was relieved he cared about cleanliness.

After his hands were clean, Emiliano bent over Armando. He laid the back of his hand on his forehead. "Mmmhmm." He leaned closer, resting his ear on Armando's chest, listening. "He's got a fever, but his heartbeat is strong. Good." He nodded toward the bandage on Armando's shoulder. "What happened?"

"The Apaches raided the cattle yesterday, and he went after them. He came back with a bullet in his shoulder."

"I reckon I better take it out. Can't afford to wait too long." Gutierrez went to his valise.

Lucero chuckled. "Nope."

"No?"

"Nope. She already done it."

The older man stared at Esperanza and frowned. "You?"

She picked up the bullet from the floor and handed it to him.

He gave it back to her, still frowning. "This happened yesterday?"

"Yes."

He went back to Armando and lifted the poultice from his shoulder. "Tell me everything you've done up until now."

While Esperanza filled in the details, he examined the red and angry wound. "You say you made this poultice with walnut bark?"

She nodded again, worried because Armando had not roused since the men came in.

"Well, young lady, it looks like you did just fine. Removing the bullet as soon as you did might well make the difference in how he does. Of course, the fever is a problem. Don't use the honey any more. or the bandage will stick to the wound. Keep using walnut bark poultices. You say you have laudanum?"

"I do, but I'm not sure I know how much to give him."

Emiliano questioned her about what she had given in how many doses and whether or not Armando had awakened afterward. He nodded at each detail.

"Do you have enough to continue regular doses— say, two drops—from time to time?"

"Yes, I think so."

"But allow him some moments of consciousness. If you can, give him time to be awake. Talk to him, and help him make sense of what happened. His mind needs to understand the same way his body needs healing."

She nodded. "Should it be stitched? I was afraid to try."

The older man shook his head. "No, I don't think so—at least not now. Don't want to trap anything bad inside. Let it heal from the inside out. He's lucky the bullet didn't shatter a bone. It'd be a whole different story in that case." He went to his valise and held up a small, corked bottle of clear liquid. "Use this to cleanse the wound from now on. The whiskey is good in an emergency, but this is pure alcohol, nothing a man might want to drink."

"Can you take him to Tucson? Would it be better for him?"

Emiliano replied, "I reckon we could, but the ride in a freight wagon would be pretty rough. Might do more harm than good." He laid a hand on her shoulder. "You've made a good start for him. Best to keep him still and quiet and let the healing progress."

"Gracias." To Lucero, she said, "Would you be able to take a message to Armando's brother for me? He'll come help."

"Of course."

Emiliano cleaned the wound with alcohol and applied a clean poultice she made for him, "As soon as you can start getting him to drink it, the walnut bark tea will help fight off the infection, too."

Esperanza wrote a quick note to Julio and another to Adelita.

Before they left, Lucero took Esperanza's hand and said, "You're a brave woman, Señora Ramirez. We'll check with you on our next trip."

"Gracias. Both of you, muchas gracias." As the two men, with Lucero's horse following, started down the trail, she whispered a prayer of thanks to Our Lady. "Goyo, let's put the chickens away now. I want you to stay with me today."

Back in the house, she gathered the dirty bandages, dropped them into a bucket to soak, and built up the fire for hot water to wash them. She put clean rags in a bucket of cold water next to the bed. After washing her hands, she made a pot of tea.

At the table, she chewed a tortilla, but she didn't taste anything. "Armando, you gave me a terrible fright this time." He had not moved since the men were here. "I don't know what I will do if you leave me."

She picked up Ha-wani's pot. "Tell me," she said. "Tell me he will be all right. Tell me I will not be left alone." She slid her thumb into the familiar thumbprint. Closing her eyes, she sensed her companion nearby. For a moment, the dark face appeared, blue mouth lines lifted with her smile.

Armando's cry shattered the silence. Hurrying to his side, she grabbed his hand. "I'm here, mi amor. I'm here." She brushed his hair back and caressed his cheek. Still hot, even hotter than when Lucero and Emiliano were here. Whispering another prayer, she wiped his forehead and cheeks with a cool cloth. He struggled against her and opened his eyes.

"Espe?"

"I'm here." She dipped the cloth in the cool water and wiped his face.

Using his good arm, he pushed her hand away. "What are you doing? Don't touch me!"

"Armando, it's me, Espe."

"No! Get away!" He tried to sit up but fell back again.

Esperanza prepared a dose of laudanum. He turned his head, but she managed to get him to drink. He sputtered, but she thought most of it went down.

When he quieted, she held his hands and wept.

Chapter 24

Fall 1866

His fever rose, and he fought with her every time she touched him during the night. Sometimes, he thought she was an Apache trying to kill him; other times, he asked where she was, why she had left him.

"Armando, I don't think I can stop giving you the laudanum. You're too strong for me, my love, even as injured as you are. Please come back to me. Remember me and don't be afraid."

As she knelt by the bed to apply a fresh poultice, he swung his fist and connected with her jaw. She fell backward, stunned, and in pain. Rolling over on her side, she curled into a ball. Goyo lay down beside her, pressing his warm body close. She wrapped her arm around him and cried herself to sleep.

She woke in the morning, cold and stiff. Goyo went to the door and waited. Because Armando slept peacefully, she went outside. The sun, now above the mountain, cast long shadows across the yard. Instead of going to relieve himself, Goyo sat, his head tilted, looking at the palo verde.

The Apache stood in the shadows, chanting. Again, his face lifted to the rising sun with both hands raised before him. It was a different song, not the one he sang before. She listened. He did not move, even his mouth did not move with the words.

Does he know?

Was his song one of hope or one of death?

She shook her head. *I can't think about that now. I can't think about Armando dying.*

Turning to her usual morning routine, she discovered the horses watching her from the turnout. She forgot to put them in the barn last night. The Apache could have stolen them. She fed and watered them and the chickens, telling Goyo to guard them. In the garden, she picked two squash, a few chile peppers, the last two tomatoes, and pulled some onions. The chanting continued uninterrupted as she went about her chores.

In the house, she washed the vegetables, seeded the chiles, and chopped everything, dropping it into the small kettle with a little lard. She tossed in a sprig of dried cilantro, a spoonful of cumin, and salt and pepper. After adding wood to the fire and stirring the coals, she swung the kettle over the blaze. She made a pot of coffee, and as the aroma filled the air around her, she thought of her father. *I want to make coffee for him again.*

Her jaw hurt when she touched it. She prepared a dose of laudanum, assuming he would wake when she changed his bandage. She laid her hand on his forehead. *Still hot—too hot.*

The small room filled with warmth from the fire, but also with the comforting smells of cooking. She tried to remember when she had last cooked. It seemed like a long time ago.

Armando awakened while she was changing his bandage and applying a clean, warm poultice. When their eyes met, she smiled at him. "Good morning, mi amor."

"*Calabasitas*," he said, closing his eyes again. He knew what she was cooking, but he seemed peaceful— too peaceful.

She washed her hands and stirred the calabasitas, covered the kettle, and wished for cheese. Gathering the vegetable trimmings, she carried them out to the chicken yard.

The Apache's chanting lingered in the open spaces around her.

Back inside, she made a cup of coffee and sat at the table watching her husband. Goyo remained outside, guarding the chickens and watching the Apache.

To Ha-wani's pot, she said, "Tell me how you managed living here." She held the cup to her mouth without drinking and waited for an answer. When none came, she prayed for Armando's recovery and for the strength to face whatever God held in store for them.

Throughout the day, his fever didn't abate. She kept him covered, cooled his forehead with cold compresses, and managed to give him laudanum along with some walnut tea.

In late afternoon, with the soft chanting in the background, she checked the horses and chickens, deciding tomorrow she would wring the neck of the small chicken to make soup. Glancing toward the bajada, she wondered how many cattle were left. The Apaches could take as many as they wanted with Armando laid up.

The chanting ceased. Startled by the sudden silence, she looked toward the tree.

He was gone. Birds flitted and fluttered in the bushes, singing, and the chickens clucked and scratched. As she started back to the house, she heard another noise. A wagon—coming up the track.

As Julio's wagon hove into sight, relief washed over her and tears began. Julio reined in the horses, set the brake, and jumped down, wrapping her in his arms. When she couldn't stop crying, he took her by the shoulders and stood back. "Armando? Is he—"

His eyes, his expression told her he feared the worst. She choked out a noise, unable to choose between yes and no. Neither would work.

After catching her breath, she said, "He is fevered, but still alive."

His relief written on his face, he hugged her again.

"I'm sorry I frightened you," she said. "It's so hard—"

"I understand, Espe."

She took his hand and led him into the house. In the dim light of the fireplace and lantern, Julio knelt beside his brother, bowed his head, said a prayer, and made the sign. He laid his hand on Armando's forehead and drew it back. "Damn."

"I keep praying it will break soon. How much longer can he take it? And he's eaten nothing for days."

"We'll bring him through this." He squeezed her hand. "Adelita sent you the things you asked for along with towels, clean blankets, bed linens, and food. The doctor sent laudanum, camphorated oil, alcohol, and fresh bandages." He had also brought dried meat, potatoes, flour, beans, and cheese. She went with him to the wagon. He lifted a bundle, and when he handed it to her, he glanced at her face and stopped short, frowning.

"Where did you get that bruise?"

"He didn't mean to."

"My God, Espe. How do you do it?"

Inside, she opened Adelita's bundle finding clean rags for bandages, and two new petticoats. There was also a new lady's rag. She smiled at finding something so personal. She carried everything to the chest, folding the petticoats and lifting the clothes to tuck the rag in the corner with her old one. The sight of it brought her up short. *When did I...?*

When Julio came in, he said, "Espe, you're pale. Are you all right?"

"Yes... I'm fine. Just tired, I think."

"Good. I'll take care of the horses and the chickens. I'll put Sofi and Pepe in the barn and mine in the turnout. You rest."

As he walked out the door, she laid a hand on her stomach. *I can't be... Not now. Not here. I chewed the seeds. For three mornings. I chewed them.*

Julio came back in, carrying a box of Adelita's empanadas. "These will make you feel better, Espe."

She prayed he was right.

Chapter 25

Fall 1866

Iasked Ochoa's men about taking him to Tucson, but they said it might do more harm than good."

She sighed, wishing for easy answers.

"We will do the best we can. He's strong. He'll survive."

She sprinkled grated cheese into the pot, stirred it, and scooped steaming calabasitas to the plates. She sat staring at her plate, unable to eat.

Julio dug in, complimenting her on the calabasitas, but she was counting the weeks since... She pulled her attention back to him. "How is Rafael?" Their son was born in July.

"He's growing fast. I think he's Adelita's entire world. Mine, too."

He ate in silence for a few moments. "Espe, I'm sorry I didn't come back with Armando on his last trip. But finding that dead body—we couldn't leave him there."

"It's all right, Julio. You did the right thing."

"He told me he knew who he was and said he got him fired from Ochoa's freight company. He was afraid he'd been here."

"He was."

"Son-of-a b—. My God, what happened?"

"Between my rifle and Goyo, we chased him away." Her smile didn't reach her eyes.

He stared at her. "You are one remarkable woman, Esperanza Luisa. Even so, I wish this wasn't so hard for you. If we'd never found the bastard—sorry—I'd have come back with Armando. I would have ridden out with him to give him cover." His eyes watered. "I could have protected him—taken the bullet myself." He pounded his fist on the table.

Esperanza shook her head. "No. You mustn't blame yourself. "She laid her hand on his fist. "We will deal with whatever God plans for Armando. We will pray, and we will bring him through this."

In the silence that followed, Esperanza prayed, this time for Armando to survive, as well as not to be pregnant.

"Thirsty." Armando's voice broke into their prayers. Esperanza rushed to him and touched his forehead. "He's not as hot."

Julio knelt beside the bed and took his brother's hand. "Welcome back, *mi hermanito.*"

Armando squinted at his brother. "What are you doing here?" His voice was barely above a whisper. Before Julio answered, Esperanza put a cup of water to his lips.

184 / Sharon K. Miller   Fall 1866

Choking on the liquid, he coughed, a violent, racking cough. Julio put his arm under Armando's shoulders and lifted him. Armando grimaced, but the coughing stopped.

"Keep him up, Julio." She rolled up a blanket and put it under the pillow. "Thanks for bringing these. My grandmother told me a sick person shouldn't lie flat for too long. We need to keep his upper body lifted now he's awake."

Julio lowered him. "Will it be enough?"

"If not, we'll use the sack of beans you brought."

Julio smiled. "You think of everything."

"Try to give him more water. I'm going to put juice from the calabasitas into a bowl. He needs nourishment. If he can tolerate it, maybe he can take solid food." For the first time, she was confident. "If he eats, he will regain his strength."

He managed the broth and even ate some of the squash, which revived him a little. She breathed a deep sigh of relief. *The worst is over*. She made the sign and uttered a quick prayer of thanks.

In the morning, before Julio stirred from his makeshift bed near the hearth, Esperanza slipped out of bed. She pulled her skirt and blouse on over her chemise, pushed her feet into her boots, and stepped out the door, Goyo at her heels. She went to the other side of the barn and squatted to relieve herself. When she stood, her stomach clenched, and she leaned over. She had nothing to come up but colorless bile followed by dry heaves she didn't think would ever stop.

Goyo came to sniff the ground where she vomited. She knelt and put her arms around him. "What am I going to do?"

He leaned into her and licked the tears from her cheeks.

Over several days, as Armando continued to take nourishment, his strength returned. Julio helped him walk around the house and even outside for a short walk every now and then. Esperanza kept his arm bound to his side so he could not use it and slow his healing. She was glad to change the bedding.

Mornings fell into a routine. Most of the time, she managed to get up before Julio roused and slip out the door. One morning when she came back in, he said, "You're not eating enough."

It was true. She had no appetite and once, just looking at the food on her plate made her dash for the door. Afterward, Julio reminded her she couldn't afford to be sick. She assured him she would be all right.

Several days later, they were all sitting at the table, Armando finally eating his first solid meal and drinking coffee. "Coffee's good, Espe."

She murmured her thanks and concentrated on not looking at the plate of eggs in front of her husband.

Armando laid his hand on his brother's arm. "How can I thank you for coming to help. How did you find out?"

"Lucero Rodriguez, Ochoa's foreman, sent word from Esperanza."

"They came by the morning after you were shot," she said. "They would have been here the night before, but they stopped north of here when it got late. He sent a rider ahead with my letters. By the grace of God, Señor Ochoa has a man who handles medical needs for the crew. I don't know what I would have done without their help."

He reached over his shoulder and felt for another bandage. "It didn't go through. Did he have to take the bullet out?"

Goyo sat with his head on Esperanza's lap. She stroked his head and scratched his ears. She didn't look up. "No."

"No? Then who—?" Armando stared at her.

Julio's eyes were wide. "You did it, Espe? You took it out?"

Tears filled her eyes. "I did what I had to do." She took Armando's hand.

He lifted her hand to his lips and brushed a kiss across her knuckles, something she had been afraid he would never do again.

To Julio, she said, "You should go back to your family. Adelita must be frantic. We will be fine now."

"You're right." To Armando, he said, "You wait until you're healed to go check on the cattle, Little Brother. And if the damned Apaches come to take a cow or two in the meantime, leave them alone. There's not a single cow out there worth your life." He went out to harness the horses.

When Armando stood, he had to grab the edge of the table to steady himself.

"You're still weak. Lie down and rest." She helped him back to the bed, drew the covers up, and kissed him on the forehead.

He relaxed into a settled sleep, his breathing even and deep. She knelt beside the bed and made the sign. "*Gracias, El Señor, por darme mi esposo.*"

At the table with Goyo curled up at her feet, she held the pot in her lap. Sliding her thumb inside the rim, she found Ha-wani's thumbprint, and a sense of peace washed over her. "Thank you, Ha-wani, for sharing your spirit with me. I will need your strength and God's help to keep the secret I am carrying.

When Julio was ready to leave, he knelt beside his brother to say goodbye. Armando awakened and said, "Help me up." When he was standing, he hugged his brother. "Gracias, *mi hermano.*"

"De nada."

Esperanza gave him letters to take to her family and his. She wrote one to Doña María and Don Jesús, leaving out the details and making his injury appear superficial. Even though she had written to them several times, they never once replied. Armando apparently ceased to exist for them.

They stood at the door, Armando holding on to the door jamb, watching Julio prepare to leave. Before climbing into the wagon, he put his arms around Esperanza and hugged her. His tears fell without shame. "Gracias, Espe. My brother is alive because of your courage."

She kissed his cheek and Armando hugged him again. They watched him out of sight, listening for the wagon to cross the wash and turn toward the Tucson Road. With Goyo by her side, Esperanza gripped her husband's hand and struggled not to give in to her terror for the child she was carrying.

Part 3: Pain and Progress

Arizona Territory 1867

Chapter 26

Late Winter 1867

Christmas and the New Year passed, as did her morning sickness. On Christmas Day, she had cramps and light bleeding, not enough to suggest a miscarriage, but also not enough to persuade her she wasn't pregnant. Lupe had done the same thing with her last pregnancy.

As much as she wanted to talk to him, to tell him about the baby, she didn't. Instead, she talked to Goyo, who listened without judgment.

"Goyo," she said, "if Armando must take me to town, will you be able to take care of the chickens and the house when he's away?"

The dog tilted his head and said nothing. He put his head in her lap, and she scratched his ears.

"You would have to be here alone. You couldn't let the chickens out of the coop or put them in at night. No, you cannot stay here if I am gone. But what will Armando do without you?"

She picked up the old pot. "Ha-wani, you had a baby here. Tell me what I must do." If she answered, Esperanza did not hear it.

To herself, she said, "I want to be happy about this child... I want to tell Armando and see him smile. But if it means leaving this place and giving up his dream, he will not smile." Repeatedly, she told herself she might not be pregnant; the morning sickness and her absent periods might be caused by something else. She told herself that, but she didn't believe it.

Armando came through the door and frowned. "I'm starved, Espe. Where's breakfast?"

She sighed. "I'll fix it now."

As she turned toward the storeroom, he stopped her. "Are you all right?"

"Yes. I'm fine." In the storeroom, she wiped her eyes with her apron and pulled herself together.

After the new year, her breasts were tender, her nipples swollen, and the morning sickness came back with a vengeance.

One morning, when she ran for the door after making coffee, Armando followed and found her bent over and vomiting behind the house. When she stood, she fell into his arms crying.

"Espe, you're sick. Come back in the house and go to bed. It's my turn to nurse you back to health."

She stepped away from him, her sobs turning into bitter laughter. "You can't do anything about this, Mando."

"I can," he said. "You didn't rest—or even eat properly—while you cared for me. Now you're sick. You work too hard. Let me do this for you. Trust me."

"No, Mando. I'm not sick." She laid her hand on his cheek. "I'm pregnant."

"You're p—?" He stared, open-mouthed. When he found his voice, it thundered in her ears. "Pregnant? How? Why?"

Angered by his outburst, she said, "I only know of one way." When she started to walk away, he grabbed her arm and turned her around to face him.

Frowning, he said, again too loud, "Don't walk away from me. I need to figure this out, figure out what we're going to do."

She pulled her arm from his grip and glared at him. "Take all the time you want. I've had plenty of time to think."

"I'm sorry, Espe." This time, he turned away. Did he mean sorry he yelled? Or sorry she was pregnant? He walked to the corner the house, where he stopped and laid a hand on the wall. For a long moment, he held his head up, looking toward La Cresta, she thought. But then, his shoulders slumped, and he lowered his head.

Goyo came and leaned against her leg. She patted his head. "You will still love me, won't you Goyo?" The dog wagged his tail. "Now, go and watch the chickens." He trotted past Armando, who didn't glance his way.

She went around the house to the garden. *I should clean this up for planting the cilantro and onions.* In the house, she washed her hands and put beans into one pot to soak for frijoles and a hunk of dried pork in another. She straightened the bedding, wiped the table clean, and brought flour and lard from the storeroom to make tortillas. She tried not to think about Armando's reaction, concentrating only on the dough. Dividing it into pieces, she rolled them, one by one, into a ball, and flattened each one on her forearm, patting and shaping it. She did this again and again, focusing only on the whiteness of the dough and the size and shape of the tortillas. When they were ready, she put a towel over them and wiped her hands.

She took feed to the chickens, and while they attacked the grain, she went into the coop to collect the eggs. As she stepped back into the sunshine, an unfamiliar sensation fluttered through her belly, as if she had swallowed a butterfly. She hurried inside, her head down. She laid one hand on her belly and waited. Nothing. Did she imagine it?

She washed her hands, heated the flat pan on the hearth, and cooked the tortillas, lifting each to a platter to cool. Again, she focused on nothing but cooking and forced thoughts of the baby and Armando out of her mind. She wondered what he was doing outside and what he was thinking.

Later, sitting at the table, she said to the pot, "Ha-wani, did you have children? Did your boys grow to manhood? Were your girls pretty?" She cradled it in her lap, drawing one finger along the painted lines, whispering, "Tell me it will be all right. Tell me Armando wants our child. Tell me he will still love me even if we have to leave this place."

As the days passed, the uneasy silence between them continued. He didn't ask how she felt, nor did he mention her pregnancy. She cried over every little thing, and she was irritable with the rooster for crowing too loud and even with Goyo for being underfoot. Most mornings she ran outside to throw up, and most mornings, Armando failed to comment. If he noticed when she abruptly placed a hand on her belly, he didn't say anything. For her, each fluttering confirmed the child was real, he was growing.

She counted the months and knew he would be born sometime in May, in four months or so; the baby was likely conceived in August when the freight wagons were camped below the ridge. She remembered the magic of that night and cried. She held the memory in her heart and longed for Armando to love her again.

After breakfast one morning, she took the rake to the garden, attacking the dried cornstalks and bean vines, pulling them out and tossing them aside. She raked through the soil, pulling out weeds and roots and adding them to the pile. When a root refused to yield after several attempts, she threw the rake into the brush, sat on the ground, and cried—again. Finally, she wiped her tears on her sleeve and stood. *I'm so tired of crying.*

Armando was on the other side of the yard, collecting stones from the old wall. She didn't know how he planned to use them, and she hadn't asked. Pepe was tied at the rail with Sofi. She tightened his cinch and untied him. Armando stopped his work and watched. Hiking up her skirt and petticoat, she swung into the saddle, pushing her feet down into the stirrups. It felt good. She couldn't remember the last time she rode.

She spun Pepe around and started down the track.

He ran toward her. "Esperanza! What are you doing?"

She kicked the horse into a trot.

"You can't go out there alone." He ran after her, but she was halfway down the hill. "Come back here!"

They splashed across the wash, and she directed Pepe northbound along the freight road. The wind roared in her ears as they flew along the dirt track. In spite of the cold air on her face, the sun warmed her back. She rocked in rhythm with Pepe's stride, listening to the four-beat pounding of his hooves. It sounded like freedom. It sounded like long ago—before Armando and this place.

She had never been this far north, so she slowed Pepe to a walk so she could examine this part of the desert. The sun glittered on the wash as it flowed southward. She passed by several ridges rising above her on the east side of the track with shadowy stands of trees and scrub in the deep gaps between them.

When the road and wash turned to the east, she rode down the bank to let Pepe drink. He lifted his head and looked behind them. She heard Sofi's four-beat stride on the hard track. She kept her eyes straight ahead, focusing on the panorama of distant ridges and hills with a scattering of saguaro and mesquites set against a deep blue sky.

When Armando reined Sofi in behind her on the bank, he shouted, "God damn it, Esperanza! Are you crazy?"

She laughed. "I was, but now I'm quite sane." She turned her horse southward without another word. When she passed him, she didn't need to look at him to know he was furious.

He rode up beside her, reaching for Pepe's bridle, and pulling him to a stop.

"I'm sorry, Armando, I thought you wanted me to go home." She took pleasure from his exasperation.

"I do, but damn it, Esperanza, you don't even have your rifle." He gestured toward the ridges looming above them. "Look where we are. The Apaches ambush people along this road. I suspect they are watching us right now."

She examined the ridgetops. "You're right. They could be up there watching. Or there." She pointed to the thick trees and scrub between the ridges. She scoured the shadows, looking for the red bandanna, but nothing betrayed a presence there.

Armando grunted. "Come on." He let go of Pepe's bridle and pressed Sofi into an easy trot. Esperanza did the same, keeping pace with him. The beat of the horses' hooves fell into a unified rhythm, each horse matching the other's stride. She believed Sofi and Pepe were soul mates, like Armando and her. Or, at least how they used to be.

She didn't want to lose him.

They didn't talk, and Armando kept his eyes on the track ahead of them, scanning left and right. Sometimes, he turned in the saddle to check behind them. When they reached the wash, he pulled Sofi up to let her drink. Pepe walked around in the water stamping his foot, splashing. Armando started up the hill, and she followed. She patted Pepe's neck and said, "You had a drink so you can wait."

Back at the rail, they dismounted, and Armando silently unsaddled Pepe and carried his tack into the house. Esperanza brushed him, combed his mane and tail. She was exhilarated by the ride and grooming him relaxed her. He enjoyed it, too, often dropping his head, his eyes half-closed, napping. Armando loosened Sofi's cinch, but he would leave her saddled, in case he had to ride out to the cattle. Throughout, they said nothing to one another.

With one last glance at Armando, she went into the house, closing the door behind her and leaning her forehead against it. *He's right. I was foolish—but it felt so good to ride again.*

She added wood to the fire and turned the pot of beans over the flames. She washed her hands, combed her hair, and smoothed her skirt. *I will apologize.*

When Armando came in, she was cutting onions and chiles to make *carnitas*. She wiped her hands on her apron, and when he started past her to the storeroom, she stepped into his path. "I'm sorry, Armando. I shouldn't have frightened you, and I shouldn't have been impudent when you caught up with me." She took his hand and pressed his fingers to the crucifix. "I pledged you my love and my loyalty when we married. I promised to help you build your home here in this place. More than anything I want to fulfill my pledge and my promise."

He wrapped his arms around her and held her close, resting his chin on the top of her head for a long moment. When he stepped back, she lifted her face to him, and he brushed her lips with his and kissed her with the passion she had missed of late. In his embrace, her desire flamed, and she pressed herself against him. He put his hand on her buttocks lifting her off her feet and pulled her against his own rising desire. She wrapped her legs around him, leaning back as he traced kisses down her neck. He loosened her blouse and lifted her breast, running his thumb around her nipple and squeezing.

"Oh!" She unwound her body from his and stood back, her hand against her breast.

"What's wrong?"

"My breasts are tender."

"Why?"

"It's one of the symptoms."

"Symptoms?" His face transformed from confusion to understanding. He turned away from her.

This time, she took his arm and turned him around. "Don't walk away from me, Armando. We need to talk about this."

"I know, Espe, but I'm afraid." His voice was barely above a whisper.

When her tears began, his own spilled down his cheek. "I am, too."

Chapter 27

Spring 1867

Spring arrived in a flash of yellow, the mesquites and palo verdes blooming, and brittlebush and marigolds painting the desert. Last month's poppies, with occasional blue lupines scattered among them, continued to carpet hillsides, and the pinks and reds of penstemon and desert verbena added rich colors. The days were warm and nights pleasantly cool. March, her favorite time of the year, brought the desert alive. Even in this place, the colors gave her optimism and hope.

Her pregnancy progressed well, and she traded morning sickness for having to urinate all the time. It annoyed her, but at least she could make coffee without running for the door. When she crawled into bed beside Armando, he would lay his hand on her round belly and smile when the child kicked him. In the dim light of the banked fire, she could see that his smile did not reach his eyes.

One evening, they carried their chairs to the yard and watched as the sun painted La Cresta and the mountains to the east with a pink glow, promising a crimson evening. Goyo lay at her feet while they talked.

"Did you find any calves today?" Armando spent longer days on the bajada because it was calving season and he needed to look for new babies. Cows were hardy creatures and could handle their own birthing, but coyotes and mountain lions, attracted by the scent of afterbirth and blood, kept the calves at risk.

"Two—probably born last night. Both were dead. I'm pretty sure it was coyotes that got them. A mountain lion would have left something to come back to later. Not much of anything left."

"And the mothers? Will they be all right?" Esperanza shuddered at the thought of losing her baby.

"They were distressed, hanging around the remains and lowing, their udders bursting with milk. They'll get over it. Their milk will dry up, and they'll go on until the next calf."

"Is it really so easy?"

He shrugged. "Like I said, they're tough."

When the baby moved inside her, she took his hand and placed it on her belly and looked into his eyes, trying to find a glint of happiness, of pleasure at soon becoming a father. If it was there, she didn't see it.

He withdrew his hand and leaned forward, resting his forearms on his knees and weaving his fingers together between them. He lifted his gaze to La Cresta and said, "I will take you to Lupe's when it's almost time."

"Are you sure?"

He pushed his hair from his forehead, took a long breath, and exhaled slowly. "I am sure, Espe. As much as I would like to have our children born here, you can't give birth with no help."

"Gracias, mi amor. But what will you do when you take me to Tucson? Will you be able to stay here to protect this place?"

"I will do my best, but there will be days when no one is here. We will lose the chickens to the coyotes and hawks because I won't leave Goyo here by himself when I go to Tucson. He will go with you to Lupe's."

She bit her lip and closed her eyes. "But what will he do without a job?"

"He will be happy herding Lupe's children."

She changed the subject. "You will be lonely here by yourself, and I will be terrified for you. What if you get hurt again?"

"I will be careful, Espe. If I must chase Apaches, I will keep my distance. I will be here for my son." Even though he smiled, she could find no enthusiasm in it. "Or my daughter."

The red ball of the sun hung low on the western horizon, painting La Cresta and the mountains red. A crimson evening.

"You are afraid we will lose this place if we don't stay."

"What will be will be. Julio will come and help. I will try to hold on to it."

Esperanza leaned the rifle against the side of the house and put her hands behind her, pushing hard on the small of her back, pressing her shoulders backward and arching slightly.

Standing with the rising sun to her back, she watched her husband as he drove the wagon down the track. Even though Julio brought supplies on his last trip, the horses needed shoes. Sofi had thrown one out on the bajada. If he had found it, he would have nailed it back on, but she had been without for more than a week. He could manage to nail one on from time to time, but he didn't trust himself to do the whole job of trimming and shaping the shoes. He had made a mess of one of his father's horses several years ago, and he was not allowed to try again. He couldn't be sure when he would be back. Everything depended on the blacksmith.

She smiled at her small protruding, round belly, but frowned as she thought about the dull backache that had been with her since this morning. She straightened up, and spread her hands beneath her belly, beneath the child in her womb. "Armando's child," she thought aloud, "our child." She looked forward to going back to Tucson and seeing Lupe and the children. She was happy about this child, but she understood the risks. Her sensible self said she shouldn't be pregnant, but her emotional self was happy. *A baby!* She would be a mother. She prayed Armando would be happy once his son was born. Somehow, she knew her baby was a boy. Lupe would sit with her through the birth. Things would work out. Mando would see to it.

The rooster crowed from inside the coop, interrupting her thoughts. She heaved a sigh and told Goyo, "*El Gallo* is demanding his breakfast." She stepped into the chicken yard and opened the coop. The hens rushed out, and the rooster marched around his ladies. Goyo took his position as sentinel.

She brought the chicken feed and scattered it in the enclosure and collected the eggs. When she stood straight coming out of the coop, the ache in her lower back intensified. She frowned and rubbed her back. *I must be more careful.*

Inside, she checked the supply of flour. She had enough to make a small batch of tortillas for her dinner. Armando would bring more flour as well as meat. She

filled the cooking pot with water. She took the sack of
beans from its hook on the wall, where it should be
too high for the mice and rats. Even so, the persistent
and clever creatures more than once chewed holes in
the burlap and compromised the bean supply. After
inspecting them for bugs, she dropped two handfuls into
the kettle. She stirred the coals and added a few sticks
of wood, watching the fire flare up and catch. A gentle
warmth filled the little room, taking the morning chill
out of the air.

She went to the door for the rifle, wondering if the
Apache would make an appearance with Armando
gone. She had grown used to his quiet presence, and,
surprisingly, when he came, she felt safe. Even as she
thought it, she worried she might be wrong. *What if he
is really dangerous? What if he is just biding his time?*
Whenever she had these thoughts, she would ask herself
why he hadn't taken advantage of her before this? *Why
would he wait?* Not sure what to think, she preferred to
think this strange Indian was her friend.

As she stepped out into the morning sun, a fierce
cramp grabbed her lower abdomen. She dropped the rifle
and clutched the doorway. Another cramp, this one more
severe than the first.

"Madre de Dios, por favor—"

Her knees buckled, and she slid to the ground. The
cramps were coming quickly now, and with them, a
terrible realization. She pulled herself up and struggled
back into the house. If she could just lie down, put her
feet up, the pain might pass.

"Breathe... *¡Respire!*" On the bed, she tried to lie back,
but the cramping grew worse. She rolled to her side and
pulled her knees to her chest. A warm rush of water and
blood, an endlessly flowing tide, washed her baby from

the safety of her womb. She struggled against her body, willing it to stop, willing the baby to stay. But she failed.

Esperanza gave birth to her child at seven and a half months. When the pain and the pressure subsided, she pulled herself up, searching for her baby in the terrible pool of blood and tissue. A boy. She laid her hand on his tiny head. She counted ten perfect fingers and ten perfect toes. With great difficulty, she pulled off her bloody petticoat, swaddled her baby and its afterbirth, and wiped his face clean. She studied him, trying to find Armando's features. He would never know his child. She wrapped him in the petticoat, as one swaddles a newborn, keeping the cleanest layers of white cotton on the outside.

She held her baby to her breast and sang to him.

> *Dulce niño,*
> *duermete ya.*
> *Es hora de descansar.*

Exhausted, she slept, holding her infant in her arms and dreaming of him playing in the yard, chasing chickens, and squealing with delight. She imagined Goyo protecting him, guarding him against danger. When she woke later, Goyo lifted one paw to the edge of the bed and rested his chin on it. "Stay with us, Goyo," she whispered. "I'm not sure I will survive."

Much later, she pulled herself from the bed, and carried her child outside, Goyo at her heels. She did not look at the rifle, still lying outside the door. Armando wouldn't be here until tomorrow, but maybe it was already tomorrow.

She stumbled across the yard to a pile of loose rocks she had tossed from the garden. She laid the precious bundle on the ground, and Goyo curled up beside it. She picked up a flat rock and began to dig. After making a shallow depression, she laid her baby in it. "I have to do this, Goyo." He sat up and cocked his head, watching her. "If I am to die today, I cannot leave my baby unprotected, unbaptized, and unprayed over."

She scrubbed her hands down the front of her skirt, stroked his cold head, and prayed.

> *Tome esto como su propio hijo.*
> *Señora encantadora y recatada,*
> *envuelto en el manto de su cuidado,*
> *hasta el día cuando en una nueva tierra,*
> *todos sus hijos se unan a usted, su madre,*
> *infinitamente misericordioso alabar y dar gracias*
> *a Dios Padre, Hijo y Espíritu Santo.*

How could she cover this child? She wished Mando were here; she needed his strong arms to hold her and tell her their child would be fine.

She laid her fingers against the crucifix. She had promised never to take it off, but she opened the clasp and held it to her lips, trying to understand why *Jesucristo y La Virgen* abandoned her. *"En el Nombre del Padre y del Hijo y Espíritu Santo—"*

Naming the baby Ángel María Ramirez Ocoboa, she prayed to *Santa Therése y La Virgen* to intercede for his spirit. She touched the crucifix to her lips again and tucked it into the folds of the bloodstained petticoat wrapping her stillborn child.

She pulled the layers up and over his face and tucked the dirt around and over him like a blanket. Still on her knees, she raised her eyes toward La Cresta.

He stood in the yard no more than fifteen paces from where she knelt. Goyo sat beside her, watching the Apache.

His dark eyes, hooded beneath the red bandanna that covered his head, his eyes, set wide apart in a hard face, betrayed little. But they penetrated the depths of her grief. Somehow, for a moment, she believed he shared her grief. Turning her attention back to the child, she said aloud, "Mando, our baby is dead, and when you return you will find me dead as well. *Perdóname por favor.*"

After covering him with another blanket of dirt, she dragged rocks from the old wall to protect him from the coyotes that would come in the night, each rock weighing on the child and on her heart. Saying a final prayer, she made the sign and struggled to her feet. Her knees almost gave way, but she managed to stand. The Apache was gone.

Before stumbling back to the house, she told Goyo, "Guard my baby. Don't let the coyotes have him."

Chapter 28

Spring 1867

Some time later she awakened. The pain lingered, and the blood flowed, puddling beneath her. She would die before Armando came back...without seeing her family again....

She tried to sit up. The fire burned low, and a faint cloud of steam rose from the kettle. A spicy fragrance filled the room. In the dim light from the fireplace, she tried to find the source. A cup sat on the chest next to the bed. She held it to her nose and breathed in the sweet vapor. *¿Té de pazotillo."* She rubbed her forehead, trying to clear her mind.

"Mando?" But only Goyo answered. He pushed the unlatched door open and came to stand beside the bed. When she did not speak to him or pet him, he lay down on the floor.

She held the cup in her hand, the strong vapor diminishing as the liquid cooled. Even though she didn't know where it came from, she knew it would relieve her cramps and slow the bleeding. Taking a sip, she felt its soothing effect immediately. She emptied the cup and drifted into a quiet restful sleep.

When she awakened from her nightmare, both the blood flow and the pain were diminished, but understanding came quickly. It was not a nightmare. Her baby was dead. She pushed herself off the bed and stood. A wave of dizziness swept over her, and she sat, her head in her hands. Goyo stood and pressed against her legs. She laid her hand on his head. When the dizziness passed, she stood again and tried to make sense of her surroundings. The bag of beans was gone, the flour was gone, but the rifle was still beside the door.

If not Mando—the Apache? Was he here? Was he in the house?

It didn't matter. Nothing mattered now. Disoriented and weak, she stumbled across the yard to the small grave. When did she lay him here? This morning? Yesterday?

Goyo followed. He pushed his head under her arm and leaned into her when she knelt. Her arm hung limply around him. She touched one of the rocks covering her child. Cold, too cold to keep my baby warm. She blinked and tried to clear her mind. But the light faded, and a choking thick, red cloud enveloped her. Scanning the sky, she found the sun low in the west.

On another evening, the deep red ball of the sun, sliding behind the low mountains to the west, its glow bathing La Cresta and the mountains to the east, would have been lovely. One of Mando's crimson evenings. But tonight, in the sunset she saw only blood—the blood of her belly against the stark white of her petticoat.

In spite of the heavy load in the wagon, Armando drove the horses hard coming up the track. The silhouette of the house loomed above him, dark against the pale night sky. No lantern light.

He had hurried home in the gathering darkness, cursing himself for being two nights away and late tonight. The deep red color of the sky—a crimson evening that would normally give him pleasure—had strangely disturbed him as he rounded the point of the mountains.

Goyo ran to meet him, barking. He dropped the reins and jumped off the wagon before it stopped.

"Esperanza!"

Goyo continued to bark.

He ran into the house and fumbled in the dark for a torch. Trembling, he stirred a flame in the fireplace and lit the tallow end. Esperanza had not tended the fire for a while—*how long has she been gone?* "Goyo!"

The dog came to the door and led him across the yard to where Esperanza lay unconscious. He did not notice the pile of rocks beside her.

"Mi amorita—"

She raised her head and looked through him.

He dropped the torch, gathered her in his arms, and carried her inside. In the darkness, he laid her on the bed and drew a blanket over her. He kissed her forehead, her cheeks, and her lips. She did not kiss him back.

Reluctantly, he left her to retrieve the torch, put the horses in the barn, and feed them. If he needed to take her to Tucson, he would need them. He left the supplies in the wagon.

Inside, he lit the lantern. Esperanza had not moved. He knelt by the bed, drew the blanket back and searched for her hand. The knot in his stomach tightened at the sight of her dirty hands, her broken and bloody nails. He brushed the dirt away and held both hands, breathing soft kisses across her knuckles. The smell of blood and something else hung in the air. She turned her head, and their eyes met.

"Espe, what happened?"

"Lo siento." She sobbed, and his understanding came with anguish, guilt, and, although he didn't expect it, relief. Their child—his child—was gone. He had promised to take her to Tucson for her lying in, and he should have taken her before now, but he feared they would end up leaving the ridge for good. They would lose the claim.

Now the child was gone. They could stay. *She will recover. We will go on.*

Paying no heed to the bloody bedding, he lay down beside her, pulled the blanket around them, and wrapped her in his arms. He prayed her tears would cleanse his selfish heart, and he would never lose this woman he loved and needed so deeply.

Esperanza wept against her husband's strong chest and drew scant comfort from the sound of his beating heart. He lulled her to sleep with soothing whispers of love and gentle kisses on the top of her head.

Sometime before dawn, she dreamed the dream.

> *A child, a dark-eyed, dark-haired naked beauty of a child, stood at the foot of La Cresta.*
>
> *She waited by the house, holding out her hand, saying "Come."*
>
> *The child, her son, laughed and ran up the mountain. He was surprisingly agile and light-footed in spite of his short chubby legs. Climbing higher, he stood on a rock ledge*

overlooking a deep canyon, a great stone tower on the other side.

Gripped with sudden terror, she shouted, "¡Venga!" The child's laughter echoed off the mountain walls, surrounding her with exquisite light and music. She couldn't breathe.

Another child, this one not unlike the first, but darker, stood on the tower across the canyon. The music faded, and the light surrounded him, his dark skin gleaming in the sun. The darker child looked at her, then at the other child.

Holding out his hand, he said to the boy, "Venga."

The boy turned to her, lifted a small hand. He stepped over the edge.

"No!" she cried, trying to run, but her legs would not obey.

Her sudden movement awakened Armando, and he tightened his embrace. She struggled, still trying to run after the boy.

She woke. In spite of the warmth of Armando's body bathing her in his strength and love, she was cold.

Not shivering cold, but soul cold.

Cold to the depths of her heart.

...cold.

She wept cold tears against Armando's chest.

Chapter 29

Spring 1867

Esperanza passed through the old wall and followed a narrow path toward La Cresta.

In spite of the sun, overhead in a pale sky, she shivered. She crossed her arms, hugging herself, hoping to fend off the icy waves coursing through her body.

When the trail melted into the mesquite scrub, she hesitated, but pressed forward, passing between the bushes, aiming for the massive ridge. Mesquite thorns and catclaw caught her skirt as if urging her to stop, to turn back. She ignored them. She stumbled down a slope into an arroyo, her boots digging into the earth and slowing her descent. She crawled up the other side on hands and knees and stood, sweeping sand from her skirt. She pushed on.

A cholla, its wicked branches hanging in her path, caught her, the joints detaching and clinging to her skirt and sleeve. She did not feel the barbs embedded in her arm or see blood blooming on the white fabric of her blouse.

Esperanza!

"Esperanza! Espe! Stop!" Armando hurried through the scrub in a headlong rush to catch up with her. He zigzagged around the mesquites and acacias, holding his rifle away from his body and pointed to the ground. Now was not the time to have it accidentally discharge.

"Esperanza!"

When he was close enough to reach it as it swept behind her, he grabbed her skirt and held on. She stopped, but she didn't turn to face him. She leaned away from his grip, trying to go forward.

"Espe, please—" He maneuvered around her and stood between her and the ridge, looking into her eyes, searching for his wife, waiting for her to see him. In a few moments, her eyes refocused on his.

"Why are you here?" Her voice was flat.

"Come home, Espe." Even though he was terrified, he spoke quietly. "Will you come home with me?"

"Home?"

"Yes. Come with me." He took her hand and led her through the scrub.

Silent, she went with him, her hand limp in his.

They had not gone far when a high-pitched buzz exploded from the brush. He stopped and scanned the ground beneath the bushes surrounding them, trying to locate the snake. He spotted it, pulling itself from an S into a tight coil beneath a hackberry bush only two strides from where they stood. With its triangular head held close to its body, it watched, it's tail still buzzing. The tongue darted in and out, tasting the air. Armando tugged her hand and stepped backward, staying clear of the cactus and catclaw behind them, while keeping an eye on the snake. As he increased the distance, the buzzing slowed to tick-tick-tick, then tick—tick—tick—silence—tick—silence. He whispered a prayer of thanks that she had not encountered the snake before he caught up with her.

When they came through the opening in the wall, he led her to the grave. The small cross he had fashioned for his son, bore the name, Ángel.

"He's here, Espe."

"Here?" She stared at the rocks covering her son, and looked at Armando, the question in her eyes.

"He's safe, Espe. He's here at home."

"Home?"

He led her to the house where he combed the cactus joints from her skirt and blouse, plucked spines from her arm, washed the scratches, and applied ointment. After helping her put clean clothes on, he sat her at the table and made her a cup of tea.

She put the old clay pot in her lap, absently tracing the painted lines with her finger.

"Come back to me, Espe," he whispered.

In time, she began going through the motions of daily life, getting up every morning and making breakfast. She made tortillas and cooked stews and calabasitas. She fed the chickens and tended the garden, carrying water to the tomatillos and squash. She tied rags to the scarecrow poles, and she pulled the weeds threatening to choke the cilantro. She helped Armando repair the roof on the chicken coop and raise the height of the surrounding wall. From time to time, she rode Pepe around the perimeter wall, but she didn't seem to take much pleasure in it. She didn't speak except when necessary, and she never smiled. Goyo refused to leave her side even though she rarely acknowledged him.

Armando had not left her alone since he came back and found her grieving for their son. He lost count of the cattle and had not ridden out to check on them, even though a couple of calves might be out there with their mothers. Between the coyotes and the mountain lions, any newborns might not have survived. He needed to fill the water barrels in the house. He brought a little up from the well each day, but he needed to take a barrel down in the wagon. Filling it took time—time he couldn't take from Esperanza. He was afraid she would go back into the desert looking for Ángel.

He wept with relief one morning when Julio drove up the track.

When his brother climbed from the wagon, Armando hugged him. "¡Gracias a Dios tu es aquí!"

"What's wrong?"

He told his brother about the baby and Esperanza's overwhelming grief. At Ángel's grave, Julio knelt, made the sign and said a prayer for his nephew. He stood and hugged his brother again.

Esperanza, pale and haggard, came out of the house and stood by the door. Julio took her hands in his and kissed them. He wrapped her in his strong arms and promised her things would get better. She stood in his arms, limp and silent. When he released her, she turned back to the house, her shoulders slumped and her head down.

Armando pleaded with his brother, asking him to do the only thing that could bring her out of her depression. "Please."

After unloading the supplies, Julio filled the barrel at the well and brought it up the hill. "I will go back to Tucson now." He leaned down from the wagon and laid a strong hand on his younger brother's shoulder. "I will do what you ask."

Chapter 30

Spring 1867

*V*enga ya! ¡Venga ya!"

Esperanza's brother-in-law, Alejandro rode into the yard on Julio's horse, Paquito, waving his hat, and shouting.

Esperanza ran out of the house with Goyo behind her, barking. *"¿Es todo bien?* What's wrong?"

"Nada. Everything is wonderful. Come with me to the wash. *Guadalupe y los niños estan aqui."*

"¿Lupe y los niños estan aqui?"

"¡Si! ¡Venga ya!" He spun the horse again, stirring up the dust and laughing.

For the first time in weeks, Esperanza smiled— tentatively at first, but then her eyes brightened. Now, she found something to smile about.

"They're waiting." Alejandro wheeled his horse and headed back down the path.

Armando grabbed her hand. "*Vámonos.* You, too, Goyo. Come!" Together they ran down the path to where the men had set up a table on the north side of the wash with benches on each side. Lupe had laid out a feast of *tamales y empanadas y mas*, along with *aguas frescas*. The children, Francesca, Lupita, and Luis splashed through the braided waters of the wash with Goyo on their heels. *El pequeño niño* clung to his mother's skirt.

Esperanza fell into her sister's arms, sobbing. Lupe wept with her. When she caught her breath, Esperanza picked up Mateo and squeezed him. He tried to squirm out of her grip, reaching for his mother. Esperanza released him into Lupe's arms, and, once safe, he looked at her with a puzzled expression.

Esperanza, her face wet with tears, touched his cheek. "*Lo siento, muchacho.* I forgot myself. You are so beautiful." Lupe hoisted Mateo higher on one hip and took Esperanza by the hand, leading her away from the others. "*Dime, hermanita.* Tell me." Lupe said. "Take me to see him."

She and Esperanza crossed the wash and started up the hill, Mateo watching his brother and sisters over his mother's shoulder as they ran and played in the wash with Goyo. The men sat at the table smoking fat cigars.

"I can't believe you're here, mi hermana. I have missed you so."

"I've missed you, too." Lupe stood slightly taller than Esperanza with the same honey-gold complexion as her sister.

"I had forgotten how much like Mamá you are. You've even inherited her gray streak."

"Since she's had it for so long, I like to believe it's not related to getting old."

Esperanza placed her hand on Mateo's head, but he turned away, burying his face in his mother's neck. "His hair was so soft."

When they reached the yard, Esperanza stopped, gesturing toward the house. "He wants this place to be our home. I don't know if I can do it anymore." She breathed a ragged sigh, "But if we leave, Ángel will be alone. I can't leave him, but I don't want to stay."

At the grave, Lupe handed Mateo to Esperanza, and he didn't object when she didn't squeeze him. Her sister knelt by the small grave and said a prayer. She stood and put one arm around Esperanza's shoulders and drew her close. "*Lo siento mucho.* I'm so sorry you are in pain."

From his position on Esperanza's hip, Mateo reached out and placed a tiny finger on the tear running down her cheek. He held up his wet finger and said to his mother, "*Tia Espe llora.*" He opened his brown eyes wide, and he stuck out his lower lip, as if he, too, were sad.

Esperanza could not resist smiling. "*Muchos gracias, Mateo*, you gave me back my smile." He giggled when she kissed his palm.

Lupe smiled at him. "You are good medicine, my son."

Together they walked to the house, and Esperanza passed Mateo back to his mother. "It had gotten better for a while, before I got pregnant, before—" She picked up the old pot and cradled it in her hands. "I found this in the garden. It made me think about those who lived here long ago. The woman who made this pot—her spirit—has lingered in this place, keeping me company. I dream about her. I even talk to her sometimes." She drew her finger along the geometric lines on the pot. "I know that sounds insane, but it helps."

"You're not insane, Espe. From the time you were small, you traveled to the Sea Ania, the Flower World, just like Abuela Tiva. You are more like her than any of us. I do not doubt your experience—or your sanity."

"But now, after—" She wrung her hands. "I can't do it any longer. I can't survive here—I love Armando, and I want to help him, but losing Ángel—"

Lupe's brows knit together, deepening the worry line she inherited from their father. "You are stronger than you think. You stood up to Doña María when she threatened your future with Armando. You did not fight for him only to turn your back now because of hardship. You will survive because you are Esperanza Luisa de la Luz Ocoboa Núñez. Do you remember why Mamá and Papá added 'de la Luz' to your name?"

"They said I brought light to them at a dark time."

"We had fled Tubac because of the Apaches. Even in Tucson, they weren't sure we were safe because Mexico was at war with the United States and they heard the Americans were coming to take the presidio. Tomás and I were small, and Mamá was pregnant with you. She had a hard time during her pregnancy, but she said when you were born, you came with such ease, she couldn't believe it. You cried only a moment or two, and then you smiled. You brought light to our family when we needed it most." She took her sister's hand. "You cannot lose your light, and you are Esperanza; you are Hope."

Esperanza held Mateo's hand, and he gazed at her with soulful brown eyes. "Gracias, mi hermana. I will try."

"You will bear more children, mi hermanita. God will give you others, and your Ángel will look after them for you. He will be with you and your children always, whether you are here or somewhere else."

"I know." Esperanza tried to smile. "But I don't want them born here. I tried to do what Abuela Tiva taught me, but it either didn't work, or I was careless. I want to lie with Armando, but—"

"You don't have to give up pleasures because you don't want children yet. I will tell you something else you can do." Lupe smiled at Mateo, saying, "Because you, my beautiful baby, are my last child."

They walked down the hill, talking quietly.

As they approached the men, Armando watched his wife. When she smiled at him, he leaped to his feet, grabbed her, and swung her around, laughing. She laughed, too.

"Put me down, Mando." She kissed his cheek. "We must eat. The children will be tired of waiting."

Standing on her feet again, she said to Lupe, "Thank you for coming. But how did you get here so early this morning? When did you leave Tucson?"

Alejandro answered. "We put mattresses and blankets in the back of the wagon. Lupe and the children slept all the way—"

"Not me," Lupe interrupted. "I couldn't sleep for the wagon's bouncing and bumping, but I think the children could sleep through an earthquake."

"They thought it was an adventure," her husband finished. "Julio and I shared the driving."

"You drove all night to get here?" She looked at her brother-in-law. "And you risked bringing your family into Apache territory?"

"We were prepared. Besides, Armando and Julio have travelled the road with no problems." He paused. "And you needed us."

Esperanza's eyes welled with tears. "Muchas gracias."

Lupe put Mateo on a blanket near the table and said, "And now we must eat and enjoy our time together."

While the adults ate, the men shared news about family and politics.

"Somebody's going to have to do something about the Apache problem," Alejandro said. "Lupe's parents have to move to Tucson."

"They will bring Abuela Tiva with them, won't they?" Esperanza broke an empanada in half and bit into it.

"They will, but she's more frail than ever." Mateo pulled on his mother's skirt, and she lifted him to her lap, stroking his dark hair. "She is staying with Mamá and Papá."

To Armando, Julio said, "Our parents are going to move as well. Reynaldo and Concepción came to town a couple of months ago. It looks like Tubac will be abandoned again."

Armando's dark eyes flashed. "Damned Apaches. I say kill them all."

Esperanza said nothing. Alejandro was about to speak when Luis, who had climbed the walnut tree, shouted, "¡Mira, Mamá. ¡Mira!"

Luis pointed to several downy feathers hanging from the branches. "Por favor, can I take them, Mamá?"

Francisca and Lupita jumped up and down, shouting, "Me, too! I want one!"

Lupe laughed. "Bien. But just one for each of you. Let's leave the others. Someone put them there for a reason."

Esperanza stared at the feathers while Luis untied three of them. She didn't remember ever seeing them when she came to the well or to the tree to collect its bark, but they must have been there. She tried to count but gave up after fifteen. Later, Julio and Alejandro packed up the wagon and loaded the children into the back with blankets and pillows. Lupe and Esperanza stood by the walnut tree and hugged one another.

"We will try to come back, Espe. I promise." Lupe climbed into the seat beside her husband and took a cranky Mateo into her lap. Julio mounted his horse to follow them.

When Alejandro flicked the reins, and the horses started out, the children shouted, and everyone waved. Esperanza turned to her husband and said, "*Gracias, mi esposo.*"

"¿Por qué?"

"They came because you asked them to come?"

"Sí. Last week, I told Julio you needed your big sister. The rest was up to them."

"She said they would come back, but I worry for their safety. It will be very late when they get home. It is dangerous to drive around the mountains—to travel between here and Tucson, especially in the dark. *¿Es no?*"

"They will be careful. Julio is armed, and Alejandro has his rifle under the seat. We will pray for their safety."

Armando picked up the basket of food Lupe left, and they started up the path to the ridge. Goyo trotted happily beside them. They were almost at the top when Esperanza caught a glimpse of red under the palo verde. She sucked in a breath and stopped. Goyo stopped, as well, but he waited, looking first toward the tree and then at Esperanza.

"Are you all right? What is it?"

"*No es nada*, Mando. I twisted my ankle." The Apache blended back into the brush and out of sight.

When they got back to the house, Armando did a quick check of the horses and the supplies, finding that nothing had been disturbed.

"Everything is as we left it, mi querida. No one has been here."

She stood by the door while he fed and watered the horses, thinking about the Apache watching her family by the wash. He had risked Armando seeing him. She patted Goyo on the head. "You would tell me if he was a bad person, wouldn't you?"

Chapter 31

Summer 1867

After her sister's visit, Esperanza's mood improved. She got up in the morning and went through her day with a little more energy. Even though the orange flowers of the Mexican bird of paradise she planted there brightened his grave, she still carried the pain in her heart. Singing his lullaby gave her a sense of peace.

> *Dulce niño, duermete ya.*
> *Es hora de descansar.*
> *Quiero que duermas feliz,*
> *… feliz.*
> *Duérmete ya.*

She pulled the weeds around the bush and told him *las flores naranjas* were for him. The small cross gave her comfort, and she began to see his grave as a place of beauty as well as pain.

One morning, after Armando rode out to the bajada, she knelt beside the grave, singing to her child and tending to the flowers. Goyo lay nearby in the shade, his chin resting on outstretched front paws, watching the chickens.

He lifted his head and whined, but he did not move.

The Apache stood between her and the house—between her and the rifle. She scrambled to her feet and backed away, touching the absent crucifix at her neck. He never came this close. Would he make his move now? *I trusted him. How could I be so foolish? Even Goyo was wrong.*

Her heart pounded in her ears, something she had not experienced for months. She glanced toward the bajada. *What will happen if Armando comes back and sees him?*

He stood motionless, watching. His expression betrayed nothing. When he took a step forward, she stepped back, nearly falling, but catching herself and increasing the distance between them. He stopped and waited. Goyo stood, but sat again, waiting.

Because he was always shrouded by shadows under the palo verde, she never saw him up close. He wore a loose shirt, the bead and bone medallion hung from his neck; a loincloth reached to his knees in both the front and the back, his muscled legs bare except for the deerskin boots reaching almost to his knees. Two pouches, a small one and one large, both with beads and fringes also hung from the belt. His tangled hair, streaked with gray, hung unevenly around his shoulders. The red bandanna, tied around his head, covered his forehead and shaded his dark eyes.

Deep lines etched his coppery brown face; his mouth stretched in a straight line, intimating neither a smile nor a frown. A light breeze carried his mildly sour body odor to her.

Even though she was still afraid to look into his dark eyes, she was drawn in against her will. He took several very slow steps forward, his eyes locked on hers. She held her breath.

Stopping, he shifted his gaze to the grave, the meager pile of rocks, and the small cross and then back to her. He closed his eyes and began to chant. For a moment, Esperanza thought she imagined it. As he sang, her heart slowed, and her breathing eased. Goyo lay down again, his black leg crossed over his white one, watching the Apache.

When he stopped chanting, he pulled the small pouch from his belt and placed it on the ground. He intended no harm.

Goyo was right.

As he turned to leave, Esperanza whispered, "Gracias."

He hesitated and turned back, and she thought she saw a sadness in his eyes, but maybe it was only the reflection of her own grief. With an almost imperceptible movement of his head, he turned and disappeared without a sound into the brush.

Esperanza stared at the small leather pouch, almost afraid to touch it. When she heard her husband riding up the track, she reached down, snatched it up, and hid it in her pocket.

Chapter 32

Summer 1867

"Are you sure?" He still worried about leaving her alone.

"Sí. I will be fine."

He needed to go to Tucson and couldn't wait any longer.

From time to time, after her sister's visit, Alejandro joined Julio on his trips to the homestead. They brought an extra half-barrel for the turnout, which they helped to enlarge, enclosing it with a rail fence. They also brought a large tank they could fill at the well, enabling them to fill the barrel in the house and the half-barrels in the barn and turnout in one trip.

Together, the three of them plastered the walls and floor in the house. When they finished, they rolled a woven mat out on the floor and hung paper flowers Lupe's girls made. Esperanza made a *ristra* with her own garden-grown chiles to hang by the door.

Now, as he prepared to go to Tucson, she put her hand in her pocket. She rubbed her fingers lightly across the beads and the soft leather, across the contours of its contents. After two weeks in her pocket, it remained a mystery.

Before he left, he put his arms around her and promised he would be home tomorrow before dark. Esperanza assured him she would be all right. She would keep the rifle with her all the time and Goyo would protect her. He kissed her goodbye and climbed into the wagon. He settled on the seat, pushed the brake off, and with a shake of the reins, he started out. She waved goodbye with one hand and kept the other in her pocket.

As he disappeared below the ridge line, she patted Goyo on the head, sent him to watch the chickens, and tried to forget what was in her pocket. In the house, she scooped water into a kettle and dropped in a handful of beans. Next, she concentrated on making tortillas. She scooped three handfuls of flour into a bowl and worked lard into it along with a bit of salt. She dribbled warm water from the small pot by the fire into the flour mixture. Again, she kneaded the dough, dripping in water until it was ready.

Watching her hands as she worked the dough, in her mind's eye she saw a darker pair of hands kneading clay and rolling out coils to shape a pot. She glanced at the pot, and, for a moment, the painted lines disappeared, and a raw brown pot sat in its place. When she blinked, the red lines reappeared against a pale brown surface. She shook her head and went back to shaping the dough for tortillas, and setting them aside for later.

Rinsing her hands in the basin, she left specks of dough floating in the water. She glanced around the room, pleased with the colorful decorations on the plastered walls. With the walls sealed, she didn't need to dust as often. She straightened the bedding, swept the mat, and knocked the cobwebs out of the corners.

She went to the door. Across the yard, the sight of Ángel's grave and his small cross pricked her heart with a sharp pain. If the day came when she did not feel the pain, would it mean she had forgotten her son? She touched her fingers to her crucifix, but it wasn't there. Her old habit made her forget she had given it to Ángel. Leaving the door open, she pushed the shutters wide, allowing sunlight to brighten the small room. She reached into her pocket.

At the table, she stared at the unopened pouch. Even though she'd carried it in her pocket for several days, weighted down by its mystery, she had not looked at it closely. With it hidden, she had touched it, ran her fingers across the beads, threaded her fingers through the fringes, and stroked the soft leather. Now, for the first time, she examined the design. Green and white beads arranged in what she first thought might be the narrow petals of a flower, but then she decided they were a suggestion of the four directions. Green pointed to the north and south, and white pointed east and west. Two pairs of beaded leaves hugged the central design, one black, one red, one green, and one white. She ran her finger across the tiny beads, taking pleasure in how so many beads, so close together could feel so smooth.

He wouldn't give my child something harmful, would he? She slid it open and gently emptied the contents onto the table. A small, polished, metal cone hanging from a short length of rawhide and a blackened, metal arrow point tumbled out.

She lifted the cone by the length of leather. Reflected sunlight danced as it turned. She didn't know its purpose, but she assumed it was somehow important to the Apache. She picked up the arrow point; its edges were honed and sharp. Scratches on the base suggested the point had been lashed to a shaft, and surface scars, along with a single crimp on one edge, suggested it had been used in a hunt or a raid.

As she slid her finger along the sharp edge, she remembered Armando's first serious injury. The same kind of point had sliced into his side. But this one had to be from a hunt. She preferred to believe it had not killed a person.

Did he mean for her son to hunt in the spirit world? Even though she knew the priest would disapprove, she was grateful. She laid the point in her open palm and closed her fist. The fingers of her other hand touching the absent crucifix, she held her breath—and squeezed. In spite of the initial surge of pain, she squeezed harder, glad to feel it somewhere besides in her heart. When she opened her hand, her pain flowed from the V-shaped cut, pooling under the edge of the point, staining it bright red. She lifted the point, watching the blood fall, drop—drop—drop—into a puddle.

At the basin, she dipped her hand in the water, letting the blood flow into it, staining the specks of dough pink. After bandaging her hand, she returned the cone to the pouch, and, without wiping away the blood, she dropped it in with the cone. She pulled the thongs tight and put it back into her pocket.

She ran the fingers of her unbandaged hand along the rim and inside the neck of the old pot. "Did you see what I did?" Blood seeped through the bandage, staining it scarlet. The image of her blood-stained petticoat came back to her, and she pressed her fingers against the stain, not to slow the bleeding, but to shift the pain from her heart to her palm.

She put the pot in her lap, wishing she could talk to Ha-wani and ask why this pot was unbroken when fragments were scattered all over the ridge. "Did you know I would find it someday?"

She rubbed her fingers again around the neck of the pot, locating the thumbprint, sliding her thumb into place. The dark face appeared before her, blue mouth lines, and straight, black hair, again gazing into her eyes, sharing her spirit.

"Tell me about your life here. I suppose you didn't have horses, but a garden? Yes, you would need a garden. You would have collected plants from the desert to nourish your family—and to heal them. You wouldn't have been alone like I am. Did you have daughters? Did your sons grow to manhood?"

That night, alone in the bed she shared with her husband, she dreamed again of the woman.

During the hungry time, too many old people and children passed into the spirit world. After three moons, her baby refused nourishment at her breast. No matter what she tried, she could not get him to suckle and relieve her painful swollen breasts of their life-giving fluid. He cried until he had no more strength to cry. The Singer-Priest sang for him, but to no avail. She didn't want to, but, desperate, she asked the Fire Keeper for help. She needed his magic.

The shaman spoke harshly. "You come to me now, Ha-wani, but only because you want something for yourself." He used her spirit name even though he had no right. The name belonged only to her and her family.

"Please, Yukui, my son has not wronged you. He is innocent." She kept her eyes downcast, careful not to meet his gaze. He would see inside and reach for her spirit.

"What will you give me in exchange for your son's life?" He pinched her swollen breast. She struggled not to react, not to let him see her pain. He put his hand to his mouth and licked her milk from his fingers. "I will come, and when your son lives, I will exact my price."

He dripped strong medicine into the boy's mouth, but the child did not swallow; he chanted over him. He burned greasewood twigs and fanned the smoke over the babe. Ha-wani could hardly breathe herself as her child coughed and gasped for breath. Yukui waved a spiny cactus joint over him, drawing the bad spirits from the child into the cactus. This he took far out in the desert to bury where the spirits would not find their way back to the child. Ha-wani prayed to the gods the bad spirits would stay there.

Even so, like others during the hungry time, her baby drew his last breath. So many funerals—so many children taken into the spirit world; the People surely were cursed.

Dazed, she wrapped her son's tiny body in the soft hide of the young deer Tonrai killed in anticipation of his son's birth. The hide was, first, a blanket for the infant and, when he was older, it would be his breechclout. She carried him to the pyre. Inside the skin, she

> tucked a small shell frog her man made for the
> child, a frog matching the one on her bracelet.
> Her spirit would stay near him. Tonrai tucked
> in two small obsidian points so his son could
> hunt in the spirit world. The Fire-Keeper
> prepared the cremation, and the Singer-Priest
> sang the child's spirit across and beyond as the
> flames erupted.
>
> Afterward, the Fire-Keeper collected the
> ashes from the pyre and put them into a small
> olla. When he placed the olla in her hands,
> she wanted to scream at him, to accuse him
> of letting her son die, but she kept her eyes
> downcast and said nothing. She and Tonrai
> carried the olla to the cemetery and buried
> him among the other lost children. Together,
> they spread the last handfuls of dirt over the
> child who left them all too soon.

Esperanza sat up in bed, clutching her aching breast and sobbing. *My baby's dead.* She swung her legs off the bed and sat up. Goyo came to sit at her feet, laying his head on her knees. She wrapped her arms around his neck and sobbed into his soft fur. *My baby's dead...her baby's dead.*

When her tears slowed, she lay down again, absently petting Goyo, whose head rested on the edge of the bed next to her. She tried to make sense of the dream.

Her dream from the night Armando came home and found her came back to her in vivid detail.

She had seen a dark-eyed, dark-haired naked beauty of a child—Ángel—standing at the foot of La Cresta. He was leaving.

Standing by the door, she had begged him to come to her.

But he laughed and ran up the mountain where he stood on a rock ledge overlooking a deep canyon.

Remembering, the terror gripped her again. In the dream, she had called to him. "Venga!" But Ángel laughed, and when his laughter echoed off the mountain walls, exquisite light and music surrounded her. *Why did I see and hear something beautiful when I was losing my child?*

Another child, darker than her son, stood on a rock tower across the canyon from Ángel. The music faded, and the light settled around the darker child, his skin gleaming in the light.

Holding out his hand, he called softly to Ángel, "Venga."

In the dream, when she realized Ángel was about to step into the abyss, terror overwhelmed her.

He raised a small hand to her and stepped over the edge.

The dream had doubled her grief as if she had lost her child twice. But now she understood. Ha-wani's child came for him. He came to take Ángel into the spirit world. He is safe. He is not alone.

For the first time since Ángel's birth, Esperanza slept in peace.

Several nights later, when they got into bed, Esperanza laid her hand on her husband's chest. He lifted it to his lips, brushed her fingers with a kiss, and said, "Goodnight, my love." When he turned his back to her, she molded her body to his and kissed him between the shoulder blades. He took a ragged breath and said, "Don't, Espe. Please."

"Why, Mando? It's been a long time. I think I'm ready."

He was silent for a few moments. "I'm not."

At one time, she believed she would never recover from her child's death, but now she knew she could go on. Did she underestimate Armando's feelings? "Talk to me, Mando. Don't turn your back, please. I want what we had before."

He rolled toward her and put his arm under her shoulders, pulling her close. "Me, too. But I'm afraid."

"Afraid?" She rested her forehead against his cheek.

He drew another ragged breath. "What if you get with child again? It happened once. It could happen again."

"I know. We followed Abuela Tiva's instructions—mostly. We were careless once."

"That's what I mean. The only way I know to prevent it is to—is not to—"

"You're right, but I miss the pleasures we shared. I miss being so close to you that we become one."

"I miss that, too." He lifted her hand to his lips again.

Uncertain how to describe to him what Lupe told her, she struggled for the right words. A wave of embarrassment flooded over her, and she remembered their awkward wedding night when she tried to explain her grandmother's advice. "I can't promise I won't get pregnant, and it's true we might again be careless, but I need you, and I want you to need me."

A tear escaped the corner of his eye and came to rest on her forehead. "I need you, Espe. I love you."

"Then I will tell you what Lupe told me."

Chapter 33

Summer 1867

Sweltering heat sapped her energy, keeping her from the chores. With the horses gone, she should muck out the barn, but in the house the heat was intolerable, and the barn would be worse. Goyo guarded the chickens from under a tree at the edge of the yard, lying on his side with his legs stretched out. The chickens scratched half-heartedly or settled into the dust, breathing through open beaks.

She forced herself to go to the garden. Yesterday's rain had flooded it. Another like that would leave nothing behind. Sweat trickled down her back and between her breasts, spreading into the waistband of her skirt while she gathered squash, tomatoes, chiles, beans, and corn. She dragged her sleeve across her forehead and carried the basket into the house.

After splashing her face with the cool water, she carried the basin outside where she sprinkled the water on Goyo and the chickens, hoping to cool them at least a little. She sat in the doorway of the house, wishing for at least a little breeze and waiting for the afternoon monsoon storm.

Throughout the day, thick, white clouds formed above the mountains. By afternoon, they turned gray along the bottoms, rising to impossible heights, and spreading their flat tops across the sky. Thunder rumbled, and lightning ripped through the heavy air. Massive curtains of rain swept along the mountains to the east. The air, thick with the fragrance of rain, pushed cool air across their little ridge, offering momentary relief before the arrival of the destructive winds that always preceded the rain.

They slammed into the ridge sooner than she expected, churning the trees and rapidly cooling the air. Her skirt whipping around her legs, Esperanza, with Goyo's help, gathered the chickens and closed them inside the coop. She hoped, this time, they would be safe and dry. Three of them drowned during a heavy rain two weeks ago when the roof leaked, and their nesting boxes filled.Armando repaired the roof and opened drains in the walls at ground level, digging trenches intended to carry the water away and down the hill behind the coop.

She unlocked the barn so Armando could put the horses away quickly if it was still raining, saying a prayer for him to beat the storm. If the wash flooded, he wouldn't be able to cross. He and the horses would be stuck until the water went down, which might be several days if the rain continued to fall in the mountains. Even if no rain fell here, rain in the mountains brought floods down below. Anyone fool enough to enter the wash when it flooded risked being swept away.

She took buckets inside for the inevitable leaks and carried in an extra supply of firewood. Hail began as a light clattering on the corrugated tin roof, followed by a deafening pounding. A steady shower of dirt and dust fell from the ceiling.

Goyo paced around, looking nervous when thunder reverberated through the little house. She rubbed his ears, telling him, "We'll be all right." When he lay down against the door, she wondered if his plan was to keep the storm outside.

Trying to be heard above the din from the roof, she shouted, "Listen, Goyo. How big do you think those hailstones are?" Curiosity got the best of her, so she opened one shutter a crack to investigate, but the wind grabbed the shutter and slammed it against the wall several times. She leaned into the hail, now pounding her and falling inside, and pulled the shutter closed.

"That was foolish of me." She picked the biggest hailstone up, and when she wrapped her fingers around it, her thumb and middle finger did not touch. "Look, Goyo." She knelt, holding the hailstone in her palm to show the dog. He sniffed and licked it. She laughed and dropped it on the floor between his front paws. "Help yourself." He pushed it around with his nose and licked it again.

"I'm glad I gathered the vegetables, Goyo. We might lose everything in this storm." Thunder shook the house, a rush of wind rattled the shutters, and rain replaced the hail. Although Goyo was busy with the hailstone, she said, perhaps to herself, "You don't have to be afraid."

She moved two buckets into place when the roof began to leak and dragged the bed into a dry corner. The fireplace spit and steamed as rain found its way down the chimney. Goyo curled up on the bed beside her while she listened to the rain pounding the roof and the wind howling through the trees.

SCREEEEEE—!! Esperanza and Goyo both jumped. She looked up, expecting the ceiling to open to the sky and rain. BANG!BANG!BANG! One of the corrugated panels blew loose. Even though the noise was deafening, it sounded as if the panel was still connected, flapping back and forth. If it blew away and they couldn't find it, they would have to wait until Armando's next trip to Tucson. He didn't have extras. New leaks fell from the ceiling and, shortly, a waterfall of sorts ran down the east wall of the house. *Oh, no. My plaster!* Sighing, she moved the buckets, pushed the chest away from the wall, and took down the paper flowers the girls had made. She stared at the floor where it was turning to mud. She sighed again.

After an hour, the wind abated, and the rain stopped. Esperanza stepped out into the yard to survey the damage. The barn survived, and the chicken coop appeared undamaged. Humidity hung thick in the air, and her clothes absorbed it and clung to her body. She walked through the mud and over flattened vegetables in the garden. The sun hung low in the west, painting a vivid double rainbow along the mountains' eastern slopes.

"I hope the rainbow means Armando will be here soon." She went around the house to inspect the roof. One of the panels had curled back above the east wall. Armando would be able to fix it and restore the roof.

When she carried the buckets out of the house and emptied them, a deafening roar rose from below the ridge. A flood. Armando would not come home tonight. He needed to make three crossings, one on the Tucson Road, another where the Cañada del Oro wash flowed across the Camp Grant Road, and here. This one usually flooded first because it drained the mountains directly to the east. The flood here would make its way to the Tucson Road and block passage there, as well.

"Come, Goyo. Let's go see how bad it is."

The wash ran fast and high, the muddy water carrying tree limbs and brush, slamming them against sturdy trees lining the banks. In some places the debris created barriers, pushing water over the bank or making whirlpools. Even if Armando made the first and second crossings, he couldn't cross here.

"The water has never been this high." She spoke to Goyo, but he probably didn't hear her over the roar of the flood.

When they started up the hill, Goyo turned and barked. Esperanza shaded her eyes against the late afternoon sun. Armando. He had made the first two crossings.

She waited. He waved to her and shouted something, but she cupped her hand over her ear and shook her head. He pointed to the walnut tree and then to himself. He would spend the night there. She nodded, blew him a kiss, and she and Goyo returned to the house.

When she awakened in the morning, she listened for the roar of the wash. It was still loud, but not as loud as the night before. She pulled on her skirt and petticoat, still damp and muddy from yesterday, pulled her blouse over her head, and put on her boots. "Vámanos, Goyo."

They ran down the muddy path. Armando was hitching the horses to the wagon. The water was not as high and definitely not as swift as the night before. Even so, Armando might not be able to cross safely. He inspected the harnesses and the traces. He walked around the wagon and examined each wheel.

He climbed into the seat and took up the reins, calling to Sofi and Pepe, who sidestepped a little when he directed them to the wash. Sofi, on the upstream side, balked, but when Pepe stepped into the water, she went with him. As the water rose to their bellies and the front wheels of the wagon rolled into the rushing water, both horses lost their footing and stumbled. Armando shook the reins, calling "Hyah," and they struggled for a foothold.

Esperanza held her breath. The rear wheels entered the water. Both horses, the wagon, and her husband were in the channel. They struggled forward against the sideward flow of water. A clump of debris slammed into Sofi, snagging her harness and swirling around her legs. She whinnied and reared. Esperanza gasped, reaching for the absent crucifix when the wheel behind the mare lifted, tilting the wagon dangerously. Armando slapped her hard with the reins. "SOFI! HYAH!" She settled and joined Pepe in moving ahead. When both horses were out of the water, and the wagon still connected, Armando reined them in, set the brake and jumped down.

He held Esperanza close. "I should have waited another hour."

"You're safe now. And the horses are safe."

While he examined Sofi's legs and cleared debris from the harnesses, Esperanza stroked their noses, murmuring, "Thank you, Sofi. You were a brave girl. Thank you, Pepe. You're a steady boy."

She climbed up beside her husband, and Goyo jumped into the wagon. At the top of the hill, Esperanza pointed out the damage to the roof and to the garden. "That's all I found, but I haven't checked the chickens yet."

After feeding and watering the horses, they let the chickens out and carried the supplies inside—two bags of beans, a bag of flour, much of which was too wet to save, dried beef, lard, canned milk, and canned vegetables. She was glad he brought lard, because, in the summer, it got rancid before she could use it all.

He helped clean up the house, putting the chest and bed back into place and the flowers back on the wall. She showed him where the leaks were, and he promised to work on the roof right away.

Suspecting he had little or nothing to eat yesterday and last night under the walnut tree, she cooked a big breakfast of eggs scrambled with chiles and onions. She made coffee and swung the pot of beans out of the fireplace.

She filled his plate and put it before him, but he didn't start eating right away. He seemed distracted. "You're not eating. What's wrong?"

"The Apaches are raiding everywhere. There have been killings, abductions, and, of course, they always steal livestock." The small pouch in her pocket grew heavy.

Armando went on. "Your parents and mine are safe in Tucson now. And the President of the United States has authorized the Territorial Governor to raise five companies of volunteers to fight the Apaches."

Esperanza sucked in her breath. "Armando, you're not thinking of—"

"No. I would, but I need to stay here to protect our home. I have letters for you. One is from your mother." He handed her a packet of letters from his saddlebag.

"Is everything all right? Did you talk to them?"

"Yes," he said, without meeting her eyes.

Armando's manner bothered her, and she trembled when she opened her mother's letter.

> *My dearest daughter,*
> *It was good to see Armando, but I do wish*
> *we could see you. We miss you terribly. We*

hated to leave Tubac, but, in the end, we had no choice.

I'm sorry to tell you Abuela Tiva died a month before we moved to Tucson. She was increasingly frail, but, most of the time, her mind stayed sharp. At times, though, she said strange things.

On the night of her death, she told me she would see "Espe's angel" in the Sea Ania. It frightened me because she always had a special connection with you. I was afraid something had happened to you, but she said, no, you were fine. I suppose when death is near, the mind strays from reality.

Your father sends his love. Tomás and Javiela are expecting their second child. Manolito is training with a small group to fight the Apaches under a new program the governor has announced. He is so passionate and will not be dissuaded, but we are terrified for him. Pray for him.

I hope you are well.
May God Be With You,
Mamá

Esperanza wept. Armando sat close holding her hand. "Abuela Tiva. She knew."

"What?"

"She knew about Ángel. Did you tell my parents?"

"No. You asked me not to."

"The night she died, Abuela Tiva told Mamá that 'Espe's angel' waited in the Sea Ania."

"I'm not surprised, are you?"

"No. She traveled the spirit world for as long as I can remember, telling stories of seeing and talking to those who had crossed over."

He was silent for a moment. "You are very like her, Espe. Sometimes I think you, too, travel in the spirit world."

"Why would you say that?"

"For one thing, you talk to the woman who made the pot."

"I pretend to talk to her."

"No, Espe. I think sometimes she talks back to you."

Changing the subject, she said, "Did they tell you Manolito is volunteering to fight the Apaches?"

"No. Good for him. Some people say the President of the United States will send the Cavalry here to help us." He scooped up a mouthful of frijoles. "Bill Oury's talking about forming his own group, and if the government doesn't come through, one way or another, they will kill them all."

"They can't mean to kill all Apaches, can they?" She slipped her hand into her pocket, searching for the peace the Apache's gifts gave her. "Surely they will make them behave. You don't really think they should all be killed, do you? Even the women and children?"

"Sí! How can you think otherwise? Look what they do to us here! And in Tubac!" He slammed his cup down. "*Son el mal—el muy mal*—They are evil."

"Armando, they cannot all be evil. There must be some good ones among them."

Armando stood, and his chair fell over behind him. "Good ones? Good Apaches? What can you be thinking, Esperanza?" He turned and started towards the door, but then came back and ripped his shirt open to show his scars. "Look. You tended to me when I came back injured. Do you forget I almost died?"

Esperanza remembered every drop of blood, every injury, small and large. She remembered her terror when he went out to chase them and her relief when he returned. Too often, he returned bloodied and bruised. She ran a gentle finger along a fresh scar, still angry and red. She wanted to tell him they might have killed him many times, but they hadn't. And to remind him the greatest danger she ever faced came from an Anglo. She wanted to tell him why they were allowed to live unmolested in this place.

He closed his shirt. "Esperanza, *es por la gracia de Dios* you are still here, still alive. You don't know how worried I am when I leave you here."

He took a deep breath and dropped to his knees beside her. "If an Apache came here, mi amorita, you would not have a chance. Even as good as you are with the rifle, you would not hear him coming, and he would slit your throat in a moment." He took her into his arms and wept on her shoulder.

She understood his pain and his concern, and she knew, now, she could never tell him about the Apache. About how often he came to watch her. She could never tell him the Apache shared her grief for Ángel when she needed Armando the most. She could never tell him about the one good Apache.

Chapter 34

Fall 1867

The sun rose above the eastern ridge, pushing cool air down the slopes and across the desert to where Esperanza stood in the yard. A brisk morning like this announced the coming of fall and an end to summer heat. She glanced at the palo verde, almost disappointed that the Apache wasn't there. Armando had left earlier because the horses needed shoes. She let the chickens out of the coop and fed them. Goyo lay down in the sun to watch them.

In the garden, she collected the corn and squash that survived the monsoon. She would soon plant again, but she wouldn't plant anything in the same place. Vegetables, especially the sisters, did better when the soil could rest from one harvest to the next. Carrying the vegetables into the house, she pulled three chiles from the ristra hanging by the door and put everything on the table for later.

She dusted the shelves, lifting the picture of her parents and touching their faces, lingering on her father's. She missed him terribly, her mother, too. Tomás would be a father again, and Manolito was fighting Apaches. She whispered a prayer for his safety and for Javiela to give Tomás another healthy child. She worried about her father's ranch and the cattle he abandoned. Don Jesús drove most of his cattle north to graze with Julio's along the Santa Cruz near Tucson. He didn't seem to care that Julio's land was not large enough to support so many cattle.

Outside, Goyo growled. When she went to check on him, rifle in hand, she saw a coyote slinking along the wall. She thought it was the same coyote she had seen a few times before, but he had kept his distance from Goyo. The chickens were inside their wire enclosure and Goyo stood between them and the coyote, growling, his teeth bared and hackles raised. The coyote looked over his shoulder toward the opening in the wall. Another coyote entered the yard. He circled around the other direction. Goyo didn't see him. They seemed to be planning a distraction. One would keep Goyo busy and the other would run in to grab a chicken.

Esperanza walked into the space between the chickens and the second coyote, the rifle at her shoulder. When Goyo noticed her and spotted the second intruder, the first one ran forward, closing the distance to the chicken yard. Goyo sprinted after him and at the same time the second coyote tried to make his move. The rifle report bounced off the mountains and both coyotes fled, one over the wall and the other through the opening.

"Good boy, Goyo. The chickens are safe—at least, for a little while from those two. But not necessarily from my soup pot." She laughed and scratched his ears. "They'll be back, I think, because I can't kill my coyote brother."

She knelt beside Ángel's grave and sang his lullaby while she swept dirt from the rocks. "Last week the Apaches tried to take five cattle, but your father managed to retrieve three. He wasn't as angry as I expected." She plucked leaves and debris from between the rocks, dropping them into a bucket for disposal later.

"I think he knows now the Apaches bargain with him for their meat, but I don't expect him to admit it. They take a certain number and let him have some back. They rarely shoot at him, and I don't think he's done more than fire warning shots lately."

The bird of paradise pods hung limp and brown. They would soon open and drop their seeds. She planned to scatter them around the yard to add more color. "I don't mean he comes back unscathed. Sometimes, his injuries are from riding through the catclaw, but other times, the Apaches fire at him once or twice, but mostly out of range. He said they must not know how far their rifles can shoot."

She put her hand in her pocket, tracing the contours of the point and the cone inside the pouch. "The Apache gave these to you. He helped me when you were born."

Goyo left his post beside the chicken yard to sit beside her. She patted his head. "Do you remember, Goyo?" The dog leaned against her. She put one arm around him and scratched his ears. "What would I do without you and my Apache?"

To Ángel, she said, "I should tell your father about him. If he knew what the Apache did for me, he would know not all Apaches are evil.... But I can't tell him, can I?"

Of course, Ángel did not answer, and Goyo offered no opinion. She believed this Apache kept her safe. He must keep the others away from the house. They stayed out on the bajada, chased the cattle, and did battle with

Armando. She couldn't remember the last time she was afraid to stay here alone.

"What do you think, my son, about those feathers on the walnut tree? Surely, the Apache put them there. But why? Do they count the number of times he has been here? Are they intended for some kind of magic? Perhaps they are meant to protect me when he isn't here."

She went inside for her sewing kit and to cut a small square of muslin from a petticoat she used for bandages, wash cloths, and flags to keep the birds out of the garden. Sitting beside her son's grave, she sewed a narrow hem around the material. Then she threaded her needle with gray and began to embroider a design, remembering how her mother labored over teaching her needlework. "Thank you, Mamá. I hope I do you proud today."

She talked to her son and to Goyo while she worked, her practiced hands drawing the thread back and forth in a subtle dance. She added dark brown at one end and white thread against the gray, creating shadows and an illusion of depth. When she finished, she held the square up to the light, pleased with a feather very like those on the tree. The shaft made a graceful, diagonal arc from one corner to the other with delicate vanes curving out. The white and brown threads imparted light and shadows giving the impression of the feather bending in a light breeze.

She opened her right hand and stared at the pale, V-shaped scar on her palm. She rubbed it, and traced its length, drawing the V with her finger. She called it her Ángel scar. She no longer had the sharp pain in her heart when she thought of him or looked at his grave; she held the pain in her hand, reminding her that both she and Ángel had a protector.

She sighed and tied a length of string around one corner of the square. "I will be back shortly, my son."

Telling Goyo to stay, she followed the path to the wash, lifted her skirt, and waded across the braided water to the walnut tree. She reached for a branch and looped the string around it. When she let it go, the small white cloth fluttered among the feathers, flashing white in the sunlight.

Part 4: Leaving

Arizona Territory 1868

Chapter 35

Spring 1868

On a day much like others on the ridge, Esperanza bent over, pulling weeds from around the squash seedlings. Generous winter rains made the ground workable, and she had tilled in aged manure. She stretched strings along the seed rows and tied strips of cloth to chase the birds away.

Armando left yesterday to pick up lumber and supplies to build a barn—a real barn—for the horses. Next year, he told her, he would start on the house.

She rarely worried about her safety when he went to town. Her confidence had grown since she faced down the Anglo, and now, she believed she could handle whatever came her way. Of course, some of her confidence she attributed to the Apache. She still wondered if he had killed the Anglo, but, since she had not seen him that day, she doubted he knew about the threat.

I have my rifle and Goyo, too.

Moments earlier, he chased a rabbit from the garden and followed it. She appreciated his help, but she needed to teach him to go around, not through, the garden. Shortly, she heard him barking from somewhere down the hill.

"Goyo, venga!" He would be back soon. He never ranged far from the yard.

She went back to pulling weeds, tossing them aside. Summer heat had arrived early, and she wiped her sleeve across her forehead. Standing straight, she massaged the small of her back with both hands and arched backward to loosen her tightening muscles.

"Well, ain't you a purty thang?"

Startled, she turned to find a man standing in the yard leering at her. He wore gray woolen pants held up by a single suspender. His dirty, white, collarless shirt was half tucked into his pants, along with a pistol. His heavy boots were scuffed and worn, and his tangled brown hair stuck out from under his ragged gray cap. One eye appeared to focus on her, and the other, partly covered by a ragged eyelid, aimed at something to his right. An ugly scar slashed across his forehead, through his eye, and down to his jawline.

When she reached for the rifle, he drew the pistol and said, "I wouldn't do that if I was you, Missy." He didn't shout, but the threat in his rasping voice was clear.

"What do you want?" Esperanza's English was good, but her accent was unmistakable. *Where's Goyo?*

"Messican, eh? Purty Messican, I'd say." His grin revealed a mouthful of rotten and broken teeth. Her stomach turned.

"Yeah, a purty Messican bitch. In a purty green dress. Wouldn't you agree, Charlie?" This time, his good eye aimed to his left, and his bad eye disappeared behind the ragged eyelid.

Another man leaned against the corner of the house.

"Ah do b'lieve yer right, Corporal Daggett. Got any orders for me?" The second man, taller than the other one, was even dirtier with blood smeared red on his trousers. He was whittling a length of wood with a large knife. Esperanza watched his hands as another sliver dropped to the ground. Judging from the pile at his feet, he had been there for some time.

The first man grinned at her. "Ah b'lieve Ah have somethin' in mind. C'mon over here, Seenyoreety. How's about a little kiss for Corporal Daggett, hero of Cap'n Quantrill's Raiders." He took a half-step forward, bowing clumsily and waving the pistol into the air.

Charlie laughed. His high-pitched cackle sent a chill up Esperanza's spine. He stepped away from the house and pointed the knife at her.

"An' when you're finished, Corporal, it's my turn."

"Poor Charlie. Y'always git my leftovers. Someday, I might let you go first." He grinned again. "But not today, Charlie." He shook his head. "No sirree, not today."

Fear, like she had never experienced, crawled over every inch of her skin. *Where are you, Goyo? I need you.*

She dived for the rifle, but Daggett grabbed her. Charlie picked it up and threw it across the yard.

When the gun landed, it discharged, and they all jumped. Charlie cackled and said, "Damn. There fer a minute, I thought ole Quantrill was here."

"Nah. 'S just us and this purty Messican bitch." Daggett tossed his pistol into the soft garden soil, grabbed her, and tried to kiss her.

She turned her head away, but he grabbed her chin and turned it back to his reeking mouth. He kept one arm around her and tried to force his tongue into her mouth, but she fought back. Grabbing her by the hair. He yanked her head backward and pulled her against him. He began grinding his hips against her and forced his tongue into her mouth.

Esperanza bit down. Hard. Daggett screamed and let go. She fell backward into Charlie, who grabbed her and cackled at Daggett's misfortune. "She's a wildcat, huh? Too much for you, Corporal. Guess I'll take my turn first."

Before Charlie could do anything, Daggett, blood dripping from his foul mouth, slapped her, and Charlie lost his grip. When she fell, she grabbed a handful of soil, throwing it in his face. She scrambled away and tried to stand.

"God damned bitch! Ah'll kill you when Ah'm finished with you!" He pinned her down and forced her legs apart.

She turned her head away and tried to press her legs together, breathless against his weight while he unbuttoned his trousers. With his trousers down, he put one hand around her throat and used the other to tear her skirt and petticoat out of the way. She struggled to breathe and keep fighting.

"God damn it, Charlie. Hold 'er down."

Charlie cackled. "I ain't givin' up my front row seat to help you, Corporal. Yer on yer own with this hellcat."

She managed to pull one leg free and kick him, but it had no effect. His heavy boot came down on her ankle, pushing it away, and opening her to his assault. He wedged himself between her legs.

Before he could push himself into her, a gunshot echoed, and Daggett's weight lifted. Confused, she pulled her skirt across her nakedness and crawled toward the house.

Charlie lay face down in the garden, and Daggett, with his trousers around his knees, scrambled for his pistol. Another gunshot and Daggett looked confused about the blood blooming on the front of his shirt. He dropped to his knees.

Esperanza struggled to her feet and backed away. Daggett's good eye met hers for a moment, a question on his lips. Before he could ask it, he fell dead at her feet.

"Armando. Thank God—"

Chapter 36

Spring 1868

He walked toward the house and leaned the rifle beside the door. When their eyes met, for the first time, his expression was unfamiliar. Only when he left the gift for Ángel, had she seen a flicker of something different. Today his dark eyes held hers for a moment, but she couldn't read them.

He turned and followed the path off the ridge.

Esperanza watched him go, trying to piece together what had happened. She turned away from the bodies in her garden and vomited. When she had nothing more to come up, she scanned the bajada for Armando. She needed him.

But he had gone to town.

She ran into the house and plunged her hands into the bucket, scrubbing them with a brush until they were raw, scrubbing her face to rid herself of his stinking breath, the taste of his saliva. Remembering his tongue in her mouth, she gagged.

Her dress was torn, the skirt ripped loose at the waist, and the bodice shredded, exposing her breasts. She ripped off what remained of her dress, petticoat, and chemise and threw them in the corner. Naked, she scrubbed herself with the caustic soap until she bled. She scrubbed every part of her body, especially between her legs where he... where he touched her. If she could rid herself of his smell, of his rough hands squeezing her breasts, of his knee shoving her legs apart, and of his weight as he started to force himself into her. If she could wash it all away, maybe it didn't happen. Maybe she could make it go away, make it unhappen.

"Madre de Dios—"

She couldn't finish the prayer. If she did, it would be real. If she gave in, she would drown in her own tears.

In spite of her resolve, she sobbed. She wrapped herself a blanket and sat on the edge of the bed rocking and sobbing, drawing ragged breath after ragged breath, struggling to forget the feel of him touching her, and trying to push the images of dead men out of her mind. When she heard a noise outside, she crept to the open door.

Armando came up the track, Julio, on Paquito, riding behind the wagon. As he drove into the yard, he saw the bodies in the garden. He leaped to the ground, shouting, "Espe! Espe!" Frantic, he ran to the house and found her hiding just inside the door. He cursed himself for leaving her alone yet again to deal with something terrible here.

He took her in his arms, but she stood wooden and unresponsive in his embrace. He led her back to the bed and sat with her. "¿Qué pasó?"

Saying nothing, she sat, her eyes blank, her mouth slack. Armando helped her lie down on the bed. He got another blanket and covered her. Tears burned his eyes as he thought about losing her. Damn him for bringing her here.

When he went outside, Julio was looking at the bodies in the garden. He said, "They are both dead, mi hermano, shot. My guess is she defended herself."

"What do I do?"

"I will unload the lumber and take these men into Tucson to the sheriff. He will know."

"No—he will charge her with murder!" Armando was terrified, but Julio insisted.

"Armando. These men were armed—one with a knife and the other—the one with his trousers around his knees—had a pistol. Esperanza defended herself." He placed a firm hand on his brother's shoulder. "The sheriff will not charge her. He cannot."

"But, Julio, I can't leave her here alone again."

"I will do it."

Armando fell into his brother's arms and wept. "I did this to her. I brought her here for my own dreams. When the Anglo came, I was not here to defend her. When Ángel died, I was not here to help her, and now, she faced these men, alone—I was not here. This evil belongs to me."

Chapter 37

Spring 1868

Two days later, Julio brought the Pima County Sheriff, Peter Rainsford Brady, his deputy, the county coroner, along with six sworn members of the coroner's jury to investigate the deaths. When he heard the commotion in the yard, Armando stepped outside. Seeing so many men with the sheriff frightened him, but Julio assured him it was all right.

"Buenas días, Señor Ramirez." The sheriff greeted Armando politely and dismounted, handing the reins to his deputy. He shook Armando's hand. "I hope your wife is recovering. Your brother told me what he believes happened here two days ago. By the laws of the Arizona Territory and the United States of America, the coroner is required to convene a jury to rule on the deaths." Sheriff Brady, a Civil War veteran, and a former Texas Ranger, was a man of substantial build with a thick mustache and a full set of slightly graying chin whiskers. He wore a well-fitting suit with a vest covering his white shirt. His gun hung from a cartridge belt below his waist, with the holster tied firmly to his leg. The sheriff introduced his deputy, the coroner, and the gentlemen of the coroner's jury.

The coroner, a short man of about sixty-five years, wearing a black suit too big for his frame and a pair of wire-rimmed eyeglasses spoke, "Mr. Ramirez, I'm sure you understand the gravity of this situation. Two men are dead. We must make a determination as to the manner in which death came to these two unfortunates. The immediate cause of their demise was by gunshot, but the question remains as to who wielded the firearm and under what circumstances." At his elbow, a member of the jury juggled a small inkwell, a pen, and a book in which he recorded the proceedings.

Pulling a handkerchief from his pocket, the coroner removed his eyeglasses and dabbed at his watery eyes. He put his glasses back on and shoved the handkerchief into his breast pocket, leaving half of it to hang out. "We must determine the nature of the crime and to what extent you and the other Mr. Ramirez," he nodded towards Julio, "are accessories to the crime."

This was not how it was supposed to go. The only crime was these men assaulting Esperanza. *Damn it. Why didn't we just bury them? No one would ever know.* Now they had no choice but to cooperate.

The sheriff administered the oath, and both men swore to tell the truth. The juror recorded their names. As part of the investigation, Armando and Julio led Sheriff Brady, his deputy, the coroner, and the jurors to the garden and described what they found when they returned to the ridge. Armando testified he and his brother came back from Tucson and found Esperanza, mute, naked, scrubbed raw, and her torn clothes in a heap on the floor. "She was wrapped in a blanket. She had scrubbed herself raw with lye soap and a brush. *Ella fue violada*. She was attacked, and she has not spoken since—" He choked back tears. "In two days, she has not said a word. She has not eaten."

Julio described the scene in the garden; he pointed out where they found each body, the knife beside one man and the pistol by the one whose pants were around his knees. "Esperanza's rifle was by the door of the house, where she always left it when she went inside." He pointed to the scattered boards in the yard. "I offloaded the lumber and put the two bodies in the wagon. I covered them with a canvas and took them to Tucson. I couldn't leave them here in the heat—and where my sister-in-law might see them." He choked back his own tears. "I had to think of her."

The coroner wiped his eyes again. "It is true leaving them here for our inspection would make our work today unpleasant." He glared at Julio. "But under the laws of the United States, of which the Arizona Territory is now a part, it is against the law to interfere with evidence of a crime. We cannot reach a credible conclusion without seeing the crime scene first hand."

The word, "crime," echoed in Armando's head. He wanted to shout, "My wife did not commit a crime!" But he remained quiet, hoping Sheriff Brady was the honorable man he was reputed to be.

The coroner continued, "From evidence collected from the bodies, both men were shot from a relatively short distance away—maybe from over there in the yard. In any case, it was not point-blank, which leads to my next question. How did your wife get away from two armed men who were presumably assaulting her and have time to get off two shots?" He squinted at Armando. "We are expected to believe she is a skilled marksman?"

"Yes. She is." Armando struggled not to lose his temper. "She was here alone. She had her rifle. Her clothes were torn—" He choked again, struggling to say the words. "One of the dead men had his pants down, for God's sake!"

The sheriff spoke. "May I inspect the rifle?"

Armando retrieved it from the house and handed it to the sheriff.

"Loaded?"

"Sí. Cuidado, por favor."

With the barrel pointing to the sky, the sheriff examined the rifle. "Anyone fired this rifle since that day?"

"*No, nadie,* señor, no one.

"Do you know how many shells were loaded that morning?"

"I check it every morning. The magazine holds sixteen."

Sheriff Brady pumped the lever to eject the remaining shells.

His deputy picked each one up. "Thirteen cartridges, sir."

The coroner sneered. "Three shells? Gentlemen, you want us to believe Señora Ramirez—a woman—gunned down two armed men in self-defense?"

"Sí señor." He resisted objecting to the coroner's use of the term, "gunned down."

The coroner harrumphed loudly.

Sheriff Brady ignored the coroner. "Did anyone besides your wife ever use this gun?"

"No sir. It's hers."

The sheriff turned to his deputy and said, "Maríano, please search the yard and the perimeter for spent shells."

He returned the empty rifle to Armando. "I don't want to make this more difficult for your wife, but we must interview her."

Looking pointedly at Armando, the coroner said, "It is my duty to interrogate your wife."

Sheriff Brady frowned at the coroner but said to Armando, "I'm sorry, Señor Ramirez, but we must speak to her."

Armando's heart sank. He escorted the coroner and the sheriff into the house where Esperanza lay still and mute on the bed. They removed their hats, but the sheriff stepped forward ahead of the coroner, who glared but said nothing. The others also removed their hats, and the recorder found himself juggling his hat along with his writing tools. They gathered around the doorway where they could hear the conversation inside the little house.

Armando knelt beside the bed. "Espe," he said softly, "this is Sheriff Brady. He'd like to ask you some questions."

Esperanza did not move. Her eyes were open but vacant. She did not shift her gaze from the ceiling.

Sheriff Brady knelt beside the bed and leaned close, speaking in a gentle tone of voice, "*Señora Ramirez, me puede decir qué pasó?* Can you tell me what happened?"

She did not answer.

"*¿Me puede decir sobre aquellos hombres?* Can you tell me about those men? Do you know who they were?"

Again, Esperanza did not respond.

The sheriff stood and turned to Armando. "Where are her clothes?"

Armando pointed to the torn dress and petticoat in the corner. He hadn't touched them, and he suspected Esperanza would throw them away.

The sheriff squatted and examined the clothes. When he stood, he turned to Armando. "You said she was bruised. Is it possible to show them without compromising her modesty?"

"Some of them, yes." He knelt beside his wife and drew the blanket down slightly.

There was a line of four bruises on the left side of her neck and one bruise on the right. Sheriff Brady held his hand as if wrapped around someone's throat. "Her assailant was a big man, right-handed. Any other bruises you can show me?"

Armando uncovered part of her left leg, revealing a dark, ugly bruise on her ankle and another one, as well as abrasions, on her shin. Throughout, Esperanza never moved, barely blinked, and seemed unaware of anyone in the room.

To the coroner, Sheriff Brady said, "She's in no shape to tell us what happened, and I would say her clothing and her bruises provide sufficient evidence to prove she was assaulted. I think we can reach a conclusion now."

The coroner frowned, but nodded towards the door and led the jury outside.

Maríano met them at the door and handed the sheriff three spent cartridges. He had drawn three Xs in the dirt to mark their location. The sheriff stood in place and faced the garden. "Your wife shoots right-handed?" Armando nodded. Sheriff Brady pantomimed shooting toward the garden where each man's body was found. He said, "Looks like she missed with one shot, but I'm satisfied."

The coroner guided the members of the jury some distance from the house where they could speak privately. The sheriff joined them and listened, even though the coroner appeared annoyed. Armando and Julio watched the proceedings.

Julio put his hand on Armando's shoulder. "Don't worry, mi hermano. Sheriff Brady is a good man even if the coroner is a fool." While they watched, the coroner spoke to the jury, and each man raised his hand, apparently in response to a question.

The sheriff and the coroner rejoined them, and the coroner spoke stiffly, "It is the decision of the jury that your wife killed these men in self-defense. We shall not pursue criminal charges."

Armando's knees almost failed, but Julio put his arm around his brother's shoulders and steadied him.

When Armando recovered, the sheriff said, "Señor Ramirez, I have reason to believe those men are the same who came through the eastern part of the territory a couple of weeks ago. We received a report from Camp Bowie to be on the lookout for two men who attacked and raped a girl at her parents' homestead not far from there. They also beat her brothers pretty badly. One of them may yet die from his injuries. The girl's father reported it, hoping the army would go after them." He waited a moment while Armando digested this news before continuing. "From the descriptions given by the father, they are likely renegades from the Confederate army. Your wife may have done the whole territory a favor."

"Gracias, Señor Brady. I am grateful."

The sheriff and the others mounted up and rode down the ridge.

Chapter 38

Spring 1868

Armando told Julio that he could not to leave her alone again. It terrified him to think something else might happen. She had handled Sam when he came and threatened her; she had survived their baby's death; and now, she endured an assault by those criminals. He couldn't gamble on another. Julio agreed to come more frequently, to bring supplies—feed for the horses and chickens, groceries, and ammunition.

After Julio left, Esperanza seemed to revive a little; she spoke a few words to Armando and prepared meals— although she ate very little of the food she made, and what she did eat usually came back up. She was listless and just wanted to sleep.

A few days later, while Armando was saddling Sofi, Esperanza came to the door. She held the door frame, her knuckles white, but she didn't step outside. She had not yet left the house.

"What is it, mi querida?"

"Where's Goyo?"

He didn't want to tell her. After Sheriff Brady and the others left, Armando realized Goyo was missing. Julio had gone to look for him while Armando stayed with Esperanza.

When Julio came to the door, Armando kissed his sleeping wife and stepped outside. He had carried Goyo's body back up the hill and laid it in the yard. "They cut his throat. He couldn't take on both of them. He probably encountered them halfway down the hill."

Armando had knelt beside his wife's beloved dog, wept, and stroked the stiffened fur. "How will I ever tell her?" One more source of pain for which he was responsible.

They buried Goyo beside Ángel, and he waited for her to ask.

Now she needed to know. He led her out the door. Once in the yard, she stopped, glanced at the garden, and turned back to the house.

"Espe, please, please come with me. You can't hide in the house."

"I can't, Armando. Don't make me."

"I won't make you, mi querida. But it's time. You are strong. You do not give up." He took her in his arms. "You saved my life. You have done what no woman has done before. You can do this now."

Looking past him, she saw the freshly turned dirt beside Ángel's grave. She sucked in her breath. "Goyo?"

"Sí."

Sobbing, she attacked, pounding his chest with her fists, and wailing. "Damn you, Armando! Damn you! Damn you!"

He did nothing to stop her assault. He deserved so much more. Her pain belonged to him.

Chapter 39

Summer 1868

I miss you both, but I'm glad you're together."
Nearly two months had passed since she lost Goyo
and a little more than a year since Ángel's birth. She sat
on the ground next to the graves, singing Ángel's lullaby
and talking to Goyo. She had put rocks on his grave to
protect him from predators. He protected the chickens—
and her—and he deserved the same. She glanced at the
chickens, scratching in their enclosure. "We've lost three
more, two to coyotes and one to a hawk. The rooster is
still here, and he's still too loud. I told Armando not to
bring me another dog, even though he thinks we need
one."

The sun climbed higher in the sky, warming the
cool morning air and promising scorching heat in the
afternoon. She sighed and started back to the house.

She glanced at the garden. It needed her attention,
but she couldn't bring herself to set foot in it. It had been

nearly two months since she had tended it. Since that day... Armando brought in the onions and fresh cilantro, but he hadn't pulled weeds. The sister crops should be fine since the corn, with the beans climbing it, was taller than the weeds. She stared at the corn. It would be ready to harvest in another two or three months. *Two or three months. I can barely think about tomorrow.*

Everything was tomorrow.

Everything was maybe.

Maybe tomorrow, she would weed the squash.

Maybe tomorrow, she would clean up the garden and prepare for fall planting.

Maybe tomorrow, she would have the energy to do her chores.

Maybe tomorrow, she would tell him...

After Daggett and Charlie's attack, little changed as they fell into old routines. Except for his trips to Tucson. He wouldn't leave her alone. Now Julio was their sole connection to town. He made regular trips bringing needed supplies. She worried her husband depended far too much on his brother.

After dinner one evening, he was about to go out and check on the horses and close the chickens in the coop when she put her hand on his arm. "Don't go out yet. We need to talk."

"What is it, mi querida?"

She poured him another cup of coffee. "We need to talk about Julio."

"What about him?"

"You applied for this homestead four years ago, and Julio has been at your side whenever you wanted him."

"I appreciate everything he does. He knows that. What's the problem?"

"Armando, they are expecting their second child. Is it possible Adelita needs him more than you?"

"He doesn't do anything for me he doesn't want to do."

"Are you sure?"

"Why wouldn't I be sure?"

"He loves you, and he would do anything for you, sacrifice anything for you. He has been there for you all your life, defending you, helping you, doing anything—everything—you ask." She laid her hand on his. "You told your father you wanted to live your own life. Don't you think he's entitled to do the same and take care of his wife and child—his children?"

"Do you think he doesn't live his own life?"

"That's exactly what I think. He's so used to being there for you, I worry about whether he's there for Adelita and Rafael. How many days a month does he spend here? Is he not in danger every time he comes here? How would you feel if you had to tell Adelita her husband was killed coming out to help you? What if Adelita thinks you're more important to him than her and their child?"

"But—"

"Just think about it, Armando. Think about it, please." She carried their plates to the basin.

As the door closed behind him, she sighed.

Outside, La Cresta and the eastern mountains glowed in the reflected light of the coming sunset. The red ball of the sun hung low on the western horizon. A crimson evening. The Pápago crimson evening that he had adopted for his own. *What if Adelita thinks you're more important to him than her and their child?*

Her words triggered a memory of something Julio once said.

In the months after he and Esperanza were married, Armando and Julio made several trips to prepare the homestead for them to move in. On their first trip, they parked the wagon beneath the ridge and began to dig the well.

When they encountered a resistant layer of caliche, they took a break under the walnut tree. Julio took off his hat and ran his fingers through his hair. "Now that we're here and you're really going through with this, there's something I need to say."

"What? Are you angry about something?"

"No, but I'm disappointed. Do you remember when we talked in the barn? The first time you mentioned doing this?"

"I remember."

"Do you remember what I said?"

"You said you'd help me."

"Yes, but I also said you should talk to Esperanza first."

Armando frowned. "I did."

"No, you didn't. You left for Tucson that night. You didn't talk to Esperanza until after you applied."

"I believed she would go along with it."

"You *believed* she would? You didn't know for sure? When you told her about it, how did she react? Was she enthusiastic?"

"Well, not at first. She didn't know enough, but after I explained it to her—"

"Damn it, Mando. What choice did she have? Would she tell you if she didn't want to come up here to this godforsaken wilderness?" He swept his arm around to encompass the surrounding landscape. "What if she thinks this place is more important to you than her?"

"She wouldn't think that."

"Don't be so sure, little brother. Don't be so sure." Julio stripped his shirt off, threw it on the ground, and grabbed the iron digging bar and a hammer.

Armando sat under the tree watching the muscles ripple across his brother's back as he wielded the hammer, chipping away at the caliche. *He's wrong. He's got to be wrong.*

Later, when they explored the bajada, he studied his brother, sitting tall on his buckskin gelding, Paquito. He envied Julio's skill in the saddle. From the time they were small, he had never fallen from a horse; Armando could not say the same. Julio directed the horse with subtle cues invisible to Armando. He would never be the rider his brother was, but, more importantly, he would never be the *man* his brother was. He said a prayer of thanks for him. *What would I do without him? I owe him so much.* But Julio's earlier words intruded. *What if she thinks this place is more important to you than her?* He adjusted his seat in the saddle before they rode up the wagon track. *She can't think that. Can she?*

Now, Esperanza's words rang in his ears. *What if Adelita thinks you're more important to him than her and their child?*

As dusk fell, he stood at the wall watching the crimson radiance fade from La Cresta, leaving shadowed granite towers and pinnacles.

Chapter 40

Summer 1868

W e're leaving?" She couldn't believe it. "We haven't stayed here five years. Will you lose the patent?"

He shrugged. "Maybe. We'll wait and see."

They were sitting in the yard on a bench Armando built with part of the lumber intended for the new barn. Except for the bench, the lumber was unused. She hadn't asked him why.

"Are you sure, Armando? This place is your dream. You're going to risk losing it?"

He lifted her hand to his lips and brushed a kiss across her knuckles. "I should have done it a long time ago, but I've been selfish." When she didn't answer, he gazed at La Cresta, sensing she was waiting for him to go on. "I never once asked you what you needed."

She took a long breath and waited before answering him. "I used to believe you were all I needed. But too many times you kept yourself from me. You let these mountains come between us." She, too, looked at La Cresta, speaking quietly without looking at him. "You did nothing after that Anglo—Sam—came here and threatened me. You did nothing after we lost our son."

"I know." He hesitated before continuing. "I won't blame you if you hate me when I tell you—but I need to confess—a part of me was glad we could stay here."

Esperanza drew in a sharp breath and stared at him, wide-eyed. "Glad our son—?" She stood and went to Ángel's grave, her back to her husband. Across the yard, a quail came through the wall, followed by her tiny fuzzy chicks—maybe only a day or two old. The father quail, his topknot bobbing, came behind them, pushing them to stay with their mother. If one strayed, he brought it back to the group, calling "chip- chip-chip."

Armando came to stand behind her. She didn't turn to face him. "You should have taken me to Tucson, to Lupe, but you didn't."

"I have no excuse. I knew what I should do, but I kept telling myself you would get over it."

Her temper rose. "You mean like the cows get over the coyotes killing their babies? Armando, I'm not one of your cows!"

He said nothing.

"And after those men, when they—" She choked back a sob. "You could have taken me away from this place—to my mother."

"Please, Espe, look at me." He touched her arm, and although she turned her body to him, she focused on the quail family. He gently turned her head until their eyes met, her tears flowing, his on the edge. "I won't ask your forgiveness. I don't deserve it. I only ask that you give me a chance to make it up to you."

"Of everything you've ever asked of me, this is the hardest."

That night she dreamed of Ha-wani.

Most of the other young families were going with them. Yukui's leadership was intolerable.

They packed their burden baskets, and she strapped the infant to her breast. They would leave most of their pots and ollas. She would take only what would be useful during their travels. She picked up the pot with the red geometric scrolls. She remembered making it and how the other women laughed at her design, so unlike theirs. Before long, though, others copied her ideas. She traced the red lines with a finger.

This village was her home; she brought her spirit here to share with Tonrai and his family. Because his parents were staying, death, for them, would come soon, but they would wait with dignity. She wanted to leave a bit of her spirit here to offer them strength and companionship. Behind their shelter, where no one could see, she knelt and scooped a depression in the ground, nestling the pot in it. She filled the pot with dirt so it would remain unbroken underground.

After covering it, she rested one hand on the mound, and the other on the back of her child's head. She gazed at the rugged ridge that had watched over the People for generations, then across the desert to the mountains beyond her parents' village.

She sang the song she sang when she molded the clay, the song the pot carried back

*to the earth, the song to comfort Tonrai's
parents when they crossed over. Her spirit
would reside here in this pot, long after she,
too, crossed over.*

*The song floated on the wind, around the
rocks, down the canyons, and across the hills
to be lifted up by other winds at other times,
a small sound, always far away, a sound only
those who really listen will hear.*

A week later, they were nearly ready to go. Armando
had already taken the chickens to Lupe's, and Julio,
Alejandro, and several others arrived early that morning
to drive Armando's bony Sonoran longhorns to Tucson,
where Bill Oury agreed to buy them. He would fatten
them up and make a tidy profit when he sold them to
the military garrison. Armando said they would not run
cattle in Tucson; he was thinking of buying land near the
river for farming.

His parents had gone back to their ranch, but
Esperanza's parents stayed in Tucson. Manuel Ocoboa
had sold his ranch to an Anglo cooperative.

Armando was nervous about leaving her alone again
for the cattle drive, but she assured him she would be all
right. She reminded him that he should not expect Julio
to manage his business dealings in Tucson.

While they drove the cattle into town, she packed
most of her kitchenware and household goods in crates
Julio brought her. She was surprised at how much they
accumulated in a few years' time. She carried a box out
to the wagon and turned to the mountains, La Cresta
and the long ridge to the east. Beautiful. No wonder the
Spanish, when they arrived here, called these mountains

L'Iglesia, the church. She understood, but it never felt like a church to her.

When she turned, he was there, under the palo verde. As always, he blended into the background with only the red bandana to mark his place. Now, he stepped out of the shadows and stopped at the edge of the yard. When she raised her hand in farewell, his gaze shifted to the scar on her palm. Again, she thought of her father. *Did you have a daughter?*

He nodded, again almost imperceptibly, turned, and walked down the path. She watched him go with a sense of loss, hoping he knew how grateful she was for his gifts. He exacted revenge on Sam for threatening her—she believed that now—and he saved her life when those men attacked her. But it was his presence she treasured the most.

She remembered the day Sheriff Brady came and questioned her. He was kind, but she could not tell him the truth. Her distress was genuine—she did not deceive them, but neither Armando nor anyone else could ever know what happened that day. If they believed she killed those men, she would not tell them otherwise.

On the day they were leaving, she put the last of the things she could carry in the wagon. She made a light breakfast using the last of the frijoles and tortillas. She picked up Ha-wani's pot and cradled it in her hands, again tracing the red lines and scrolls. She saw the dark face, the corners of her mouth lifted in a smile, blue lines curving out. "Thank you, Ha-wani, for leaving a bit of your spirit here to help me survive in this place."

On her way to the wagon to add it to the box of kitchen goods, it tumbled from her hands. Pieces, large and small scattered across the ground.

"Oh no!" She knelt and examined the fragments of the pot that meant so much to her. She picked up some, trying to see how they might fit back together. She would never be able to fix it. She dropped all but one, a rim piece, the one with the thumbprint. She placed her thumb in the depression. "Gracias, mi amiga. I was never alone as long as I had this gift of your hands."

She slipped it into her pocket along with the small buckskin pouch as Julio and Armando rode up the hill. They had been at the well shoring up the sides and nailing boards over the top to protect it. Armando would restore it if he came back to re-establish his ranch.

"I am ready."

The men dismounted, tied their horses to the rail and went into the small house. They carried out the table and chairs, the bed frame and mattress, loading them on the wagon. Finally, they brought out the pots, kettles, and the fireplace tools. They stabilized the load with ropes, tying them securely to the sideboards. Armando unsaddled Sofi and put the tack into the wagon. He brought Pepe out of the barn and harnessed both horses.

When he took Esperanza in his arms, she leaned away from his embrace and looked into his eyes—his green eyes. "You are sorry to be leaving?"

"*Sí y no.* A little of both. I love it here, but I'm sorry for the pain you have suffered because of me—and because of this place. You are not sorry, are you?"

"To be honest, no. But I am sorry that we have failed to build your dream here."

"And I'm sorry we must leave our son behind."

Esperanza's face clouded. She walked to the grave. She knelt and smoothed the soil around the rocks and replaced some that had tumbled from the mound. Armando stood behind her, his hat in his hands. She touched her fingers to the absent crucifix and sang Ángel's lullaby softly.

> *Dulce niño,*
> *duermete ya.*
> *Es hora de descansar...*

Julio waited by the wagon, and when the soft melody drifted to him, he took his hat off and bowed his head. When the song was finished, Esperanza reached for Armando's hand, and he knelt beside her. Together they prayed to La Virgen to watch their child, making the sign before rising.

Adiós, m'hijo hermoso. My beautiful son, I will think of you every day."

To Goyo, she said, "Gracias, my friend. Take care of my baby." She went directly to the wagon, her back straight, her shoulders lifted, and her step purposeful. After she climbed into the seat, she slid her hand into her pocket and waited. *Maybe tomorrow I'll tell him about our baby.*

Julio untied his horse as Armando took up the reins. "Hyah!" The horses started down the track for the last time, with Julio following on Paquito.

Esperanza focused on the track ahead of them. Had she looked back, she might have caught a glimpse of red in the shadows of the palo verde.

If you enjoyed this book, please consider leaving a review at Amazon, Barnes and Noble, other online book retailer's sites, and Goodreads. Even if it's only a line or two, it would be a huge help.

The Clay Sustains

Book 3 in The Clay Series

Stone Towers Village, 1158 CE

"They come! They come!"

Ha-wani's voice rang through the midmorning air. Everyone in the small village came running. She turned and dashed back through the opening with most of the village following.

They were coming. Finally, they were coming home. She ran with the others down the path, her sister running just behind her. Catching sight of them, she stopped with several other women and watched.

Where is he? She felt her heart stop beating momentarily and then start pounding again when she saw him, his unmistakable broad shoulders, his brown skin glistening in the sunlight. Her breath exploded from her lungs, and she shouted for joy.

When she reached him, Tonrai swung his burden basket to the ground and swept her into his strong arms. He covered her face with kisses, and she clung to him, her heart singing words of thanks for his safe return. He pushed her away, gazed into her eyes, and pulled her back into his arms. In that moment, she saw something unspoken in his dark eyes, something fearful, something dreadful. His spirt was troubled. A shiver ran down her spine.

"Please," she prayed, "please let all be well. She could not know that her life, along with the lives of everyone on the ridge, was about to change.

On the day the men departed, Ha-wani, her mother-in-law, and her sister, along with all of the village, had seen them off with a sense of hope. It had been two cycles of seasons since they had taken such a trip. After the first year of the drought, the council had decided that the trip would put excess strain on the village food supplies because such a trip required extra rations for each man. They wanted to be sure there was enough to see them through the hungry time. After the second year, they had become even more desperate. The hungry time had been hard. When they entered the third year of the drought, the council decided it was their failure to obey the traditions that had worsened the drought. Perhaps they had been wrong not to go to the Great Water. Perhaps the rains had failed because they had not sent songs to the sea and brought back the blessings of the water.

They would send trade goods with a party who would sing the songs and bring back salt and shells. When the shells were here, the waters would follow. All would be well; they would be one with the Earth again. With this hope, the village greeted the men.

Knowing he would share the news of the journey with her when the time was right, she asked no questions. They joined the great procession, noisy and joyful, moving in a body toward the compound wall.

Youngsters and the men who had stayed in the village relieved their fathers and brothers of their baskets. For the first time in two turnings of the moon, the men walked lightly upon the ground, feeling relief and pleasure in their homecoming.

Nevertheless, as they walked along the ridge toward the compound, Ha-wani felt a tension among the men. She pushed it behind her and thought only of Tonrai's return. Other than the day her mother had given her to him, this was the happiest day she had known, and she desperately wanted nothing to ruin it.

When they reached their family courtyard, she paused her excited chatter to catch her breath. Clinging to her husband's strong arm, she looked around for the rest of her family expecting their joy to match hers. An-nat, dusty and tired like Tonrai, stood talking quietly to her mother-in-law and sister. When he walked away, Ranaä collapsed, sobbing.

She looked wide-eyed at her husband, the question refusing to form in her mouth.

He looked into her dark eyes for barely a moment and then looked at the ground at their feet.

"It was on the way out. On the day of the third sunrise, we were crossing the Valley of Burned Rock." Ha-wani tried to still the fierce beating of her heart as she imagined that awesome place. For generations, her people had told stories about the frightful things that happened to travelers and traders in that scorching land. Anyone who wanted to travel to Great Water had no choice. They had to cross it. She said nothing as Tonrai continued.

"We met a band from several days west of here. They had given up their village and, bringing almost nothing with them, they were going south in search of a new homeland. They were hungry and tired, and their children and old were dying." Tonrai's voice shook. "We gave them what we could, but we had to think of our obligation to the People, to our own families. We had to complete our journey."

"Yet what of your brother? Was it because of these people he has not returned to us?"

"Yes, but they were only a part of it." He took her arm and pulled her to the outer edge of their courtyard. They stood in the shadow of the hut near the compound wall. It was here they had first pledged their devotion to one another. In his eyes she saw his troubled spirit, and although she was afraid, she gazed into them, offering her spirit to share his burden. In times of trouble, they must be one.

In that moment, the combined strength of their *sedaku* shone in their eyes.

Look for *The Clay Sustains* coming in 2017.

The Clay Remembers

Book 1 in The Clay Series

Reviews

★★★★★ A first volume that compels from the outset

In the Arizona desert, Anna Robinson sifts through layers of the past, bringing lost objects to the light of day. But she'd prefer it if her own past stayed below ground. Husband Foster has demeaned and assaulted her, even interfered with her work. Yet the artifacts she unearths, which women before her have shaped and woven, give her the strength to evade him for now.

The treasures Anna lights upon are no fabulous devices, nor is she a mere 'psychic' archaeologist. Her empathy, her bond with our forebears, is a gripping metaphor for the need of women down the years for recognition of their joy, skill, and creativity, which enrich the lives of all. Sharon K. Miller shows how pressing that need can be, ranging against Anna a belittling archaeologist husband whose family is incapable of seeing beneath the surface, and whose greatest talent, ironically, consists of burying secrets. That's but one of the subtle oppositions that set this novel apart, like the skyward reach of the Robinsons, living well above ground on the fourth floor of their property, or Foster's inability to appreciate the simple and natural (such as Anna's need for a child) in telling contrast with Nick Anderson—with whom Anna falls in love—and his easy connection with a world of real things about him: soil, animals, a woman who knows who she is, the birth of new life.

The Clay Remembers honors that continuity—the positive, the intimate, the beautiful and sustaining. The voices of the past, caught with deftness and sensitivity, guide Anna in her quest to restore balance to the present—to find her place in a tradition she can see and hear, and happiness with a man whose past is as haunted as her own. Alive with the light, scent, and grit of the desert, this first volume compels from the outset. Its successors promise to uncover more of time, craft, and enduring love.

David Neilson, Author of *The Prussian Dispatch,*
Book One of theSophie Rathenau Vienna Mysteries
http://sophierathenau.weebly.com/

★★★★★ **Masterful Storyteller**

We all hope to meet and fall in love with our soul mates, but for Anna Robinson, her husband, Foster was not that person. Abusive, cruel and controlling Foster silenced Anna as only a man of his demeanor does well.

An intelligent woman, Anna escapes and finds a home in Arizona. Doing what she loves most, Anna joins an archaeological team and begins to dig for remnants of the past—not hers but the Native Americans' long gone. Her unique gift allows her to connect with those long-ago people; her preternatural ability to touch sherds of pottery allow her to connect to the past through touch, sight, and smell.

As her friend tells her, "You did touch her. The clay brought her to you. Every piece of ancient pottery on this land has a maker, and a story, and a song. They say the clay remembers the hands that made it. You don't need to be Native American, and you don't need to know why it happens. Celebrate it. Open your mind and heart to the stories the Earth wants you to hear."

Although Anna is able to give voice to the silent women of the past, she struggles to overcome her abuser and begin life anew. She knows how important it is to her to find her inner voice and strength; it could mean life or death!

The Clay Remembers is a touching, positive, and insightful story with emotional depth that a reader cannot help but experience. Every woman should have her voice and power; Sharon Miller demonstrates the importance through Anna. A masterful storyteller, Miller makes powerful connections to her readers through her book.

Miller does not allow her readers to become bogged down with negative feelings; there is laughter, love, and lightness to the story that does not take away from her message.

Miller's inclusion of historically accurate information is a treat. Well written with superb character development; plot development is excellent as well. Her insight into different personalities is strong.

This is an excellent book. Methodical, Miller builds a story, and it plays out smoothly and meaningfully. A first-time author, Miller hits a homerun. A true storyteller, Miller will continue to wow her readers.

Charla White
WordsAPlenty Blog
http://ow.ly/oNr73o1dupY

Visit www.sharonkmiller.com
to join my mailing list. Look for announcements about
upcoming book talks/walking tours of the Romero Ruin
site at Catalina State Park.

Other Sites:
www.theclayremembers.com
www.buckskinbooks.com
sharon@buckskinbooks.com
about.me/sharon.miller

Social Media:
@authorskmiller

Blogs:
authorsharonkmiller.com
boxeldersandblackberries.wordpress.com

Pinterest
www.pinterest.com/buckskinbooks/the-clay-remembers/
www.pinterest.com/buckskinbooks/the-clay-endures/

Author Notes

Many Tucson residents will recognize the Ramirez homestead as the Romero Ruin in Catalina State Park. Sometime in the mid-1800s, Francisco Romero (1822-1905) and his wife Victoriana Ocoboa (1833-1908) established a homestead some fifteen miles north of Tucson in the Territory of Arizona. Romero built a simple home on the site of an ancient Hohokam village.

Certain events in the lives of my fictional characters, Armando and Esperanza Ramirez, are based on historical accounts of Francisco and Victoriana Romero. For example, while they lived at the site, the Apaches constantly raided, stealing cattle and threatening their safety. Romero did, indeed, chase after them armed with pistols and a rim-fire carbine, which gave him an advantage over the weapons of the Apaches. His son reported that he bore multiple scars from his battles with them. They built their house from rocks and cobbles from the ancient Hohokam compound.

The history of their time there is confounding, with different sources suggesting different dates. Some sources place them there as early as the late 1850s and others around 1879. I chose to place Armando and Esperanza at the site in the mid- to late 1860s and to provide a fictional backstory for them.

The Romero Ruin site has been the subject of archaeological interest for more than one hundred years. In the early 1800s, the site was marked on the map as *Pueblo Viejo* (ancient village), and the first description was written in 1910 with photographs by geographer Ellsworth Huntington.

It is among the largest and most important ancient sites in the Tucson area. Data from various archaeological studies suggest that the site was occupied by the Hohokam from approximately 550 CE through 1450 CE. Book 3 in the Clay Series, *The Clay Sustains*, takes place on the same site during the twelfth century.

PROLOGUE

TIN-NE-ÁH: The Apache people. Current usage generally includes the Chiricahua, Jicarilla, Lipan, Mescalero, Plains Apache, and Western Apache bands. The Apaches engaged in warfare with Spaniards and missionaries during the colonial period, other Native American bands (e.g., Pimas, Pinals), Mexico, and Anglo settlers. The Apache in this story would have been a member of the Aravaipa band in Arizona living at túłtsog *hadaslin,* Where the Yellow Water Flows, near the northern end of the San Pedro River.

N'AÍÍ'EES AND WHITE CHANGING WOMAN: The Apache Sunrise Ceremony or *na'ii'ees* is an arduous communal four-day ceremony that Apache girls of the past and present experience soon after their first menstruation. Through numerous sacred ceremonies, dances, songs, and enactments, the girls become imbued with the physical and spiritual power of White Painted Woman, or White Changing Woman, and embrace their role as women of the Apache nation. (See Chapter 15 notes for more detail.)

A WOMAN'S DEATH MEANT NOTHING: In his 1868 account, *Life Among the Apaches*, John C. Cremony reported the following event that took place in 1864. "One day an Apache woman died in camp, and I asked Gian-nah-tah if there would be much lamentation. He simply smiled at the idea, and replied: "It was a woman; her death is of no account." Whether that was an accurate observation, I'm not sure. I have found nothing in more recent literature to confirm it as a general belief. My guess is that, at a time when men constituted the largest part of the warrior force, the death of a man resulted in a weakened offense or defense. The Apache did have women warriors, though. Lozen, Victorio's sister, fought valiantly beside her brother and later beside Geronimo.

APACHE DEATH BELIEFS: The Apache were very superstitious about death. In general, they believe that everyone is allotted a specific time on Earth unless the person is taken too soon by an act of violence or witchcraft. There is contradictory information regarding a belief in an afterlife. Some sources say they did not; others say it is vague; and other say that a life after death mirrors the one lived on this earth. Specifically, though, the Apache feared the dead and everything connected with them. When people died, they were buried immediately and as far away as possible. The personal belongings of the dead and their wickiups were burned or destroyed, and the family moved to a new site immediately to trick the ghost. They never approached graves and the name of the dead was never mentioned or even thought about because it would bring the ghost back. Note that, in Chapter 31, the Apache does not approach the grave; he approaches Esperanza.

PART 1: THE BEGINNING

Chapter 1

VELVET ASH: A tree of substantial size that grows along stream sides, canyon bottoms, wash sides, and gullies. For medicinal purposes, collect bark from younger branches. Bark tea is used for indigestion with liver sluggishness and mild constipation. A poultice/oil/salve can be made and used externally for skin conditions.

CAÑAIGRE TUBER: Also known as wild rhubarb and dock. This plant is found throughout the desert in sandy and moist soils. It may be used as a topical astringent to lessen irritation and redness from burns, rashes, and scrapes, and to staunch bleeding from superficial cuts. As a mouthwash or gargle, it soothes mouth sores, bleeding gums, and sore throats. It is collected in late winter or early spring when the leaves first show themselves. Dig the older tubers and leave the younger ones to grow later.

PAZOTILLO: Also known as Colt's tail, Horseweed, Canadian Fleabane, and Erigeron. It is found in disturbed soil along ditches and areas where water tends to collect. An infusion is useful in treating intestinal inflammation and ulcerative colitis. The essential oil of Canadian Fleabane works to slow mild to moderate hemorrhaging, internal bleeding, and uterine bleeding after childbirth.

CRUCIFIXION THORN: A leafless shrub or small tree displaying branches with pointed thorn-like branchlets. It is commonly found throughout the Sonoran Desert. Collect small clippings from spiny tips of outer branches, leaving the younger, fruit-bearing branches. It is used for diarrhea, dysentery (from ameobic or protozoal infections), or as a sitz bath/douche for vaginitis.

DEYAA: Western Apache meaning "Leave" or "Go."

GRACIAS, EL ÁRBOL: The tradition of showing respect to the natural world involves asking permission to take what you need and expressing gratitude for the gifts.

CURANDERA: *Curanderismo* includes four specialties, beginning with the *yerbera* (herbalist) and continuing with the *partera* (midwife), *sobadora* (folk chiropractor), and *curandera espiritual* (spiritual healer). Some practitioners specialize in only one area, but all make use of herbal *remedios* (remedies). All of these folk healers are known as curanderas. Abuela Tiva's specialty was working with herbal remedies.

Chapter 2

EL DIA DE SAN JUAN: June 24 is *El Día de San Juan,* St. John the Baptist's Day, in the Catholic calendar. It was St. John who baptized Jesús in the River Jordan, thus marking the beginning of his ministry. This is why so many of the Mexican traditions associated with this day involve water, especially running water. If the summer rains start on the June twenty-fourth, that is a sign that they will be long-lasting and copious. But if it rains before El Día de San Juan, it is considered a warning of something bad coming.

PÁPAGO VILLAGE: The name "Pápago," or "tepary bean eaters," was used by the Spanish conquistadores to refer to a Native American tribe dwelling in southern Arizona and northern Sonora. In 1986, when the Papago tribe formed their own nation, they reclaimed their name, "Tohono O'odham," which translates as

"Desert People." The Tohono O'odham are believed to be ancestors of the Hohokam. The name, "Pápago," is now considered offensive, but during the time of this story, they had not yet claimed their cultural name.

CALL DOWN THE CLOUDS (SING DOWN THE RAIN): The saguaro wine ceremony is an important observance—a seasonal cleansing that restores the people and the land. Contemporary Tohono O'odham carry on the centuries-old process, preparing the wine and gathering together for song, dance, and ritual drinking. *I'itoi*, the Creator of the Tohono O'odham, taught the Desert People their sacred wine ceremony so they could summon the rain *(ju:kˇi)* they needed to survive.

NICOLÁS RAMIREZ: Fictional ancestor of Armando Ramirez, based on the historical ancestor of Francisco Romero, on whom Armando's character is loosely based. Nicolás Romero settled south of Guevavi in 1751. His ranch was called Buenavista.

THIS RANCH/LAND GRANTS: During the 1820s and 1830s, Sonoran ranchers tried to colonize the grasslands of southeastern Arizona through grants from the Crown. These ranches commonly raised longhorn cows, whose descendants roamed the range as feral survivors long after the land grants were abandoned or passed legally to other owners by 1840. For this story, I have chosen to allow Don Jesús and Manuel Ocoboa to hold onto their lands. An 1860 map of Arizona Territory shows some identified mines and towns between Tucson and the Mexican Border. An 1876 map shows a large number of ranches.

DOÑA (FEMININE) / DON (MASCULINE): From the Latin, Dominus, meaning Lord. Historically, *don* was used to address members of the nobility. Later, it was reserved for persons of the blood royal, and those of high or aristocratic birth. Although originally reserved for royalty, select nobles, and church hierarchs, it is now used as a mark of esteem for a person of personal, social or official distinction, such as a community leader or a person of significant wealth. The title is used with the given name, as in Don Jesús and Doña María. Note that Esperanza addresses Doña María, as Señora, which is correct.

SPANISH NAMING CUSTOMS: Based on historical traditions for naming children practiced in Spain, a person's name consists of one or two given names followed by two family names (surnames). The first surname is the father's paternal surname, and the second the mother's paternal surname. The first surname is considered primary. Women keep their names when they marry. Doña María's given names are María and Dominga. Her first surname, from her father, is Castillo de Vega; her second surname from her mother is Reyes. Sometimes surnames are connected by y, meaning "and." With Doña María's name, the "and" clarifies that "de Vega" belongs with Castillo. Don Jesús's given names are Jesús and María (commonly given to male children). His first surname, from his father, is Ramirez; his second surname, from his mother, is Gonzales de Bonillas. The additional appellation, "de Vega," and "de Bonillas," reference the family place of origin. The use of "de" does not necessarily denote a noble family, but its usage was popular for denoting noble heritage. Many people, regardless of their true origins, used additions such as, "de Vega" and "de Bonillas" to imply an aristocratic background.

SPANISH DESCENT: Settlers on the frontier, imitated the social and racial rankings of metropolitan Mexico. Residents who may have been of mixed-blood origin often sought the higher social status of Spanish origins. By the end of the colonial period, many settlers identifed as *gente de razón* and claimed to be Spanish. Father Ignaz Pfefferkorn, an eighteenth-century Jesuit missionary in Sonora, observed very few true Spaniards living in Sonora and "scarcely one who could trace his origin to a Spanish family of pure blood." Practically all those who wish to be considered Spaniards are people of mixed-blood. This certainly would have been the case for Don Jesús and Doña María. Armando has a realistic view of his family's heritage.

MESTIZO: A person of mixed racial or ethnic ancestry, especially, in Latin America, one of mixed American Indian and European descent.

OCOBOA FAMILY: Historically, they were a Yaqui family from the Tubac/Tumacácori area who gained *vecino* status, that is, landowner status, at the end of the colonial era and moved upward socially through intermarriage. They are likely the ancestors of Victoriana Romero on whom the character of Esperanza Ramirez is loosely based.

GOVERNOR OF TUBAC: Rámon (Raimundo) Pamplona, born in 1783 at Tumacácori, was the son of Miguel Antonio Pamplona, a Pápago, and Josepha Ocoboa, a Yaqui. He served as the native governor of Tumacácori. Josepha Ocoboa would have been an ancestor of Victoriana Romero. Interestingly, the Francisco Romero papers at the Arizona Historical Society contain a note that Alvino Ocoboa, Victoriana's father, was born in Spain. There is no evidence that such a claim is true. I have interpreted it as an effort by the elder Romeros to legitimize Francisco's marriage to someone of Yaqui descent.

VERACRUZ: In 1824, Veracruz became a federal state in Mexico. The state experienced political and social instability during much of the 19th century with conflicts between centralists and federalists and between liberals and conservatives. When his liberal government was attacked in Mexico City in 1857, Mexican President Benito Juárez governed from Veracruz.

BENITO JUÁREZ: National hero and president of Mexico (1861-72), who for three years (1864-67) fought against foreign occupation under Emperor Maximilian and who sought constitutional reforms to create a democratic federal republic.

NEW MEXICO TERRITORY: The boundaries of the New Mexico Territory at the time of establishment (September 9, 1850) contained most of the present-day state of New Mexico, more than half of the present-day state of Arizona, and portions of the present-day states of Colorado and Nevada.

ARIZONA TERRITORY: The creation of the Arizona Territory by the "Arizona Organic Act" on February 24, 1863, removed all the land west of the 109th meridian from the New Mexico Territory, i.e. the entire present-day State of Arizona plus the land that would become the southern part of the State of Nevada in 1864. Arizona became a state in 1912.

MEXICAN INDEPENDENCE: The Treaty of Córdoba established Mexico as an independent constitutional monarchy under Agustín de Iturbide. Eighteen months later, Antonio López de Santa Anna and Guadalupe Victoria ousted the emperor and established the first Mexican Republic.

L'IGLESIA/SANTA CATALINA MOUNTAINS: Father Eusebio Kino is credited to have named the Santa Catalina Mountains (Sierra de la Catarina) in 1697.

Early Spanish settlers also called the mountains "L'Iglesia," the Spanish word for church since the looming mountains looked like a cathedral. One of the visible peaks from Tucson is Cathedral Peak, which resembles church towers.

Chapter 3

YAQUI/YOEME: The sixteenth century missionaries brought "civilized" natives as teachers and inspirations for the indigenous people they encountered during their mission work in New Spain. In the Pimería Alta, they used Ópatas and Yaquis as model families to enter into ceremonial kinship with the unbaptized natives, serving as godparents and becoming compadres. With the influx of *gente de razón* in the early nineteenth century, Yaquis came fleeing oppression in their homelands. They worked as servants and miners.

COLLARED LIZARD DID PUSH-UPS: It is the male lizard that does push-ups in order to attract attention of prospective mates and to direct other males to steer clear of his territory. As noted in the *Tucson Weekly*, "If the push-up ruse works according to plan, all female lizards within viewing distance will suddenly swoon and have the urge to mate with this push-up pounding He-Man. All other male lizards will steer clear — unless, of course, they are bigger and badder than the push-up lizard king, in which case they'll beat him up or eat him."

THE RIVER DISAPPEARS: The Santa Cruz River, with headwaters in Arizona north of the current border with Mexico, flows south into Mexico and then turns, flowing northward through the Santa Cruz Valley, past Tucson, and, finally, flows into the Gila River. Currently, unless it is flood season, somewhere

north of Tubac, the river flows into an underground
channel before rising to the surface west of Tucson.
Historically, it is believed to have flowed on the
surface a greater distance year-round.

Chapter 5

GENTE DE RAZÓN: Literally, "people of reason" or
"rational people." A Spanish term used in colonial
Spanish America and modern Hispanic America to
refer to people who were culturally Hispanicized.
Indigenous peoples and mixed-race people were
generally considered not to be *gente de razón*. Before
the end of the eighteenth century, the terms *vecino*
and gente de razón included Christian Indians,
as well as persons of European descent. Mission
(Christianized) Indians also received the "rational
people" ranking. As members of gente de razón
society, they increased their chances for social
mobility. Missionaries gave new converts Christian
first names and Spanish surnames as permanent
symbols of their new spiritual and cultural identity.
As the number of converts grew, colonial officials
found it necessary to distinguish the Christianized,
tribal Mexicans from the non-Christian ones. The
gente de razón identity was, at first, commonly used
to designate the crown's Christianized subjects
regardless of racial background. In the eighteenth
century, Father Ignaz Pfefferkorn, a Jesuit missionary
in Sonora, observed very few true Spaniards living in
Sonora and "scarcely one who could trace his origin
to a Spanish family of pure blood. Practically all who
wish to be considered Spaniards are people of mixed-
blood." During the Mexican period, an influential
wealthy group of large landowners emerged to
provide the frontier with an "aristocratic-like"

society. Cultural advancement to a *gente de razón* status became synonymous with a Spanish heritage. By Mexican independence, the upper class associated *gente de razón* standing with a non-Indian or non-Mexican biological posture. Allegiance to Spain, while politically severed, gave the upper class social benefits as descendants of "Spaniards." Many were preoccupied with "Castilian" ties.

LOST MISSION OF CIRU: In the 1920s, long-time residents said that what is now known as the Romero Ruin was the site of the *Lost Mission of Cirú*. For many years, people believed a fortune in gold that had been left behind when the mission was abandoned. Because that mythology persisted into the 1950s, the site was frequently vandalized by both pot hunters and gold hunters. The site lies between Montrose and Alamo Canyons near the Cañada del Oro Wash. These ruins, ultimately proved to be the site of a prehistoric Hohokam village on which Francisco Romero built a homestead in the nineteenth century. Historically, Francisco Romero and a friend prospected in the area, looking for the legendary mine and its treasure.

PUEBLO VIEJO: Literally "ancient village," this is the name given to the area where Francisco Romero (historically) and Armando Ramirez (fictitiously) built his homestead. The ancient ruins of a Hohokam village generated speculation about the origin of the house blocks and walls.

HOMESTEAD ACT: The Homestead Act of 1862 specified that any U.S. citizen, or intended citizen, who had never borne arms against the United States could file an application to claim 160 acres of surveyed government land. Applicants were required to live on the land for five years, build a 12 x 14 dwelling, and grow crops. Note that the law specifies "surveyed" government land. An 1876 map shows several surveyed sections south of Tucson, but none north of the Catalinas. In fact, records of homestead applications in Arizona during the time of this story are rare. It is believed that many ranches (that were not long-held land grants) were "informal" homesteads. Hartley's 1865 map identifies a large number of ranches in the area south of Tucson. There is no record of Francisco Romero's application; however, his heirs were granted the patent (deed) for the land in 1911.

I'ITOI OR ELDER BROTHER: The Akimel (Pima) and Tohono O'odham consider I'itoi the creator of the human race. The creation story explains that a child called "First Born" arrived on Earth while it was not yet completed. First Born sang a song about the Earth Medicine Man as he worked, an invocation to assist in completing the Earth. First Born asked the Earth's creatures to name the light that would allow them to see each other. They agreed on "Sun." After he had made all the preparations, First Born left. From this point, I'itoi arrived, then Coyote, Buzzard, and others. Working together, but devising their own creations, they finished Earth. I'itoi created people out of clay, gave the desert people the "crimson evening," and instructed them to live there always, at the center of creation. The people see Elder Brother as the spirit who resides at the center of all things.

Chapter 6

GADSDEN PURCHASE: When the Gadsden Purchase made southern Arizona a part of the United States in 1854, almost all the land in the region became part of the public domain, subject to federal laws regarding its appropriate use, including the laws that regulated the transfer of public land to private parties. An important exception to the status of public domain was any grant of land made by the Mexican government or the Spanish colonial government, to a private citizen before southern Arizona became U.S. territory. Mexican troops remained in Tucson until March 1856, but when they headed south, only a few civilians went with them. U.S. troops rode into southern Arizona in late 1856 to take possession of the region, and Mexican, as well as Anglo immigrants, began to trickle into the area.

TUCSON LAND OFFICE: In 1881, the Government Land Office was located at 301 N. Main Street. John Wasson was U. S. Surveyor-General. H. M. De Hart was his Chief Clerk. I've found no record of a Land Office or Surveyor General in Tucson before this. I have taken the liberty of moving Mr. Wasson's assignment, along with his clerk's, back in time by seventeen years.

LA SIERRA DE LA CATARINA: The Santa Catalina Mountains, Tucson's "signature" mountains, lying north of the city.

Chapter 7

HENRY RIFLE: The original Henry rifle was a .44 caliber rimfire, lever-action, breech-loading rifle designed by Tyler Henry in the late 1850s. Production ended in 1866. Manufactured by the New Haven Arms Company, the Henry evolved into the famous Winchester Model 1866 lever-action rifle. With the introduction of this new model, the company was renamed Winchester Repeating Arms Company.

SIEGE OF TUBAC: More than two-hundred Apache warriors attacked Tubac sometime in early August 1861 and initiated a siege on one side of the Presidio. Mexican bandits occupied the other side but stayed out of the fighting. The townspeople fought for three days, sending a dispatch rider to Tucson, requesting reinforcements. Twenty-five militiamen, carrying a Confederate flag, arrived at the town and fought off the final assault. On the last night, the Arizonans left Tubac to be burned by the Apaches and plundered by the Mexican bandits.

Chapter 8

EIGHT-REALES COINS: Bars of silver and gold mined in Northern Sonora were hacked into chunks of proper weight and struck with heavy hammers between crude, hard-metal dies. The strike imprinted a Spanish pattern into the coin. The size, shape and impression of these coins were highly irregular. The silver coins were called *reales*. The Spanish dollar is a silver coin worth eight reales and contained 0.08 troy ounces of silver, hence, the term "*peso de ocho*" or "piece of eight." Coins were minted in the Spanish Empire after 1598. The Mexican eight-reales coin eventually became the one peso coin.

NICOLÁS RAMIREZ TREASURE: The discovery of the silver was made by a Yaqui Indian in 1736. Prospectors arrived, creating Arizona's first mining boom, but Spain tried to take ownership of the riches. If the silver was a buried treasure, it belonged to the king; if it was a natural deposit, the king was entitled to one-fifth of the treasure. Since it was natural, many prospectors and soldiers, who hired Yaqui miners, acquired a fortune from the mines. Historically, the owner of a huge 2500-pound chunk of pure silver, Lorenzo Velasco, became Sonora's largest rancher. For this story, this is how Nicolás Ramirez gained his wealth; the coins in the story would have been the crudely formed pieces of eight passed down through generations.

Chapter 9

PHAINOPEPLA: A black, silky, crested flycatcher-like bird with a long tail and white wing patches that feasts on the berries of mistletoe. The male of the species is black; the female is gray. Courtship for the phainopepla begins as early as January and can last through April. One of the first indications of the breeding season is the building of a nest by the male. Nest construction is the male's responsibility alone, and if his creation is accepted, a female takes up residence.

LA CRESTA: In Spanish, the word "Cresta" means ridge. To avoid confusion in the text between the small ridge where the homestead is built and the massive ridge standing between them and Tucson, I needed to give it a name. Today, it is called Pusch Ridge, but George Pusch, for whom it is named, came to the area many years later.

WILD CARROT SEEDS (QUEEN ANNE'S LACE) FOR CONTRACEPTION: Dried seeds are chewed. One teaspoon of seeds, dried or fresh, can be chewed well and swallowed with water or juice. This is the method used most commonly and with the longest historical record of contraception.

PART 2: LA CRESTA

Chapter 10

ROAD TO CAMP GRANT: See Map 1 for the location of the road to Camp Grant.

CAMP GRANT: Built by troops in May of 1860, Camp Grant lies at the confluence of the San Pedro River and Aravaipa Creek. Its purpose was to protect area settlers and emigrants against hostile Indians. In early 1871, when Pinal and Aravaipa Apaches requested sanctuary near the fort, they were allowed to hunt and farm the area and start a camp nearby. Unfortunately, during this time, other Apache bands continue to raid the territory, and though unfounded, many settlers blamed those bands living near Camp Grant. On April 30, 1871, a mob of angry citizens from Tucson and their Pápago Indian mercenaries clubbed, shot, and mutilated one-hundred and forty-four Aravaipa Apache people, mostly women and children near Camp Grant. The Apaches massacred at Camp Grant were not responsible for the hostilities the attackers blamed them for. According to historical records, Francisco Romero participated in this raid.

CORDONES: From the Spanish, these are long, finger ridges.

METATE: A flat stone that has a shallow depression in the upper surface for holding maize or other grains to be ground with a *mano* (hand tool). They might be described as a very large mortar and pestle.

THREE SISTERS: Corn, beans, and squash in the garden help each other to survive. The squash provides shade for the roots of the corn and beans; the corn provides stalks for the beans to climb; the beans provide shade to the growing ears of corn. They also attract pollinators to the garden. Sunflowers and amaranth are also considered sisters.

AMARANTH: Also known locally as pigweed, amaranth was cultivated by the Hohokam and continues to grow abundantly in the Sonoran Desert. Comparable to spinach, it is a popular green vegetable among the Yaquis. It should be collected while it is young and green. Once it goes to seed, it is very bitter,

Chapter 11

CHILE RISTRA: An arrangement of chile peppers hung together to dry. Today they are considered more decorative than functional.

Chapter 12

CATCLAW: *Acacia* greggii is a small tree or deciduous shrub with vicious thorns (shaped like a cat's claw) that grab and don't let go. It grows largely in the desert southwest. The sharp thorns literally tear clothes and lacerate flesh. It is also called "wait-a-minute bush."

APACHE METAL ARROW POINTS: The Apaches made points from discarded tin cans and barrel hoops, which had become ubiquitous during the middle of the nineteenth century.

Chapter 13

GOYO: A diminutive of Gregorio, meaning watchful, vigilant, guardian.

Chapter 15

QUAIL SAYING LOS PÁPAGOS: I first learned this description in Eva Wilbur-Cruce's memoir of growing up in early Arizona, *A Beautiful, Cruel Country*. She describes the Gambel Quail's four-note call as sounding like "Los Pápagos." Mary Austin, author of *The Land of Little Rain*, describes the three-note call as "Cuidado! Cuidado!"

WIKIUP: An 8-foot-tall frame of wood held together with yucca fibers and covered in brush usually in the Apache groups in the highlands.

WHITE CHANGING WOMAN: The first woman, White Painted Woman (also known as *Esdzanadehe*, and Changing Woman) survived the great Flood in an abalone shell, then wandered the land as the waters receded. Atop a mountain, she was impregnated by the sun and gave birth of a son, Killer of Enemies. Soon afterward, she was impregnated by the Rain and gave birth to Son of Water. Guided by spirits, she established a puberty rite to be given for all daughters born to her people. When she became old, White Painted Woman walked east toward the sun until she met her younger self, merged with her, and became young again. Thus repeatedly, she is born again and again, from generation to generation.

WHITE CHANGING WOMAN'S DRESS: The buckskin dress worn by an Apache girl during her ceremonial initiation into womanhood is important for her ritual transformation and in the life of the community. It represents Changing Woman and the way in which the girl is ceremonially transformed. It is an elaborate white buckskin dress, never before worn. It is often made by the girl's father after he ritually kills the deer and prepares their hides. The fringes on the dress represent the rays of the sun. Colored ribbons on her cane represent the four sacred directions. An abalone pendant attached to the girl's forehead symbolizes her ritual transformation into Changing Woman. Changing Woman's power makes the dress and other paraphernalia potent enough to bring healing and longevity to the gathered community. The living presence of Changing Woman gives the young Apache the spiritual strength and sense of cultural identity necessary to face with uncommon fortitude the challenges of life in two worlds.

USSEN: The Apache people believed that they existed because their god, Ussen, placed them on the Earth.

Chapter 16

FLEA-BITTEN GRAY HORSE: This is a color consisting of a white coat with small speckles, or "freckles," of red-colored hair throughout. Most horses who become flea-bitten grays still go through a brief period when they are pure white.

Chapter 17

SEA TAKAA: Sea takaa is part of a person's being, and the Yoeme believe if one has sea takaa, the person will be well protected from evil people and spirits during their lifetime. In order to keep it, the person must follow the "right path," respecting all living creatures, plants, the elements, and the mountains.

Chapter 18

DUTCH OVEN: During the seventeenth century, the Dutch perfected the process for producing cast metal cooking vessels. They became common in Europe and in the New World. They were commonly used by the Lewis and Clark expedition and westward bound settlers. The name of this cooking vessel has been in use since 1710.

Chapter 19

TULLY-OCHOA FREIGHT COMPANY: Estevan Ochoa was a Mexican-born American businessman and politician who helped build the Arizona Territory. Tully, Ochoa & Co. was one of the premier freighting organizations in the Southwest—before the railroads laid their tracks through town. Ochoa established the connection to Tucson from Missouri along the

310 / Sharon K. Miller

Sante Fe Trail, fighting Apache raiders along the way. They supplied Army posts, mines, ranches, Indian reservations and the many towns and cities along their routes. Coming to Tucson in 1860, he was a short, soft-spoken businessman, a leading citizen in the latter nineteenth century. His mule teams traveled with well-armed men through a wild landscape. Freight wagons could carry a five- to eight-ton load and may have been pulled by teams of eighteen to twenty mules or oxen. Wagon transportation was slow and expensive, costing up to $350 a ton and averaging no more than twelve to fifteen miles a day. Before the advent of the railroad, it was the only means of moving goods and freight across Arizona and the west.

MULESKINNERS: The animals pulling freight wagons were controlled by a single "jerk line" handled by either the driver or a muleskinner who rode to the left, or "near" wheel animal.

Chapter 21

YOEME BIRD OF PARADISE SONG: The song is a traditional Yoeme song. The Wilderness World or *Huya Ania* is where every plant, animal, and rock are one and communicate. The Yaqui approach the *Huya Ania* in a spiritual way. They don't just hike into the desert, but they first ask permission to enter and to bless their way. It's a very practical thing to do. It's good to have the blessing and permission of rattlesnakes, Gila monsters, and puma when you invade their territory. The *Yo Ania* is another enchanted world associated with caves that are a source of power to the *Surem*. The *Tuka Ania* is the Night World filled with unusual occurrences. The Dream World or *Tenku Ania* is a private world that involves the dreams of each individual Yaqui. Finally, there is the *Sea Ania* or Flower World, the world beneath the dawn. The flowers in Sea Ania are metaphors for all that is good and beautiful for each individual.

Chapter 22

TREATING GUNSHOT WOUNDS: A bullet that did not shatter a bone or injure organs was usually removed if the doctor could see it or feel it under the skin. Most doctors probed for bullets using their fingers. Once it was found, they might use a bullet extractor or knife to cut it out. Afterward, the wound was allowed to bleed to wash out any cloth and in hopes of preventing infection. Finally, the wound was sewn up, if necessary, and bandaged.

WALNUT TREE BARK: Soaked, softened, and pulverized into a paste, it was used for pain.

WALNUT TREE TEA: Used for infection.

Part 3: Pain and Progress

Chapter 27

DULCE NIÑA, DUERME YA: Translated: Sweet baby, sleep now. The lullaby that Esperanza sings to her child is, in fact, not from the nineteenth century. It is a modern lullaby, written by a man who identifies himself only as Pablo, to the tune of the theme from "Pan's Labyrinth." I found his lullaby in an answer to a Yahoo request. He describes himself as a native Spanish speaker. (For the rest of the lyrics, see the glossary.)

Chapter 28

TÉ DE PAZOTILLO: Tea made with fleabane; used to slow internal or uterine bleeding.

Chapter 29

CHOLLA: A cactus also known as the Jumping Cholla. When you get too close, you may find yourself painfully stuck to a spiny section which seems to have "jumped" from the plant. Pieces will even "jump" whenever stepped on and attach themselves to your leg. Because they have tiny barbs on the ends of the spines, they can be difficult and painful to remove from skin and clothing. The best way to remove cholla joints from clothing or skin is to use a comb.

POST-PARTUM DEPRESSION: A mental illness that often follows childbirth during which the mother experiences depression, sadness, anxiety, lack of motivation, restlessness, moodiness, ennui, and "empty" feelings that don't go away. These feelings may be mild to severe. Post-partum depression may sometimes follow live births; it is not limited to women who have given birth to stillborn babies.

Chapter 32

SPIRIT NAME: In the ancient Yoeme culture, when a child was born, negative things could harm her. Her real name was kept secret and she was given a flower name, or a name from something in nature to protect her real name from harm. Real names may be known to family and loved ones, but not to outsiders.

EYES: Even today, many people believe that the eyes are windows to the soul. Many native cultures teach their children to never look into the eyes of others because it is considered an act of intimidation. It may be thought as an assault on the person's spirit, an attempt to steal the spirit.

Chapter 33

FRAGRANCE OF RAIN: In the desert, rain releases the pungent scent of creosote, often carrying that fragrance on the wind ahead of a storm sweeping across the land. Desert dwellers are familiar with the fragrance and look forward to it every monsoon. As we say, "The desert smells like rain."

MONSOON: Summer weather in the Sonoran Desert brings the winds that carry heavy thunderstorms and destructive lightning. There are five seasons in the Sonoran Desert, because summer is divided into two seasons: fore-summer is in May and June when it is hot and dry. Summer monsoon season is from July to mid-September, bringing soaking rains.

BILL OURY: Prominent Tucson citizen, William S. Oury served as the first Mayor of Tucson in 1864, sheriff of Pima County from 1872-1877. He led the Camp Grant Massacre in 1871. In 1836, in Texas, he served at the Alamo garrison but missed the famous battle because he had been sent out as a courier.

PART 4: LEAVING

Chapter 35

CAP'N QUANTRILL'S RAIDERS: Leader of perhaps the most savage fighting unit in the Civil War, William Quantrill's guerrilla warfare terrorized civilians and soldiers alike. By 1864, Quantrill had lost control of the group, which split up into small bands. To his supporters, he was a dashing, free-spirited hero. Several ex-Raiders—the James brothers, Frank and Jesse, and the Younger brothers, Cole and Jim—went on in the late 1860s to apply Quantrill's hit-and-run tactics to bank and train robbery, building on his legacy of bloodshed.

Chapter 37

PETER RAINSFORD BRADY: An American military officer, surveyor, and politician. Following a short service in the United States Navy he joined the Texas Rangers, where he served during the Mexican-American war and along the western frontier. From Texas, he moved westward where he became an early settler and political office holder in Arizona Territory. He spent much of the Civil War in Sonora gathering supplies and intelligence for Union forces. At the end of the war, he returned to Tucson where he served as an Indian interpreter and two terms as sheriff. Governor Anson P.K. Safford also appointed him a military adviser at the rank of major. In 1871, Brady represented Pima County, Arizona as a Council member during the Eighth Arizona Territorial Legislature.

Chapter 39

CALICHE: Layers of calcium carbonite, a natural cement, may be found in the desert soil. It is impermeable and must be broken up for water to reach the surface or for the roots of plants to reach deeply enough to access moisture.

Chapter 40

LEAVING: The historical record reveals little evidence that Francisco and Victoriana Romero stayed at the homestead as long as my fictitious characters. Archaeological evidence does not support the number of historic structures described in this story. However, if they had, I'd like to believe that they may have had experiences not totally unlike those in the narrative.

Glossary

Spanish and Apache Words Used

ABUELA— Grandmother

ACONTECIÓ EN AQUELLOS DÍAS QUE SALIÓ UN EDICTO DE PARTE DE CÉSAR AUGUSTO, PARA LEVANTAR UN CENSO DE TODO EL MUNDO HABITADO...— It happened in those days that a decree went out from Caesar Augustus that a census of the whole inhabited world...

ADIÓS, M'HIJO HERMOSO.— Goodbye, my beautiful child.

AGUAS FRESCAS— Fruit drinks, like lemonade

AH, DIOS.— Oh, God.

¡AHORA!— Now (imperative)

ANTES DE DIO— Before God

AQUI— Here

AYÚDAME, SEÑOR, A SER UNA MEJOR ESPOSA. DÉME LA FUERZA PARA DURAR.— Help me, Lord, to be a better wife. Give me the strength to endure.

BAJADA— Geological term for a foothill slope generally made up of alluvial fans that have formed into a single apron of deposits against the slope

¡BASTA!— Enough! (imperative)

BIEN— Good

BIENVENIDO.— Welcome.

BUENAS DÍAS, MI AMORITA— Good day, my love (feminine)

BUÑUELOS— Doughnut-like pastries; churros, fritters

CALABASITAS— A stew made from squash, onions, tomatoes, and spices

CAÑAIGRE— Dock, or wild rhubarb

CARNITAS— Pork with tomatillo sauce

CASA— House

CAZUELA— Meat/vegetable soup or stew

¿COMO ESTÁ?— How are you?

CORDONES— Long finger ridges

CUIDADO.— Be careful.

DAȷ̂IDȷ̂L(APACHE LANGUAGE)— The Apache's name, He Moves Lightly

DE NADA.— It was nothing.

DEYAA! (APACHE LANGUAGE)—Leave! or Go!

DIME, HERMANITA— Tell me, Little Sister

DÓNDE ESTÁS?— Where are you?

DULCE NIÑO, DUERMETE YA— Sleep now, sweet baby. *ES HORA DE DESCANSAR*— It is time to sleep. *QUIERO QUE DUERMAS FELIZ*— I want you to sleep happily. *DUÉRMETE YA*— Sleep now

EL AMOR ES PACIENTE Y AMABLE— Love is patient and kind

EL ÁRBOL— The tree

EL CIUDAD— The city

EL DÍA DE SAN JUAN— San Juan's Day, June 24

EL GALLO— The rooster

EL NIÑO PEQUEÑO— The small boy

EL PÁJARO NEGRO— The black bird (Phainopepla, a crested black bird that resembles a cardinal)

ELLA FUE VIOLADA— She was violated/raped

EMPANADAS— Filled pastries

ENCANTADA DE CONOCERTE.— Nice to meet you.

EN EL NOMBRE DEL PADRE Y DEL HIJO Y ESPÍRITU SANTO— In the name of the Father, the Son, and the Holy Ghost

ERES BELLA.— You are beautiful.

¡ES ESCANDALOSO!— It is scandalous!

¡ES IMPERDONABLE!— It is unpardonable!

ES MUY BELLA.— It is very beautiful.

¿ES NO?— Is it not; Isn't it?

ESO ESPERO— I hope

Es por la gracia de Dios— It is by the grace of God

¡ESTANCIA!— Stay! (imperative)

ESTE ES GOYO— This is Goyo

¿ES TODO BIEN? — Is everything good?

ESTOY AQUÍ.— I'm here.

ESTOY BIEN.— I'm fine.

ESTOY SEGURO.— I am sure.

FELIZ NAVIDAD.— Merry Christmas.

FRIJOLES— Beans

GENTE DE RAZÓN— Men of reason, of a class higher than the indigenous peoples encountered by the missionaries and Spanish explorers and conquistadores

¡GRACIAS A DIOS TU ES AQUÍ!— Thank God you are here!

GRACIAS.— Thank you.

GRACIAS, EL SEÑOR, POR DARME MI ESPOSO.— Thank you, Lord, for giving me my husband.

GRACIAS, MI HERMANO.— Thank you, my brother

GUADALUPE (LUPE) Y LOS NIÑOS ESTAN AQUÍ.— Guadalupe and the children are here.

HERMANO, HERMANITO— Brother, Little Brother

HERMANA, HERMANITA— Sister, little sister

HIJO DE PUTA.— Son of a bitch.

HOLA.— Hello.

I'ITOI (TOHONO O'ODHAM LANGUAGE)— Elder Brother, who created the earth for the Tohono O'odham

JESUCRISTO Y LA VIRGEN— Jesús Christ and the Virgin (Mary)

LA CASA DE RAMIREZ — The Ramirez House

LA CRESTA— The ridge, now known as Pusch Ridge, north of Tucson at the western end of the Santa Catalina Mountain range; used as a geographic name in the story to distinguish it from generic desert ridges.

LA SIERRA DE LA CATARINA— The Santa Catalina Mountains

LAS FLORES NARANJAS— The orange flowers (Mexican Bird of Paradise)

L'IGLESIA— The church; the name given to the Santa Catalina Mountains by the Spaniards

LO SÉ.— I know.

LO SIENTO.— I'm sorry.

LO SIENTO MUCHO.— I'm very sorry.

LO SIENTO, SEÑORES.—I'm sorry, gentlemen.

LO VOY A HACER.—I will do it.

LOS BASTARDOS—Bastards

MADRE DE DIOS—Mother of God (a prayer to the Virgin Mary)

MASA—Short for masa de maíz, a maize (corn) dough made from freshly prepared hominy It is used for making corn tortillas, tamales

¿ME PUEDE DECIR QUÉ PASÓ?— Can you tell me what happened?

¿ME PUEDE DECIR SOBRE AQUELLOS HOMBRES? — Can you tell me about those men?

METATE— Grinding stone

M'HIJA— My child (feminine)
M'HIJA LINDA— My pretty daughter
M'HIJO— My child (masculine)
MI AMIGA— My friend (feminine)
MI AMIGO— My friend (masculine)
MI AMOR— My love (masculine)
MI AMORITA—My love (feminine)
MI ESPOSO— My spouse (masculine)
MI HERMANA— My sister
MI HERMANITA— My little sister
MI HERMANITO— My little brother
MI HERMOSA HIJA— My beautiful daughter
MI NIETA — My granddaughter
MI NIÑA— My little girl; my girl
MI QUERIDA— My dear (feminine)
MI QUERIDO— My dear (masculine)
MIERDA— Shit
¡MIRA!— Look!(imperative)
MUCHAS GRACIAS, MI QUERIDA.— Many thanks, my
    dear. (feminine)
NADA— Nothing
N'AÍÍ'EES (APACHE LANGUAGE)— Apache puberty/
    womanhood ceremony Each girl assumes the role of
    White Changing Woman
NO ES NADA.— It is nothing.
NO NADIE.— No, no one.
OLLA— Pottery jar, usually large
ORIÓN — The constellation Orion
PAZOTILLO— Daisy-like flower, Canadian fleabane
    (Erigeron); used for intestinal inflammation,
    diarrhea, hemorrhaging
PERDÓNAME, POR FAVOR.—Forgive me, please.
POR FAVOR.— Please.
¿POR QUÉ?— Why?
PUEBLO VIEJO— Ancient village

¿QUÉ ES?— What is it?

¿QUÉ PASÓ?— What happened?

¿QUE QUIERES?—What do you want?

QUESADILLA—Tortilla with cheese

¡RESPIRE!— Breathe!

RISTRA— Rope

SALA— Living room

SANTA THERÉSE Y LA VIRGEN— St. Theresa (Saint Therese of Lisieux is the patron of the sick. She received a vision of the Child Jesús just before her fourteenth birthday) And the Virgin Mary.

SEA ANIA (YOEME)— Flower World, one of several spiritual worlds of the Yoeme Others are *Huya Ania*, Wilderness World; *Yo Ania*, Enchanted World; *Tuka Ania*, Night World; *Tenku Ania*, Dream World

SEA TAKAA (YOEME)— *Sea takaa* is part of a person's being, and the Yoeme believe if one has *sea takaa*, the person will be well protected from evil people and spirits during their lifetime. In order to keep it, the person must follow the "right path," respecting all living creatures, plants, the elements, and the mountains.

SERÁ NUESTRA AVENTURA.— It will be our adventure.

SÍ. AYER FUE EL DÍA DE SAN JUAN.— Yes. Yesterday was *SAN JUAN'S DAY*.

SIEMPRE ESTOY CONTIGO.— I will always go with you.

SON EL MAL, EL MUY MAL.— They are bad, very bad.

SOY FINO.— I'm fine.

SOY UN IDIOTA.— I am an idiot.

SUCIO— Dirty

TAMALES Y EMPANADAS Y MAS— Tamales, empanadas, and more

TE ADORO.— I adore you.

TE AMO. / Y TU.— I love you. / and you.

***TÉ DE PAZOTILLO*—** Tea made from oil derived from Canadian fleabane (Erigeron), a daisy-like flower. Used for diarrhea and to constrict uterine lining and slow hemorrhaging.

***TENGO QUE HACER PIS.*—** I have to piss.

***TIA*—** Aunt

***TIA ESPE LLORA.*—** Aunt Espe is crying.

***TIN-NE-ÁH (APACHE LANGUAGE)*—** Meaning The People

***TOME ESTO COMO SU PROPIO HIJO, SEÑORA ENCANTADORA Y RECATADA, ENVUELTO EN EL MANTO DE SU CUIDADO, HASTA EL DÍA CUANDO EN UNA NUEVA TIERRA, TODOS SUS HIJOS SE UNAN A USTED, SU MADRE, INFINITAMENTE MISERICORDIOSO ALABAR Y DAR GRACIAS A DIOS PADRE, HIJO Y ESPÍRITU SANTO.*—** Take this child as your own Lady lovely and demure, enfolded in the mantle of your care, until the day when in a new land, all your children join with you, their infinitely merciful mother, endlessly giving praise and give Thanks to God the Father, Son and Holy Spirit.

***TU ERES MI ALMA / Y TU ERES MIO.*—** You are my soul. / and you are mine.

***TU ERES MI VIDA. / TU ERES MIA.*—** You are my life. / You are mine.

***TÚŁTSOG HADASLIN (APACHE LANGUAGE)*—** Where the Yellow Water Flows, the Apache encampment at Aravaipa

***USTED SOBREVIVIRÁ.*—** You will survive.

***VÁMONOS.*—** Let's go.

***VAYA CON DIOS.*—** Go with God.

***VENGA.*—** Come. (imperative)

***¡VENGA YA!*—** Come now!

Book Club Discussion Questions

1. What is your initial impression of Esperanza? Of Armando? Of Julio?

2. Discuss Esperanza's encounter with the Apaches at the river. What do we learn about her through this experience? If the Apache leader knew she was there, why didn't he capture or kill her?

3. Discuss the role of spirituality in Esperanza's life. How does it serve her in times of need? Does it ever fail her? How do we see her faith reflected in her behavior and her relationships with other characters?

4. In what ways do her Yoeme/Yaqui heritage and her relationship with Abuela Tiva contribute to the development of her character?

5. Discuss Esperanza's relationship with Abuela Primitiva. What is her role in the story?

6. Discuss her relationship with her parents, her sister, and her brothers.

7. By visiting the Pápago village, Armando demonstrates his desire to know more about the beliefs of Pápago people and their relationship with the world around them. In what ways does he succeed or fail?

8. Contrast the families of Armando and Esperanza. In what ways did their different childhood experiences shape their characters and provide insights into their marital relationship at the homestead?

9. Discuss Armando's parents: their motivations, their relationship with others and with each other. To what degree might they be described as "aristocratic?"

10. Armando's parents try to maintain a façade of frontier "nobility." Is it likely their ancestors managed to keep their "Spanish blood" pure?

11. Armando has very clear notions about his heritage and his citizenship. How do these notions give him direction?

12. In what ways is Esperanza a product of the time and the culture of that period in Territorial Arizona? In what ways does she depart from what might be considered the cultural norms? How can you account for these departures?

13. Esperanza never leaves the homestead, except for her wild ride on Pepe, during the four years they are there. Why didn't she demand that Armando take her with him to Tucson? Why didn't she demand that Julio come and stay so she could go with her husband? Why didn't Armando offer her the chance to get away from there?

14. To what degree is Esperanza's self-sacrificing nature admirable? To what degree is it a weakness?

15. Discuss Armando's relationship with his brother. What is Julio's role in the story?

16. Armando "believed La Cresta, the massive ridge, called him to linger beneath its magnificent rock towers and in the embrace of L'Iglesia." On the other hand, "Esperanza wanted to share his devotion to this place, she struggled to understand why it was somehow alien to her." Discuss these opposing viewpoints and how they influence the actions and behaviors of the characters.

17. In Chapter 12, Armando says, to Esperanza, "...there is nothing in this world I need more than you. Not this ranch, not those cattle...not these mountains." Is he being truthful to her? to himself?

18. Discuss Esperanza's relationship with the Apache, who watches from the palo verde. Is "relationship" the right word? How would you describe his interest in her and her interest in him?

19. What is the Apache's role in the story? Why does she never tell Armando about him? Why does she not fear him? What is your interpretation of the feathers on the walnut tree?

20. Discuss the portrayal of Apaches in the story.

21. Discuss the role of *eyes* in the relationships between Armando and Esperanza, within Armando's family, in Esperanza's connection to Ha-wani, and even in regard to the intruders with whom Esperanza must confront,

22. Discuss the scene between Esperanza and Doña María and the scene between Doña María and Don

Jesús. What do you learn about each of them from these interactions.

23. Discuss Esperanza's connection to the Hohokam woman through the pot. How does it help her deal with living at the homestead?

24. Esperanza always calls the homestead "this place." Why?

25. Discuss how Esperanza deals with the following events: Sam's threatening arrival at the ridge, Armando's bullet wound, her pregnancy and the death of her baby, and the assault by Charlie and Daggett.

26. In Chapter 28, after Armando discovers their baby died, "he prayed her tears would cleanse his selfish heart," and, later, he admits he has been selfish. Were there clues to his selfishness early in their relationship? In his relationship with his family?

27. In Chapter 34, Armando says, "I did this to her. I brought her here for my own dreams. When the Anglo came, I was not here to defend her. When Ángel died, I was not here to help her, and now, she faced these men, alone...I was not here. This evil belongs to me." Given that he allows two months to pass before he tells her they will leave the ridge, do you think he really believed what he said? What keeps him from acting on her behalf?

28. Does Armando really love Esperanza? Discuss.

29. Discuss Esperanza's dreams. What is their role in Esperanza's experiences and in the story?

30. In Chapter 38, Esperanza learns of Goyo's death and physically attacks Armando, swearing at him. Why do you think she reacts so viscerally?

31. In Chapter 39, Esperanza asks Armando, "What if Adelita thinks you're more important to him [Julio] than her and their child?" Her question triggers his memory of something Julio asked him when they were digging the well: "What if she [Esperanza] thinks this place is more important to you than her?" What have been Armando's priorities throughout the story? How have those priorities affected his relationships with Julio and Esperanza?

32. In Chapter 40, after Armando's confession, Esperanza tells him, "Of everything you've ever asked of me, this is the hardest." What does she mean?

33. Also in Chapter 40, she remembers the day Sheriff Brady came and questioned her. "He was kind, but she could not tell him the truth." Compare this with events in Chapter 37 when the sheriff questions her. Is there a disconnect?

34. Discuss the role of the natural world in the story: birds and animals, the river, the wash, the mountains, the weather.

35. In what ways does the inclusion of Spanish and Apache languages contribute to the story?

36. If you have read *The Clay Remembers: Book 1 in The Clay Series*, have you found parallels in the characters or the events?

About the Author

Sharon K. Miller is an author and editor. The Clay Series has been a long-time project for which she has done extensive research into the archaeology and prehistory of the Tucson Basin and the history of the Spanish *entrada* into Southwestern United States.

Her affinity for the Sonoran Desert led to the development of the character of Anna, the protagonist in *The Clay Remembers*. Her fascination with the Romero Ruin in Catalina State Park led to an investigation of Francisco and Victoriana Romero. She expected to find some insight into the woman who had lived there, but, other than her Yaqui background, very little was available about her. As a result, Esperanza Ramirez, the main character in *The Clay Endures*, was born. Book 3, *The Clay Sustains*, tells the story of Ha-wani, a twelfth century Hohokam woman who made the pot featured in Books 1 and 2.

One pot. Three women. Eight-hundred years.

References

All Books in The Clay Series

Alcock, John. *When the Rains Come: A Naturalist's Year in the Sonoran Desert*. Tucson: University of Arizona Press, 2009.

Arellano, Anselmo F. *Las Curanderas: Traditional Healers in New Mexico, Mother Earth Living*, 1997. www. motherearthliving.com/health-and-wellness/new-mexico-shealing-tradition.aspx? PageId=3.

Ashmore, Wendy, and Robert Sharer. *Discovering Our Past: A Brief Introduction to Archaeology*. Mountain View: Mayfield Pub., 1996.

Bahr, Donald M., Juan Smith, William Smith Allison, and Julian Hayden. *The Short, Swift Time of Gods on Earth: The Hohokam Chronicles*. Berkeley: University of California, 1994.

Baldwin, Gordon C. *The Warrior Apaches: A Story of the Chiricahua and Western Apache.* Tucson: D.S. King, 1965.

Ball, Eve, with Nora Henn, and Lynda A. Sánchez. *Indeh, an Apache Odyssey.* Provo: Brigham Young University Press, 1980.

Barnett, Franklin. *Dictionary of Prehistoric Indian Artifacts of the American Southwest.* Flagstaff: Northland Press, 1973.

Barter, G. W., ed. *Directory of the City of Tucson for the Year 1881.* San Francisco: H.S. Crocker & Co., Printers, 1881.

Baylor, Byrd. *And It Is Still That Way: Legends Told by Arizona Indian Children.* El Paso: Cinco Puntos Press, 1998.

Baylor, Byrd. *When Clay Sings.* New York: Aladdin, 1987.

Bennett, Robin Rose. "Wild Carrot (Daucus Carota): A Plant for Conscious, Natural Contraception, USDA Plant Profile." *Sister Zeus,* 2009. www.sisterzeus.com/qaluse.htm.

Bernard-Shaw, Mary, Henry D. Wallace, Linda Mayro, and William H. Doelle. *Archaeological Testing at Los Morteros North and a Mitigation Plan for the Site of Los Morteros,* Technical Report No. 87-10. Tucson: Institute for American Research, 1987.

Bezy, John V. *A Guide to the Geology of Catalina State Park and the Western Santa Catalina Mountains.* Tucson: Arizona Geological Survey, 2002.

Bowden, Charles. *Frog Mountain Blues.* Tucson: University of Arizona Press, 1994.

Boyer, Jeffrey L. "Is There a Point to This? Contexts for Metal Projectile Points in Northern New Mexico. *Papers of the Archaeological Society of New Mexico*, No. 38, Albuquerque: Archaeological Society of New Mexico. www. academia.edu/4160733/Is_There_A_Point_To_ This_Contexts_ for_Metal_Projectile_Points_in_ Northern_New_Mexico.

Colwell-Chanthaphonh. *Massacre at Camp Grant: Forgetting and Remembering Apache History.* Tucson: University of Arizona Press, 2007.

Cornett, James W. *Indian Uses of Desert Plants.* Palm Springs: Nature Trails Press, 2011.

Cornett, James. "Mistletoe Depends Upon Bird." *The Desert Sun,* 2014. www.desertsun. com/story/life /home- garden/james- cornett/2014/12/06/mistletoe-depends-upon- bird/20039567/.

Cremony, John C. *Life Among the Apaches.* San Francisco: A. Roman and Company, Publishers, 1868. (Digital reproduction by Digital Scanning, Inc., 2001.)

Crider, Destiny L., Cathryn M. Meegan, and Steve Swanson. *The Hohokam Preclassic to Classic Transition Part II: Modeling Socioeconomic Changes.* Tempe: Arizona State University Department of Anthropology. n.d.

Dancey, William S. *Archaeological Field Methods.* Edina: Burgess, 1981.

"Depression During and After Pregnancy." U.S. Department of Health and Human Services, Office of Women's Health. www.womenshealth. gov.

Doelle, William H., and Deborah L. Swartz. "Hidden Times: The Archaeology of the Tortolita

Phase, *Archaeology in Tucson: Newsletter of the Center for Desert Archaeology*, Vol. 11, No. 2. Tucson: Center for Desert Archaeology. Spring, 1997.

Ferg, Alan, ed. *Western Apache Material Culture: The Goodwin and Guenther Collections.* Tucson: University of Arizona Press, 1987.

Fish, Suzanne K., and Paul R. Fish, eds. *The Hohokam Millennium.* Santa Fe: School for Advanced Research Press, 2007.

Fontana, Bernard L. *Entrada: The Legacy of Spain and Mexico in the United States.* Tucson: Southwest Parks and Monuments Association, 1994.

Gargulinski, Ryn. "Why Lizards Do Push-Ups? And Other Tucson Wildlife Tidbits You Need to Know Before You Die." *Tucson Weekly*, May 20, 2011. www.tucsonweekly.com/TheRange/archives/2011/05/20/why-lizards-do-push-ups-and -other-tucson-wildlife-tidbits-you-need-to-know-before-you-die.

Giddings, Ruth Warner. *Yaqui Myths and Legends.* Tucson: University of Arizona Press, 1959.

Gregonis, Linda M., and Karl J. Reinhard. *Hohokam Indians of the Tucson Basin.* Tucson: University of Arizona Press, 1979.

Griffith, Jim. "El Dia de San Juan," Special to the Arizona Daily Star, June 14, 2013. http://tucson.com/news/blogs/big-jim/big-jim-el-d-a-de-san-juan/article_1963ed22-cb14-11e2-8346-0019bb2963f4.html.

Gronemann, Barbara. *Hohokam Arts and Crafts.* Scottsdale: Southwest Learning Sources, 1994.

Hanson, Roseann Beggy, and Jonathan Hanson. *Southern Arizona Nature Almanac: A Seasonal*

Guide to Pima County and Beyond. Tucson: University of Arizona Press, 1996.

Hatch, Stephanie. "Traditional, Processual, and Post-Processual Archaeology." *Archaeology, Art History, Religion, Ancient Cultures, Anthropology, and Nature*, 2010. http://stephaniehatch.blogspot.com/2010/02/traditional-processual-and-post.html.

Hayden Papers. *Francisco Romero Documents*. Arizona Historical Society. Tucson.

Heilen, Michael. *Uncovering Identity in Mortuary Analysis: Community Sensitive Methods for Identifying Group Affiliation in Historical Cemeteries*. Walnut Creek: Left Coast Press, 2012.

Hernandez, John. *Blood Along the Cañon del Oro— Tully & Ochoa Wagon Attack*. April 4, 2013. www.copperarea.com/pages/blood-along-the-canon-del-oro-tully-ochoa-wagon-attack-2/

Hester, Thomas R., Harry J. Shafer, and Kenneth L. Feder. *Field Methods in Archaeology*, Seventh Edition. Mountain View: Mayfield Pub., 1997.

History.com Staff. "Struggle for Mexican Independence," 2010. http://www.history.com/topics /mexico /struggle-for-mexican-independence.

History.com Staff. "Veracruz." http://www.history.com/topics/mexico/veracruz.

"Homes in the Gold Coast Historic District of Chicago." http://www.74elm.com/photo-gallery/.

"Honey." http://www.dermnetnz.org/treatments/honey.html.

"How to Grow a Three Sisters Garden." Native Seeds SEARCH, Tucson. www.nativeseeds.org.

Huckell, Lisa W. *Archaeological Assessment of the Proposed Catalina State Park.* Arizona State Museum Archaeological Series, Tucson: University of Arizona Press, 1980.

"Illinois Grounds for Dissolution of Marriage." www.divorcesource.com/ds/illinois/illinois-divorce-laws -674.shtml,http://www. illinoisdivorce.com/family_law_articles/grounds_ for_divorce.php.

Kallevang, Britta. "Beliefs of the Pápago Tribe." http://classroom.synonym.com/beliefs-papago-tribe-6515.html.

Kane, Charles W. *Medicinal Plants of the American Southwest.* Boston: Lincoln Town Press, 2011.

Kessel, John L. *Friars, Soldiers, and Reformers: Hispanic Arizona and the Sonora Mission Frontier, 1767-1856.* Tucson: University of Arizona Press, 1976.

King, Dan. *General Hohokam Pottery Descriptions,* July, 2004. www.rarepottery.info/protect / articles.htm.

Lavin, Patrick. *Arizona: An Illustrated History.* New York: Hippocrene Books, 2001.

Malville, J. McKim, and Claudia Putnam. *Prehistoric Astronomy in the Southwest.* Boulder: Johnson Books. 1993.

Marks, Tracy. *Becoming Woman: Apache Female Puberty Sunrise Ceremony,* 1999. www. webwinds. com/yupanqui/apachesunrise.htm.

Martin, Patricia Preciado. *Beloved Land: An Oral History of Mexican Americans in Southern Arizona.* Tucson: University of Arizona Press, 2004.

Martin, Patricia Preciado. *Images and Conversations: Mexican Americans Recall a Southwestern Past*. Tucson: University of Arizona Press, 1996.

McNamee, Gregory, ed. *Named in Stone and Sky: An Arizona Anthology*. Tucson: University of Arizona Press, 1993.

Miranda, G. "Racial and Cultural Dimensions of 'Gente de Razón' Status in Spanish and Mexican California." *Southern California Quarterly*, *70*(3), 265-278, 1988. www.jstor.org. ezproxy2. library.arizona.edu/stable/41171310 doi:1.

Molina, Felipe. Yoeme History and Culture, personal communication, 2014.

Muehrcke, Phillip C. and Juliana O. Muehrcke. *Map Use: Reading, Analysis, Interpretation*, 4th Edition. Madison: JP Publications, 1998.

Nahban, Gary Paul. *The Desert Smells Like Rain: A Naturalist in Papago Indian Country*. San Francisco: North Point Press, 1982.

Nabhan, Gary Paul. *Gathering the Desert*. Tucson: University of Arizona Press, 1985.

National Register of Historic Places. *Registration Form: Ghost Ranch Lodge*. U.S. Department of the Interior, 2012.

New Perspectives on the West, "William Clarke Quantrill." *The West Film Project*. Public Broadcasting System, 2001. www.pbs.org/weta/ thewest/people/i_r/quantrill.htm.

Officer, James E. *Hispanic Arizona: 1536-1856*. Tucson: University of Arizona Press, 1987.

Olin, George. *House in the Sun: A Natural History of the Sonoran Desert*. Tucson: Southwest Parks and Monuments Association, 1994.

Overstreet, Daphne. *Arizona Territory Cook Book: Recipes from 1864 to 1912*. Phoenix: Golden West, 2004.

Pablo. "Duerme Ya" (Sleep Now), *Lullaby written to the theme from "Pan's Labyrinth,"* 2008. https://answers.yahoo.com/question/index? qid=20080918 102717AAFdsjU.

Phillips, Steven J., and Patricia Wentworth Comus, eds. *A Natural History of the Sonoran Desert*. Tucson: Arizona Sonoran Desert Museum Press, 2000.

Pirate Medicine: "Gunshot wounds." *Pestilence and Pain During the Golden Age of Piracy*, n.d. http://pirates. hegewisch.net/Pestilence_Pain.html #gunshots.

Pluralism Project, Harvard University. "Apache Initiation Dress." http://pluralism.org/religions/ native-american-traditions/native-peoples-experience/apache-initiation-dress/.

Potter, Lee Ann, and Wynell Schamel. "The Homestead Act of 1862." *Social Education*, Vol. 61, No. 6, (October, 1997) 359-364.

Record, Ian W. *Big Sycamore Stands Alone: The Western Apaches, Aravaipa, and the Struggle for Place*. Norman: University of Oklahoma Press. 2008.

Redish, Laura. "Native American Vocabulary: Apache Words" www.native-languages.org/ apache_ words.htm.

Reid, J. Jefferson, and David E. Doyel. *Emil W. Haury's Prehistory of the American Southwest*. Tucson: University of Arizona Press, 1986.

Reid, Jefferson, and Stephanie Whittlesey. *The Archaeology of Ancient Arizona*. Tucson: University of Arizona Press. 1987.

Saguaro Sings Down the Rain, Tucson: Tohono Chul Park, n.d.

Saxton, Dean, Lucille Saxton, and Susie Enos. *Dictionary: Papago-English, O'otham-Mil-gahn, English-Papago, Mil-gahn-O'otham*, Second Edition. Tucson: University of Arizona Press, 1983.

Scholes, Walter V. "Benito Juarez." *Encyclopedia Britannica Online*, 2016. www.britannica.com/ biography/ Benito-Juarez.

Shelton, Richard. *Going Back to Bisbee*. Tucson: University of Arizona Press, 1992.

Shelton, Richard. *Hohokam*. Tucson: Sun/Gemini Press, 1993.

"Spanish Dollar, Pieces of Eight," 2016. https://en .wikipedia.org/wiki/Spanish_dollar.

Spicer, Edmund H. *Cycles of Conquest: The Impact of Spain, Mexico, and the United States on the Indians of the Southwest, 1533-1960*. Tucson: University of Arizona Press, 1962.

Stein, Pat H. *Homesteading in Arizona, 1862-1940: A Component of the Arizona Historic Preservation Plan*. Phoenix: Arizona State Historic Preservation Office, 1990.

Stockel, H. Henrietta. *Women of the Apache Nation: Voices of Truth*, Reno: University of Nevada Press, 1991.

Sutton, Mark Q., and Brooke S. Arkush. *Archaeological Laboratory Methods: An Introduction*. Dubuque: Kendall/Hunt, 1998.

Swartz, Deborah L. *Archaeological Testing at the Romero Ruin, Technical Report 93-8*. Tucson: Center for Desert Archaeology, 1993.

Swartz, Deborah L. *Archaeological Testing at the Romero Ruin, Technical Report 91-2*. Tucson, Center for Desert Archaeology, 1991.

Thiel, J. Homer. "People of the Presidio: Family Records from the Tucson Presidio." *Supplemental Media Content for Archaeology Southwest*, Vol. 24, Nos. 1-2. Tucson: Center for Desert Archaeology, 2010.

"UA Engineers Help Save and Reconstruct the Past." *Arizona Engineer* 20.1 (2006). University of Arizona College of Engineering and Mines.

Underhill, Ruth Murray. *Papago Woman*. Prospect Heights: Waveland Press, 1979.

Underhill, Ruth Murray. *Singing for Power: The Song Magic of the Papago Indians of Southern Arizona*. Tucson: University of Arizona Press, 1993.

Underhill, Ruth Murray. *People of the Crimson Evening*, Palmer Lake: The Filter Press, 1982.

Van Ness Seymour, Tryntje. *The Gift of Changing Woman*, New York: Henry Holt and Company, 1993.

Wagoner, J.J. "History of the Cattle Industry in Southern Arizona, 1540-1940." *University of Arizona Bulletin, Social Science Bulletin No. 20*. Tucson: University of Arizona Press, 1952.

Ward, Andy. *Palatkwapi: True Southwest*, 2014. www.palatkwapi.com.

"Weatherby 9 Lug/Magnum," n.d. http://en.wikipedia.org/wiki/Weatherby_Mark_V.

Weaver, Donald E, Susan S. Burton, and Minnabell Laughlin, eds. *Proceedings of the 1973 Hohokam Conference*. Ramona: Acoma Books, 1978.

Wechel, Edith te. *Yaqui: A Short History of the Yaqui Indians*, n.d. www.manataka.org/ page129.html#YAQUI%20HISTORY.

Weiser, Kathy. "Arizona Legends: Fort Breckinridge, Built Again and Again," 2016. www.legendsof america.com/az-fortbreckinridge. html.

Yetman, David. *Sonora: An Intimate Geography.* Albuquerque: University of New Mexico Press, 1996.

Zucker, Robert. "Treasures of the Santa Catalina Mountains: Naming the Santa Catalina Mountains." n.d. *Entertainment Magazine.* www.emol.org/treasurescatalinas/santacatalinas. html.

Zucker, Robert. "Lost Mission of Ciru." *Entertainment Magazine,* n.d. http://www.emol.org/treasures catalinas/missionofciru.html.